CW01558533

A Kind of Sleep

by the same author
ROAD LINES

CHRIS OULD

A Kind of Sleep

ANDRE DEUTSCH

To Joe Pagett,
true Irishman

For a free Ireland

First published in Great Britain 1986
by André Deutsch
105 Great Russell Street, London WC1B 3LJ
Printed in Great Britain by
Ebenezer Baylis and Son, Worcester

ISBN 0 233 97931 X

Shade

ONE

The afternoon heat settled out dust on hot steel. There had been no rain for two weeks and the track that led from the shed and the dark red gridded plates of the weighbridge into the scrap-yard was so dry it was beginning to crumble in places. The moulded ruts of the crane's caterpillar tracks broke off and were gradually ground to grey dust that would stir with the slightest breeze.

Beside the track the scrappers, the wrecks, sat low and defeated and dead; dented door panels, windows without glass, unclosable bonnets, slow rotting tyres and rusty, studded wheel hubs. There was no life in their paint and their chrome plating was pitted. The heat only shimmered above, without seeming to touch.

Beneath the cars the rust slowly flaked rough and fell. In places where nobody trod long stalked weeds pushed around holed sills and grew against the curves of front wings. Inside the closed cars the trapped air gradually took on the smell of rotting seats and rotting steel and enclosed dampness evaporating. Once in a week one wreck perched on the roof of another might sag and settle by a couple of inches.

Larne sat in a faded, frayed deckchair in the doorway of the shed. The overhang of the roof kept the sun out of his eyes, but the rest of his body had no shade and was wet with sweat that glistened in the folds of his arms. Beside him the sandy brown mongrel lay in part of the shade he made, its tongue lolling. It was too hot to sleep and Larne's blued green eyes moved slowly over a stack of old tyres, the first, most serviceable of the wrecks, the rusty chain-link fence and then the steep bank behind it which led up to the railway line and where the long grass and docks had dried and turned brown. His eyes seemed to move because he was awake, but for no other reason.

It was cooler inside the shed, and there the smell hung: old, dark oil, congealed and thick with dirt as it leaked away from the sumps of the black, heavy-resting engines collected together with gear boxes, transmissions, starter motors and axles.

Partitioned off from them by unplaned wooden boards, the office was dark enough to widen eyes from the sun until they got used to it. There was a yellow wooden desk against the partition with an old cash register at one end. The cash register's keys were smudged with the same oil that leaked from the engines; like the door handle, the desk top, the chipped filing cabinet drawers and the half-plastered walls. Whatever was touched kept its mark like a tide line above and around and over the litter and junk that sometimes hung from nails in the wall.

Larne stayed outside, moving his hand just a little in the sun, as if easing out tightness or dull aching. It was his left hand and it lay across his dirty-jeaned thigh. Its fingers were twisted; the middle two each with an extra knuckle, and the lines of the scars on its back ran up and down over knotted tendons and caved-in bone. He didn't look at his hand as he moved it, but if he had his face said it would have been in the same way that he looked at the scrappers and the chain-link fence and then at the noise-sudden train on the line to Waterloo station.

The noise of the train covered that of a van pulling up by the gate, but when the train had gone a door swung closed and the dog beside Larne lifted its head. Larne looked too, moving a piece of bluntly cut hair across his forehead. It was damp with sweat, dark, and a few strands were grey.

The van was a Ford, lightweight, white and not clean. A young man, twenty-four or five, came around its front end and into the yard. He was short and fit-looking and wore a white T-shirt like an old-fashioned vest, unbuttoned in a V below his neck. The straps of braces came over his shoulders and clipped to the waistband of khaki drill trousers with large pockets. His hair was light, almost blond, and his face was pale except for a pair of heat-flushed red rings below his eyes and above his cheekbones.

He walked sure-footedly as he came up to Larne, looking around. He stood for a moment, then hooked a thumb through the belt loop on his trousers. 'Joe Larne?' he asked.

Larne's eyes rose to the young man's. He nodded slowly.

'My name's Hagen. You've got a blue S reg Cortina for sale.'

Larne's face became vaguely thoughtful. 'Who told you that?'

With a shrug and a slight shift of balance Hagen said, 'I forget; I just heard.'

'Well you can look, but there's nothing like that. Help yourself.'

He pushed himself out of the chair without looking at Hagen, moved it aside and went into the darkness of the shed.

He was seated again, on a battered grey typist's chair, when Hagen's foot scuffed the concrete floor and he came into the doorway of the office. Larne had a tin of tobacco open on his leg and was rolling a cigarette.

'Look,' Hagen said, his voice harder than it had been.

'Did you find it?' Larne said without taking his attention from the cigarette.

'Look,' Hagen repeated slowly, slipping into the faint trace of an accent. 'You know who I am, you know what I want. Don't fuck me about.'

Larne looked up, putting the lid back on his tin. 'I won't fuck you about, son, but I don't know you. What d'you want for that?'

'You know; you're holding.' But the edge in his words had no effect on Larne. Hagen took a step forward and put the knuckles of one hand on the edge of the desk. 'Who do you *think* I am?'

Larne lit his cigarette and didn't reply.

Glancing down and then up as the dog slid past his legs and went on to a drinking bowl Hagen drew a breath through his teeth, glaring. 'McGiven sent me,' he said. 'For a short. Will *that* do you?'

Larne looked thoughtful again, compressing his lips, then drawing on the cigarette. He looked round at the dog, got up and went to a plastic water can by a tap in the wall. He hooked the index finger of his left hand through the can's handle and used his right to tip water into the dog's bowl. 'Are you working for McGiven?' he said.

Hagen shifted impatiently. 'I just said I was.'

'You said he sent you.' Larne straightened but he kept hold of the water can and it swung slightly on his finger. 'Where's Mallon?'

'Away.'

Larne kept the water can swinging with a small movement of his wrist. 'Where?'

'What's it matter. He's away so I'm here.'

Larne faced Hagen straight on now. 'It matters to me,' he said. 'Mallon knows how it works.'

'So?'

'So you'd better know too.' He lowered the can to his side and jerked his head. 'Outside.'

Larne led the way along the track through the yard and Hagen walked on his right, slightly behind. The direct sunlight was harsh after the dimness of the office and the heat was trapped by the steel and made hard. As they came to the brown wooden side of an old goods wagon piled with rags, a dog began to bark, persistent and bass.

At the back of the wagon there was a tall pen of large steel-mesh caging an Alsatian on ten square feet of bare earth. The dog barked with its muzzle through the mesh, pushing and rattling the cage as Larne went towards it, ignoring the noise.

Hagen hung back and watched suspiciously as Larne opened a latch on a gate and slid through into the cage. As soon as he was inside the Alsatian stopped barking, but it stood ready to start again as Larne poured the last of the can's water into an enamel bowl.

'Too hot for dogs,' he said. 'Makes them irritable, and this one's a bastard anyway.'

He came out of the cage and dropped the empty can by the gate. 'What kind of short do you want?'

'Whatever you've got. McGiven didn't say, but he wants some spare ammunition to go with it.'

Larne nodded. 'Up here.'

Further into the yard the wrecks gained a sense of permanence; dumped too far back to be dragged out easily; left and forgotten. Some of them could have been twenty years old, their parts too out-dated even for spares. From somewhere the mongrel appeared, but it knew the wrecks too well to bother to sniff and search in amongst them.

Larne picked up a short crowbar from the bonnet of one as he passed. 'Are you out of Belfast?' he asked Hagen.

After a flick of his eyes, damp now where they were flushed, Hagen nodded. 'In and out.'

'How long this time?'

6

'A few months.'

Larne made no reaction to that and he stopped beside the front end of a leaning transit van. It was caught by an angular piece of shade from two stacked cars, its bonnet and windscreen gone and its cylinder head on the ground beside it. Larne gestured at a dark patch of oil between the van's front wheels.

'Oil and petrol,' he said. 'It puts sniffer dogs off. Got it?'

Hagen nodded again.

Larne got down on one knee and thrust the crowbar into the soil at an angle. He levered and broke up the earth but nothing else came to the surface. He tried again in a spot a few inches away. He used his right hand to ram the bar in and both to lever it up. The third time it was harder and a flat biscuit tin came up with the earth. He pulled it out and stood up.

Putting the crowbar aside he held the tin in the crook of his left arm and worked the rusting lid off. Inside there was a dark greasy package of cloth. He tossed the lid away, skimming to rattle out of sight, and balanced the tin on the ledge of the van's front grill.

Hagen came to his side as he opened the cloth out. There was no awkwardness from Larne's crippled hand. The thumb and first finger worked slightly pincer-like and at an odd angle, but that was all.

The cloth had wrapped a blued, short barrelled revolver and two Swan Vesta matchboxes. Larne picked the gun up, turned it in his hand, examining the metal, then snapped the cylinder out. It was empty and clean. He clicked it back into position and put the gun back on the cloth. He turned to Hagen.

'There's a dozen bullets, six in each box. McGiven won't need more.'

'Okay,' Hagen said. He reached out and took the pistol. After a moment feeling its weight he cocked the hammer with his thumb. When he pulled the trigger the hammer fell sharply. 'What calibre is it?'

'Three fifty-seven.' Larne held out his hand and the other put it there.

'When do you see McGiven?'

'Tonight.'

'It needs cleaning and oiling. Tell him or do it yourself. Wipe it down anyway, get rid of your prints. Give it him clean.'

7

'I know the job.'

'The job's just delivering. Passing it clean is your life.'

'Yeah, and what about you? Your prints are there.'

'I didn't leave prints; I didn't play with it.' He flipped the cloth back over the gun, picked it up and tossed it the short distance to Hagen. 'Take it to McGiven,' he said flatly.

For a moment Hagen was still, then he turned – still holding the gun to his stomach as he'd caught it – and moved away down the track. A little dust rose at his heels and Larne tossed the tin after its lid. He waited until he heard the Alsatian bark as Hagen went past it and then he pushed back the soil he'd disturbed with the steel toe of his boot.

TWO

At twenty to eight the phone rang while Larne was shaving. He stopped in midstroke and lowered his hand from his chin to look at his watch, then he finished the stroke to his jawbone and stirred the plastic head of the razor in the sink. He made another scrape through the foam, his head cocked, stretching the skin. The final patch was under a sideburn and when he'd cleared it he pulled the plug in the sink, rinsed the razor-head in a hard brief stream of cold water and put it on the side of the bath. The phone stopped after the fifth ring.

Larne cleaned off his face with a towel and then ran cold water to wash away the tidemark around the sink. The phone rang again. He stepped round the bathroom door to the stair landing, went down and into the back room on the right. The curtains in the room were still closed and the light was grey. There was a vague smell of old cigarette smoke and detergent or soap from the adjoining box kitchen.

The green telephone ended its second chime and started a third. Larne took a step to its small side table, held back briefly, then picked up the receiver while the third bell still echoed.

He listened to a coin being pushed in at the other end, then: 'Joe?'

'Yes?'

'It's Danny.'

'Yes Danny,' Larne said.

'Come over to the café for breakfast. All right?'

'Are you there now?'

'I will be.'

Larne glanced at the window and frowned slightly. 'Okay.'

'Twenty minutes.'

'Right.'

He listened to the phone being hung up and the purr, then hung up himself.

He rubbed his chin with a knuckle and went over to draw

9

the curtains. The room lightened. Outside the sun was bright, but not high enough yet over the high brick wall on two sides to catch the patch of grass at the rear of the house. The yard was empty and clean except for a piece of bone left close to the dustbin by a wandering dog.

Larne gave the yard a cursory look and went to pull back the curtains in the kitchen. From there he went through to the front room where the curtains were already drawn and white nets hung behind them. The furniture in the room was old-fashioned and squarely uninviting; a moquette-covered settee and two armchairs, a gas fire on the chimney breast with a mirror above it and a television set in the corner, nothing else.

He stopped a couple of feet behind the regular folds of the nets, stood still and looked through them. It lasted a minute and then without any shift of expression he moved to the glass-panelled front door, twisted the stiff key in the lock and opened it.

For a moment he seemed to judge the temperature outside, combining this with a brief look at the length of the quiet terraced street, working his shoulders in a shrug. He bent and picked up a milk bottle from the step. The movement stretched three short, irregular scars between his left shoulder blade and the belt of his jeans and emphasised a shallow, unnatural hollow in the back of his left arm as it hung forward.

He took the milk bottle inside and left it in the rack of the fridge door before going back upstairs. He put on a clean, wash-faded T-shirt and a pair of desert boots and paused to roll a cigarette. When it was lit he descended the stairs, lifted a scuffed brown leather jacket from a coat hook as he passed and worked himself into it before he opened the front door again.

Outside his movements were open and unhurried. He locked the door behind him and breathed the fresh air for a moment before setting off to his right.

The street was still; a short dead-ended terrace with no through way for traffic. A few unwashed cars stood with their wheels in the gutter, waiting, and higher up sparrows chipped without purpose.

On the other side of the street the houses had bay windows and yard-wide gardens behind low walls and grey privet, but on Larne's side the houses were flat-faced with only a stone step between them and the pavement. Some of the steps were painted and clean and most still had milk bottles on them.

Larne walked to the open end of the street, smoking at intervals. The air was cool and shadows were long and there was a mixture of clarity and haze that said another hot day without rain. By ten the sun would have burned out any life in the air.

At the corner Larne dropped his cigarette in the gutter and glanced back. A woman he knew by sight was coming out of a house below his. She began to follow his path, already dressed for the weather in a light cotton dress which exposed her shoulders and arms. She carried a flat straw shopping bag and walked quickly, but Larne wasn't interested.

He turned right again, walking easily with one hand resting in the pocket of his open coat. The streets were still quiet and withdrawn, with curtains still closed and only a few cars grinding past from cold starts. He followed a route he knew, crossing from one pavement to another and taking corners at economical angles without looking back.

Finally he turned out on to a main road which ran north towards London and south through the centre of Croydon. It was brighter there and more open and the sun caught the road's full width from just above roof level. The sky was a soft light blue, wisped with white, but the pavements were hard, grey and arid. Soft dust accumulated in brickwork cracks and clung evenly to paint and windows. Crisp packet and sweet wrapper litter moved in the wake of speeding lorries that made Larne squint as their wake blasted him with grit and diesel fumes.

He walked against the broken stream of traffic for thirty yards or so, then crossed at a quick jog in a gap behind a bus. He slowed at the kerb, took a couple of steps and pushed open the door of a newsagent's shop with a wire rack of papers outside it.

Inside the shop there was only a small space to stand in in front of the freezer cabinet and sloping chocolate displays. An old man in a trilby had stationed himself to one side of the door with a rough-haired dog by his feet. As Larne entered he pulled the dog back against his legs and the shop-owner broke off their talk with a nod of greased hair.

'Morning sir. Lookin' nice again.' The man had a scrubbed look apart from his fingers which were stained with newsprint.

Larne ignored the familiar tone and asked for tobacco and

papers. As the owner got them Larne scanned the overlapping newspapers in front of him. 'Sorry, no *Express* today.' The man laughed sharply. 'Ask me, they're only on strike 'cause of the fine weather.'

From the side the man with the dog grunted. 'Bleedin' unions.'

Larne pulled a *Mirror* from the rows and held out two pound coins.

'Thank you.' The shopkeeper rang in the money and counted change. Larne let him drop it into his palm, took his things with a nod and left the shop.

On the pavement outside he paused in the open for the first time since the corner of his street, clearly scanning the road and the traffic in both directions as he folded the newspaper and pushed it into the back pocket of his jeans. The inspection lasted several seconds, then he set off again at the same place.

The Traffic Café was a two-minute walk from the shop, on a side road faced by semi-detached houses interspaced here and there by impoverished shops that sold tropical fish or hired out fancy dress costumes. A couple of times Larne looked back; once as he left the main road and again as he stepped between two parked cars, crossing to the café on the opposite side. The glances seemed more in the way of confirming something than out of suspicion.

The café was glass-fronted with a wooden-framed door in the centre. Above it a sign as wide as the building gave out its name in bulbous letters, with the 'i' in Traffic painted to look like a traffic light. The paintwork was dirty and dry like the windows. Behind them net curtains were tied back in large loose curves. Larne pushed the bar on the door and went in.

It was five to eight, and although a sign on the door said the café didn't open until seven thirty the air was already hung with the acrid smell of burnt fat. There were two rows of pine tables, three on each side of the room, with a central aisle to the counter at the back. Two tables were occupied; one by a gang of four workmen eating fried breakfasts, the other by one man alone: Danny Mallon.

Mallon was facing the door at a table close to the counter but half-screened from it by a partition that shielded a side exit through into the rear of the café. He waited until Larne had taken the glances of the workmen as the door closed behind him, then lifted his hand in a small salute. Larne acknowledged the greeting with a dip of his chin and went to the counter.

The woman behind it was middle-aged, dressed in a pink nylon housecoat. A thin curl of dark hair fell over her forehead and every minute or so she pushed it back with the back of her hand. She already looked hot and tired of the fat in the air.

Larne glanced at a menu of yellow peg-in letters on a board, then ordered a coffee. The woman made it with a neutral acceptance, adding steam from the coffee machine to the air, carefully holding the cup by its handle. When she put it down in front of him Larne gave her the right money without being asked, picked up a plastic spoon from a glass on the counter and went to join Mallon.

The space between the varnished edge of the table and the chairs was narrow and Larne had to shuffle sideways to get in. He worked his way to the chair by the wall, directly opposite Mallon, and there was a slight look of vexation in his face as he did it. When he finally settled Mallon nodded. 'Joe.'

He was a medium-sized man, with sand-coloured hair that was quite long and curly round the sides but going thin on top. He wore a gold earring in his left ear and his face showed his thirty-odd years. At times his expression would drift back to a slow, natural look of amusement and contempt for whatever was around him, but as Larne tore open a packet of sugar and tipped it into his coffee Mallon seemed to have lost that distance from things. He looked tired. By his hand there was an empty plate scattered with crumbs and a half finished mug of tea.

'All right, Joe?' he asked.

Larne nodded, stirred his coffee and raised his eyes. 'As far as I can tell. Except you can't tell till they drop on you. Where did you call from?'

'A box down the road.'

'Couldn't it wait?'

'For what? I just carry, Joe; you know that. I don't hold. I picked the stuff up and now I'm delivering. You aren't the only one, but you're the last, and then I'm going home to my bed.'

Larne took out his tobacco tin and began to make a cigarette. He cast a glance at the woman behind the counter but she had her back turned and the four workmen and the drone of a radio were enough to cover his words.

'Where's it from?'

'The States I suppose.'

'Where did you pick it up?'

'Oh. Amsterdam.' He lit a cigarette, a Gauloise, and looked sharp for a moment, as if he'd been reminded of something.

'Is there much?'

'Just the one case. Six in it.'

'Have you checked it?'

'Yeah.' He finished his mug of tea. 'Let's go.' But he didn't move and neither did Larne.

'You aren't in that much of a hurry,' Larne said and put the cigarette in his left hand so he could pick up his cup with his right. 'Why didn't you come to the yard?'

Mallon looked past the older man's shoulder, at the door. 'The stuff's in the van. I didn't want it sitting around for another couple of hours till you got there. I've been waiting since seven already.'

He broke off as the door opened and a man with a large beer gut and a grubby white shirt came in. He paid no attention to anyone as he went to the counter, ordered and then took a mug of tea to a table by the window. He sat looking out at the road. In the silence between them, Larne drank some coffee and smoked and seemed to be waiting for Mallon to stop watching the fat man.

'Who's the kid - Hagen?' he asked then.

Mallon frowned a little, took a drag on his cigarette, then spoke breathing the smoke out. 'You've met him?'

'He came for a short a couple of days ago. He said McGiven had sent him because you were away. What's he doing?'

Mallon didn't answer the question directly. Instead, after a moment, he said: 'You've heard of Paul Hagen, the one doing life in Wakefield? Hagen's his brother, called David.'

'Bacon sandwich!' The woman behind the counter put the plate out and the fat man got up again and came for it. Mallon looked at his watch and when the fat man had gone back he stood up.

Larne took a last sip of his coffee, then stood up as well and the two men worked their way out from the table towards the door.

Outside the street noise had increased and there was more passing movement. Mallon angled right across the narrow forecourt of the café. He dropped his cigarette and trod on it and somehow being outside seemed to lighten his aspect. They walked twenty yards along the road and turned a corner by a hairdresser's shop into a street where Mallon's blue Bedford van was parked by a lamp post. An electric milk float rattled over a pot hole and jerked to a halt at the far end of the street.

'Is Hagen carrying for McGiven?' Larne said as they approached the van.

Mallon rattled his keys. 'Not full time. Somebody told me he'd come to run a unit. I don't know. They say he's a good sniper; got it from his brother.'

'Paul Hagen was jailed for bombing,' Larne said.

'Yeah.'

Mallon opened the passenger door, then went round and opened his own. He started the van as soon as he was settled, pushing the ignition heater with one hand while twisting the keys. When the diesel engine fired he revved it, let off the brake and accelerated fast in first to the street junction. He paused only briefly and pushed the engine again, slipping out into a narrow break in the traffic.

He handled the van well, getting the most work from the engine before changing gear, watching the traffic in front and turning the wheel deftly. There was a compressed feel of economy in the way he drove; workman-like, but perhaps slightly too tight to be called relaxed. And for a while he followed a course that kept him moving, sometimes away from where he was heading, rather than have to wait and give way at junctions. Larne made no comment on that, though he watched the corners and turns. And when Mallon eventually did come on to the road that led to the scrap-yard Larne turned in his seat to look in the back of the van.

The chipped paint and battered plyboard lining the sides and floor, combined with cement dust spilling out of a paper sack and the remains of a load of sand, were just like any working van. A bucket of bricklayer's tools was wedged behind a wheel arch and behind the seats there was an up-turned wheelbarrow and a couple of shovels over a pile of old polythene sacks. Larne turned back, apparently satisfied.

'Are you still driving for Gillespie?'

'Same as before,' Mallon said factually. 'When he needs me, or when there's a load to bring in.'

'Tell McGiven, I don't want him sending strangers around to collect.'

Mallon glanced at him, then back at the road. 'You mean Hagen?'

'Anyone I don't know.'

Mallon turned off the main road, past a cemetery, close to the railway line now. After another bend he slowed the van and pulled in alongside the scrap-yard gate. He watched the mirror for a moment, leaving the engine running. No other car came past and the narrow road was deserted. He turned to Larne who was waiting.

'I don't know what happened,' he said, lighting a cigarette. 'I haven't seen him since Monday. If he needed it in a hurry while I was away he'd have to send somebody else. Hagen should be all right.'

'He's not a carrier,' Larne said, uncompromising. 'He knows fuck all about it. I don't work like that. Tell McGiven: next time he sends someone who knows what they're doing or he gets nothing.'

He paused. Mallon examined the filter of his cigarette before drawing on it, then nodded. 'Okay, Joe.'

Larne opened his door and got down from the van.

The Alsatian and the mongrel were waiting inside the gate as he came round the van, and the Alsatian barked twice through the steel grill until Larne gave a brief whistle to silence it. He unlocked the padlock and went into the yard, leaving the gate closed behind him. The mongrel came close to his leg to be patted but the Alsatian stood off, then followed them to its cage, knowing the routine and speeding up to a trot at the last moment and slinking in through the gate, as if to prevent usurpers.

Mallon watched from the road, and as Larne latched the cage the carrier edged the van forward, nudging the gate open with its bumper. When he was clear of it he accelerated, bumping over the ruts, following Larne's outstretched hand towards the top of the yard. After a look at the road Larne followed on foot.

When he got to the van Mallon had killed the engine and opened the back doors. He had also moved the wheelbarrow aside and pulled a shallow rectangular wooden box from beneath it. The box was made of soft fibrous white wood, tacked together with staples and six inches of it stuck out past the end of the van. Mallon held a large screwdriver with a sharp blade and with his cigarette in his mouth gave Larne a questioning look.

'Want to check?'

Larne nodded and Mallon began levering up staples. 'Second time today,' he said, thumping the butt of the screwdriver with his palm. 'These bloody staples are rubbish.'

'How long have I got them?'

'A few days, a month, I don't know; depends where they're going. Keep them handy.'

'Together?'

'Yeah.'

Larne said: 'I'll give it a week, then I'll move them out somewhere.'

Mallon paused his work with the screwdriver. 'They might want a quick turn round – in and out.'

'It'll be fast enough.'

'Okay, that's your business.'

He slid the blade under the lid of the box and jerked it. There was the sound of wood and drawn metal. The staples on one side of the box bent and the lid came up as if it was hinged. Mallon pushed it right back until more wood broke and it stayed upright, out of the way.

There were six assault rifles in the box – Kalashnikov AKMs – packed in layered pairs, muzzle to butt, their forward curving magazines overlapping in the middle. A rough attempt to cushion them had been made with shredded paper, but the stuff did little except fill spaces. The rifles themselves had an appearance of slight use; the odd mark on the wood of a stock and the past-new greyness of the stamped-steel sides.

'All right?' Mallon asked.

'All right for me. Are they loaded?'

'Shouldn't be; no one said they were. I can check.'

'No, leave them be,' Larne said, looking at his watch and then at the wrecks beside the van. 'We'll put them back there. I'll cover them when you've gone.'

Mallon pushed down the lid of the box and then the two men slid it out of the van and carried its dead weight between them. They manoeuvred it between two cars and put it down in long grass behind them. Larne went off and came back with a warped sun-beaten bonnet and dropped it over the box. He looked at it critically for a moment, then moved away.

On the track Mallon closed the van's doors. 'Do you still want me to tell McGiven what you said?'

'He should know it already. I'm known. What happens if Hagen walks in and a couple of coppers are doing a spot check?'

A shade of suspicion moved across Mallon's face, but briefly. 'Are you worried about the police?' he asked.

'I am when McGiven sends little boys on pick ups.' He dug in his pocket for his tobacco tin. 'A man makes a mistake and someone else pays. You know what I'm talking about.'

'Yeah. Okay,' Mallon said with a nod. He shifted his feet, then tapped the van door lightly, ending the meeting. 'I'll be around, Joe.'

'Okay.'

Mallon got into the van and started the engine. He followed the track round where it made an island of scrapped cars and went out of sight, grinding in first gear. There was still a trace of dew on the ground, so only a little dust rose in his wake. The Alsatian barked as he passed, but the van's engine noise faded quickly as he turned out into the road.

For a while after Mallon had left Larne didn't move. He stood with his head down, rolling a cigarette, and only looked up when it was lit. It was quiet in the yard, secluded where he stood, and his eyes moved absently over the broken, bent frames around him. He had a half-present look of dissatisfaction now that he was alone, as if his sense of it was too indistinct to define, but something about Mallon had been out of tune.

The second drag on his cigarette caught in his throat and made him cough. He hawked and spat on the dry ground. There was half an hour before the yard normally opened and the place seemed quieter for that, but he moved then, pushing himself out of the stillness.

He went down the yard, fed the dogs from a store of tins in the office and put on a pair of steel-capped boots. A train passed on the line and he carried a shovel back to the long grass where the rifles had been dumped. He worked steadily for twenty minutes. Once or twice he paused and looked across at the flat empty sidings beyond the fence, with spear-shaft weeds between the rails. Further on, a line of houses looked out over the same thing from a different angle. Nothing moved and nothing disturbed him and by nine o'clock he'd buried the rifles two feet down and disguised the place with replaced turfs and a heap of old doors and body panels. When he walked away he seemed satisfied.

THREE

August blazed without rain for another week and the prolonged heat seemed to run one day into another like an arctic summer when the sun didn't set and the division of time was somehow false and unnatural and meant nothing. The scrapyard was quiet because it was a holiday month and when there was no work to do Larne passed the time doing nothing. Being still seemed to come easily to him and he didn't try to fill his time with either people or things.

There was that same sense about him when he sat in a pub called the Flagship eight days after he'd seen Mallon. It was lunch time and the door of the pub was propped open. Most of the drinkers were outside in the sun, sitting on heavy pine benches only a couple of yards from the traffic on a main road, kept distant from it by their beer and their talk.

Inside it was cooler and quieter. A few people leaned on the bar and the air was still and stratified by thin cigarette smoke. Larne was alone in a side room with a pint of beer on the unvarnished table top in front of him. He sat with a foot on the cross bar of the table's cast-metal base, his knee drawn up slightly. He was in his work clothes and his hands were only rinsed clean. He watched a couple of flies circle a dusty hearth and its grey-metalled gas fire that hadn't been lit since April, then looked away.

He had a view of part of the bar through a door frame; a man in shorts and another stripped to the waist, the barmaid in a large Indian shirt. He watched them without interest and then Hagen came in.

He stood at the bar where Larne could see him, but until he'd ordered a drink he didn't look round. When he did he saw Larne and then, as if surprised at being watched, his eyes flicked away. They were gone for a moment, then came back and stayed there. Larne didn't move.

The barmaid put Hagen's drink down and he turned, spoke to her and waited, pulling money out of his jeans. Finally he paid the woman and picked up two pints of beer.

Hagen walked into the side room and nodded, but Larne still didn't shift. His eyes were studied and cool as they followed Hagen's movements. Hagen put one of the glasses down by Larne's other and sat facing him. He nodded again, said 'Cheers' and drank.

Larne leaned forward, taking his foot off its rest as Hagen lowered his glass. 'That better be the last drink you buy me,' he said with his voice low. 'And the last time I see you, because you're either stupid or careless, and whichever it is I don't want you round.'

For a moment Hagen's face was a mixture of puzzled and surprised, but as Larne continued to stare at him the expression became harder.

'This is business,' he said. 'It doesn't matter what you want.'

'Who told you that – McGiven?'

Hagen didn't reply.

'Did he tell you I'm known, too?'

'Listen—' Hagen said shortly.

'*You* listen. I told Mallon for McGiven; I don't work with strangers. He knows that and if he doesn't like it he can find someone else to do his holding. Tell him.'

'That's shit. You know who I am.'

Larne sat back slowly and relit his cigarette. He stared at Hagen through the first draw on it. 'Where's Mallon?' he asked then, his voice passive.

'Gone away.' The tough edge was still in Hagen's voice.

'What d'you want?'

Hagen took a slightly crushed packet of cigarettes from his back pocket, withdrew one and lit it. 'The load Mallon left with you,' he said.

'Okay. When?'

'I'll bring the van to the yard in an hour.'

Larne shook his head. 'Tonight, half-past nine. Don't be early or late.'

'They're needed now. Get rid of the old man and it'll only take five minutes.'

'They're not in the yard.'

For a second Hagen was still, then he spoke with a hiss. 'Jesus *Christ*. Mallon told you we might want them fast. Where are they?'

Larne watched his anger neutrally. 'They're safe enough.'
'That's not—' He broke off. 'When did you move them?'
'Last night.'

'You couldn't have waited a day? Bloody hell. Who're you supposed to be working for anyway. D'you know you've screwed up a whole bloody schedule? McGiven won't like it.'

Larne put his glass down and leaned forward slightly. 'If you planned your jobs properly there wouldn't be any rush.'

Hagen gave him a contemptuous glare and made to get up, but Larne's left hand moved faster and banged down on Hagen's forearm, pinning it to the table top. His crooked fingers didn't grip it but the pressure was enough.

'Nine thirty,' he said. 'By yourself. Stop at the gate and wait. If you think there's someone following you keep going and crash a gear as you pass, then ring the yard tomorrow.'

Hagen looked up from Larne's hand, then nodded. The older man relaxed the pressure and drew back his hand. Hagen got up, straight, turned and walked out. When he'd gone Larne sat back, unconsciously flexing his fingers.

Just after one Larne left the pub and walked back to the yard. The sun had burned off any cloud and it was hot and unpleasant. The air was acid, stinking and dead from exhaust fumes. It was a short-tempered day of sweat and glare and poison drawn out of the bricks, and even Larne seemed to feel it. As he followed the road he glanced round once or twice, perhaps in case Hagen was still hanging around, but if he was Larne didn't see him.

The yard gate was open and he went in past an old Scammel tow truck to the office. Wally Osbourne was still on his chair in the corner, hunched up, reading yesterday's *Standard* and eating a sandwich. He was the yard's owner, at least sixty-five; a small wiry man wearing a greasy deerstalker pushed back on his head and a stained plaid jacket over his shirt. His face was hawk-like and bellicose and he wore brown, plastic-framed glasses on a hook nose.

He looked up with crumbs in his untrimmed, cigarette-stained moustache as Larne came in. 'Fuckin' coppers,' Wally said and reached out to turn off a radio on the floor beside him.

'What about them?' Larne sat on the typist's chair by the desk and turned it so he could look at the old man.

'Comin' pokin' round 'ere, that's what.' He sounded as if he'd been saving it up. 'Ten minutes after you'd gone – two of 'em, *and* one was a bleedin' woman. Jesus Christ! Says they're checkin' the records on new cars been scrapped, write-offs. Supposed to be a gang usin' the plates on stolen cars, so can they see the books. Then he says, *what about a cuppa then?* Fuck me! I told him, I don't buy tea for no fuckin' plods to drink, bleedin' tax we pay. I tell ya kid, some of 'em want fuckin' jam on it.'

Larne nodded and began to roll a cigarette. 'How long did they stay?'

'About five minutes, and that's too bloody long for me.' He rushed a cigarette of his own from a tin case, lit it and puffed hard. 'Nothin' for you, though,' he added.

'Sure?'

'Yeah. I've 'ad fifty years of coppers, kid. I can *smell* what they want, but they wouldn't get nothin' from me. I told ya, I don't care a fuck.'

Larne struck a light and let that go with just a nod of acknowledgement because it was true. Two years before Wally had found a cached pistol by accident and shown it to Larne. He could have guessed by the way it was hidden that Larne had put it there, but when Larne took it away again without comment Wally had done nothing. Larne hadn't asked why, and after a week of added wariness he'd just accepted that that was how it was. The old man didn't care, and the only times the subject was mentioned were like now, through an oblique reference, when sides could be drawn.

Wally leaned over the arm of his chair, crushing the newspaper on his lap. He picked up a mug of tea from the floor and had it half-way to his mouth before he remembered something else. 'Oh yeah, a bloke rang. Wanted to know where you were. Business he said. Did he find you?'

'Yeah, I saw him.'

Wally drank noisily and changed the subject. 'So who's goin' to fetch that fuckin' wreck from Slaney's? I 'ad 'im on the blower an' all. It's gettin' to be a bleedin' answerin' service in 'ere. You want me to go?'

Larne shook his head and stood up. 'I'll fetch it. He's got a couple of new ones to look at. Do you want me to put in a bid?'

'Please yourself, kid. I ain't goin' to stop you. Fuck it, you've got the cheque book.'

'Did you get some more meat for the dogs?'

'No, and I ain't goin' to. I'm starvin' 'em for if them coppers come back. Give 'em a taste for the bastards.'

Larne chuckled. 'Just mind it's not you they start tasting. I'll be back.'

He waved a hand and went out.

Slaney's garage was on the edge of West Wickham, built in whitewashed concrete going grey; neat, with rounded corners and square, steel-framed windows. It was a style that looked sharp and modern in British films of the postwar decade, but now its age and design gave it a look of an old toy, emphasised by newer buildings that had gone up around it. When it was built it had stood alone by the road, almost in the country, but only a few trees at the back showed any sign of its past. It still had a couple of petrol pumps on the forecourt, but it had lost most of that trade to a plastic, self-service discount station further along the road.

Larne had reversed the tow truck round to the back of the garage where there was a strip of tarmac between the building and a wall-edged grass bank a few feet high. Five or six trees at the top of the bank cast permanent shade on the ground and the roofs of three cars which were spaced out in a line.

Larne was on his back, half under the first car, manoeuvring a hook and chain around a displaced suspension arm. The whole front end of the car and part of its roof was caved in and buckled by impact but he had already managed to secure a similar hook on the other side, ready to tow.

Finally he got the thing as he wanted it and edged out and sat up as John Slaney came out through the barn-like doors at the rear of the garage. He was about the same age as Larne, but he was fatter and looked older. He had his shirt sleeves rolled up and a loose tie round his neck. As he came out of the garage he made a show of arching his back and stretching. The movement briefly removed his double chin.

'All right, Joe? Got it fixed up okay?'

Larne stood up and dusted himself down as Slaney made to shake hands. The gesture was automatic and didn't mean very much.

'It'll hold,' Larne said, looking in through the car's empty windscreen to check that the handbrake was off.

'Towing or carrying?'

'Towing.'

'Well come and look at these two first. See what you reckon. Might be some good to you.' Slaney held out a guiding hand towards the other two write-offs.

The first was a red Mini, it's paintwork still new; but like the one Larne had hooked up its front was an impact-destroyed tangle, almost unrecognisable. There were small chips of glass littering the dashboard and the floor inside, and dried blood on the driver's seat. The off-side door was missing and there were marks from emergency cutting gear around the door pillar.

'Head on smash,' Slaney said. 'Near Leaves Green. The police said he overtook blind and a lorry caught him. Christ knows what happened then. He got pushed sideways into that thing.' He nodded at the third car, a Lada Estate. 'Woman and two kids in that. The bloke in the Mini was dead when they got him to hospital. No bloody wonder. Which d'you fancy; one or both?'

Larne looked at the Lada, caved in all the way down one side. 'How much?'

'Three. The Lada's all right except for the shell. I was thinking about buying a new shell and rebuilding it but I haven't got the time.' He paused and waited without pressure while Larne thought about it.

Then Larne shook his head. 'The Lada's no good. There aren't enough around to get rid of the spares. People who've got them go to the dealers. Fifty for the Mini.'

'Fifty? Do me a favour. It isn't that bad.'

'Chop it yourself then, you'll find out.'

'Eighty.'

'No.'

A mechanic whistled from the garage. 'Phone! Someone for Joe.'

Slaney waved an acknowledgement. 'If that's Wally you ask him about the Lada.' Then he laughed and huffed in an imitation of the old man. 'Fuckin' Ladas. Jesus Christ, kid, fuck me.'

'I'll tell him,' Larne said with a mild grin and moved off towards the garage.

Inside a radio was echoing round the work bay and an air compressor was ticking over in a corner. The mechanic had gone back to work on the underside of a car on a ramp but he called across as Larne came in. 'How's life, Joe? Stella's got the phone in the office. Tell her to put the tea on.'

Larne tipped his head. 'Okay.'

The office was a cube in the front corner of the building, with a window looking out over the road and another in at the workshop. Inside it was divided in two by a thin wall – one side for a secretary, the other for Slaney. The door between was propped open.

A girl of about twenty-five was typing out an itemised bill in the first half of the office, but she stopped and turned on her chair, smiling, as Larne walked on to the thin carpet. She had dark red hair, wore a flimsy-looking blouse and had a face that was pleasant but pale. She said, 'Hi, Joe. Phone for you.'

'Who is it, Stell? Wally?'

'No, someone called Presley or Plessy, I didn't catch it properly. He's in a phone box. Here.' She gestured to a phone with a lighted hold button.

Larne paused for a second, then said, 'Can I take it in there?'

'Sure. Trade secrets?'

'Everything's secret with your boss around.' He moved towards Slaney's office. 'Oh, and Dave says he's thirsty.'

'That's nothing new. I'll put it through.'

Larne went into the office, pushing a door-stop away with his foot. The door swung closed on its own.

The office was tidy and bare, as if it wasn't used much. Its walls were plaster painted light blue instead of the wood-effect wallpaper in the outer office. It was more open, but it felt empty, like somewhere ready to be sold.

With his back to the door Larne picked up the phone on Slaney's desk. He didn't sit down or even rest against the desk and his eyes stared out of the window at the road. 'Yes Danny,' he said.

'Joe. Listen. Two things.' Danny Mallon's voice was clear and clipped. It sounded concentrated but not excited. 'There's going to be some events soon, so get your stuff put away. Follow me?'

'Yes. What else.' Larne's voice matched Mallon's; toneless.

'Have you moved the stuff I gave you?'

'Yesterday.'

'Is it okay—' The pips went, cutting him off, but he immediately pushed more money in and when it fell his voice came back. 'Is it okay where it is?'

'Yes.'

'All right. I'll be round to collect it tonight. I'll pick you up.'

'When?'

'Late. I've got some other things to do. After twelve. I'll come to the house.'

Larne was silent.

'Joe? Okay?'

'Okay. Are you all right, no trouble?'

'No. Listen, I meant it about the stock. The blues'll be checking.'

'I'll see to it.'

'Right. I've got to go. I'll see you tonight.'

'Yeah.'

Larne hung up and after a second he went back to the other office. Stella was putting tea into mugs beside a filing cabinet, on top of which a kettle was coming to the boil. She stood with a cigarette between the very ends of her fingers, held away from her side as if she didn't like the smoke. 'Like a cuppa?' she asked.

'No, thanks, I've got to go.'

'Trade secrets all right?'

'Still secret. See you, Stell.'

'Bye, Joe.'

The garage was filled by the rip sound of an air driven drill and Slaney was watching the mechanic work. As Larne went over to them the sound stopped and the mechanic swore. He looked round as Larne approached. 'Tea ready yet, Joe? I'm pissed off with this.'

'Just about,' Larne said, and to Slaney: 'Did Wally pay you for the wreck?'

'Yeah, all settled.'

'Okay, I'll see you next time.'

'Here, what about the Mini then? You want it?'

'For fifty?'

'Jesus Christ, you're worse than that miserable old sod you work for.'

'Yes or no; I've got things to do.'

The humour dropped out of Slaney. 'Okay Joe, fifty, but you're not doing me any favours.'

Larne nodded and gave a perfunctory smile. 'I'll pick it up tomorrow.'

'Need a hand with the winch?' the mechanic offered.

'No, I'll manage. Thanks. See ya.'

He walked out of the garage and Slaney shook his head. 'See what it gets you?'

FOUR

Larne turned the Scammel into the yard with the engine in low gear and noisy. Just past the office he hauled the wheel in a tight turn so that the car behind was between the two tracks without blocking them. He stopped the engine and got down.

Wally had created an area of shade by raising the bonnet of an Escort and working beneath it at the bottom of the railway embankment. He'd stripped to his braces and shirt and rolled up his sleeves. His jacket and hat hung on a wing mirror and his bony, vein-standing arms were deep into the car's engine compartment. On the ground beside his open tool box were the radiator and starter motor.

'You 'ad my bleedin' ratchet?' he demanded as Larne came over. He turned his head but stayed bent over.

'No.'

'Well some fucker 'as.' He looked back at his work, turning a spanner, 'You 'ad another call while you was out. I gave 'im Slaney's number.'

'Yeah, I got it.' Larne squatted down, resting his back against the side of a slightly shaded car, facing Wally. The mongrel was there, lying on its side with its legs stuck out. He patted it a couple of times but it only rolled its eyes. 'Slaney's got a Mini. I said we'd take it.'

'How much?'

'Fifty. The engine should be all right. It's a year old.'

Wally grunted meaninglessly. 'What about the other one?'

'A Lada.'

'Bloody Russian crap.'

'Yeah, well it's a rebuild job anyway.'

Wally extricated himself from the car and tossed his spanner into the tool box with a clatter. 'Fuck it. What's the time?'

'Quarter to three.'

'What time you finishing tonight?'

'Late.'

The old man gauged that, then nodded once. 'Let's get that

29

thing off the truck. I said I'd take the old woman shopping. The fuckin' sales is on again.'

Larne stood up and the two men went to the tow truck. When they'd lowered the car behind it and detached the chains Wally got into the cab and took it up one side of the yard and back down the other so it was facing the road. He left the engine running while he collected his hat and coat.

'Lock my tools up will ya, kid. I'll see ya tomorrow; that's if I ain't bankrupt by then.'

Larne waved a hand and the old man drove out of the yard.

At five, with the sun burning orange and a slight breeze out of nowhere but still no clouds in the sky, Larne stopped work. He'd had a couple of customers since Wally had gone and had started to strip the wreck from Slaney's, but when he began to pack up he still hadn't got as far as removing the engine.

He gathered his tools methodically, but instead of putting them away in the shed he left them outside and went to close the gate on to the road. He did it from the inside but deliberately pushed the padlock and chain through the mesh so they hung on the outside, as if he'd gone home. He took a look at the road but there was nothing there.

The mongrel followed him, waiting to be fed. He put dog food on two enamel plates, gave one to the dog in the office and took the other to the Alsatian's cage, collecting his tool box on the way. The Alsatian was also waiting for the routine and didn't bark as Larne let it out to eat. He left it and went on up the yard.

It took him just over an hour to collect all his stock. There were eleven pistols – revolvers and semi-automatics – each with enough ammunition to load them at least once. Their hiding places varied, though; from oil sump pans and exhaust baffles to small, unmarked burial places. Larne had put thought and care into hiding them, and he was equally careful to leave no sign that they had been removed. He handled them all as little as possible and when he had them together in a hessian sack he left them in the boot of a car close to the place where he'd first cached Mallon's rifles, and went back to the office.

The light faded slowly outside, but in the office it became a dim half-presence more quickly. Larne didn't put the light on. He had made tea and then settled with it and half a packet of biscuits and a newspaper. He didn't smoke much, and when it became too dark to read he sat with his eyes lightly closed, resting and waiting.

It was nearly half-past eight when he came out of his stillness and he seemed to judge the light and the temperature of the air as if they were new to him. Then he struck a light to half a cigarette and stood up.

The mongrel was lying across the doorway but it got up and followed him, as if it had been waiting too. He took a shovel from the shed and went back to the place where he'd left the sack of pistols. The Alsatian didn't show itself and by now it was too dark to see into corners. Even in the open the blue dusk light robbed things of detail. The sun had gone and it was cooler.

With the shovel and sack Larne moved along the fence until he came to a place where two pieces of mesh met at a concrete post. On the other side the ground dropped away in a dry weed-grown slope to the railway sidings. In the background the windows of half a dozen houses put out squares of yellow light.

Larne untwisted three pieces of wire that held the fence together and then pushed one side inwards. He passed the shovel through the gap he'd made, dropping it on the other side, then ducked through himself. The wire links rubbed his shoulder and he pulled the sack after him, but when the mongrel looked like coming too he said 'Stay' and pushed the wire back, closing the hole.

He went down the bank at an angle with brittle-stemmed weeds rustling against his legs, giving out a dry dusty scent. At the bottom he turned, away from the yard and the houses and paralleled the bank, walking quickly. The ground there was covered in purple-black cinders which crunched under his boots.

About twenty yards on the bank cornered inwards to his right for ten or twelve feet before going forward again. He followed the corner and stopped out of sight of the houses and everything else except the lifeless, converging railway tracks. It was so dark now that even things close to were difficult to distinguish.

31

Larne stopped where a piece of Victorian brickwork protruded from the bank like a partially exposed ruin. Once it could have been a drainage outlet or some other form of culvert, but now only part of the roof and two sides were exposed because it had filled up with cinders and soil. Yesterday had been the first time he'd used it and he peered at its shape in the darkness as if he still wasn't sure about its safety. Then he put down the sack and began to work.

The angle of the slope made it awkward. He had to bend forward to get the blade of the shovel into the earth in the culvert and his crippled left hand couldn't grip well enough to do more than guide the blade. Despite that, using the weight of his body to push the shovel in, he took nearly a shovelful each time, turning and dropping it in a pile behind him. He dug about a foot into the soil, making a square hole, then knelt down and put his hand in, scraping and searching. There was only a faint light from a low quarter moon, but his hand found a piece of rope and pulled it out as far as it would easily come.

He stood up and pulled harder. The weight on the other end of the rope moved and he stepped back, keeping up the pressure. He took two paces and then the box with the rifles inside slid out and down the slope.

Larne unfastened the rope, which was looped lengthways around the box, and retied it round the neck of the sack. Leaving the box where it was he used the shovel to push the sack right back into the hole and it seemed to slide down at the last, as if the culvert was unblocked further back. He left the rope trailing and filled in the hole with the earth he'd removed, finally tamping it down with his hand and scattering dead weeds and cinders over the place. With his boot he scuffed the cinders where the soil pile had been.

He straightened and tilted the face of his watch to see the faintly luminous hands. After a moment he dropped his arm with a glance down the railway lines and squatted beside the box. In the darkness its wood was a blurred patch of whiteness and he brushed soil from it, as if gauging its size and the best way to lift it.

It wasn't easy; it was low down, had no handles and weighed nearly sixty pounds. He worked his right hand under one long side and gripped the wood as best he could with his left. He paused for a second, then heaved, straightening his legs and bringing the box in against his body. The weight tried to pull him off balance but he kept the lift going, quickly changing grip so both his forearms were under the thing, then heaving again and dropping his shoulder to catch it. For a moment the box was tilted but he manoeuvred it level and kept it that way, supporting it with a hand. He pulled the shovel from the ground with his free hand and started back the way he had come.

His footsteps were heavy and by the time he reached the bottom of the bank below the gap in the fence his breathing was hard and his face was strained. Facing the bank he paused for a second, shifting the weight as if to ease his shoulder, then pushed forward, using the shovel to steady himself.

He grunted with effort after three steps but made another two up the slope before the dead weight of the box finally pulled too far forward to hold and fell, a couple of feet short of the top. He let it go and stood with his head bowed and his hands on his knees, rasping air back to his lungs.

After a while he straightened slowly, as if waking, and spat to clear his mouth. He seemed to be listening, but there was nothing to hear. He bent again to the box and in a final effort against its uncompromising weight he shoved it to the top of the bank.

The Alsatian barked as he brought the box through the fence but he silenced it with a couple of hard words and re-sealed the gap. It was twenty-past nine, and by the time he'd lured the dog back to its cage he was waiting for the sound of Hagen's van.

When it came it was soft; an engine being guided not driven, almost coasting. The road was quiet and it was exactly on time.

Larne was standing back from the gate, out of sight behind a column of tyres, with the key to the padlock in his hand. The engine sound came closer, then the beams of dipped headlights swung across the gate and into the yard and there was a faint squeak of brakes. Larne shifted slightly but held back. The headlights died and then he stepped out. In their faint after-glow it was just possible to make out the van's shape and colour and also the faint blur of a face at the wheel.

Larne moved quickly, unlocked the padlock and rattled the chain free. He pushed the gate open and Hagen edged the van forward, halting five yards inside. Larne went to the passenger door and spoke through the half-open window: 'Follow the track to the top and wait. I'll be there.'

Inside Hagen nodded and switched on his sidelights. His face became visible in the half light of the dashboard. 'Have you got the stuff?'

'It's up there.'

'Okay.' He pushed the car into gear and drove on. Behind him Larne closed and relocked the gate.

Hagen stopped the van where the track turned. He sat across the seat with the door open and the interior light on. The radio was playing very quietly between fades in the reception and his cigarette smoke drifted idly until it was lost from the weak light in the van. When Larne came up and stood by the end of the door Hagen made no move to rise. He seemed to study Larne for a while and then he said: 'How long've you been here?'

Larne gave a small shrug. 'Since I closed up.'

'Want a smoke?' He flipped the lid of a packet and held it out.

Reaching forward Larne took one with his left hand, and Hagen's eyes followed it until it withdrew. Larne struck a light and as he breathed smoke he looked round briefly and backed up to rest against the boot of a wreck. 'Thanks,' he said.

Hagen dipped his head. 'How's your hand?'

The look on Larne's face shifted in the dead yellow light. He frowned, but it was a questioning look – as if the enquiry surprised him because the answer was self evident. 'It's all right,' he said.

'McGiven told me about it. I asked him.'

Larne grunted.

'Is that why you don't carry any more?' His eyes were fixed on Larne with no trace of self-consciousness.

'No, I've got a record.'

'But you're holding.'

'Yeah, and the stuff's over there if you still want it. I thought you were in a hurry.'

'We changed the times. I've got to be in Watford by two. There's no hurry, they're going north.'

'With Mallon?' Larne drew on his cigarette and flicked ash.

'He hasn't been around for a while.'

Hagen pulled his own cigarette down to the filter and

flipped it away. He lifted his head to blow out the smoke and looked at the sky. 'It's a nice night,' he said, then lowered his gaze. 'Listen, I'll be around for a bit. I'll need to drop some things and pick them up later on, like this lot. So I'll be coming to you sometimes, okay?'

'How long and how often?'

'I don't know. A few months.'

'For McGiven?'

'Some of it.'

'What about the rest?'

Hagen cocked his head and looked shrewd. 'It'll be properly used.'

Larne was still for a moment, then he dropped his cigarette and trod on it, standing upright. 'Did you give McGiven the short you picked up?'

Hagen smiled. 'No, I kept that one for myself.' He reached under the dashboard and took it out. He held it at an angle, resting on his leg, but the muzzle was pointing at Larne. There was silence and Larne didn't move. Hagen was still watching him, but when the older man did nothing he laughed shortly, turned the gun and put it away.

'Listen, Joe,' he said. 'I don't work for Johnny McGiven, I work *with* him. That's how it is. We both get orders and sometimes they're the same. If you want to check, go and see him, he'll tell you. I don't mind. You don't want mistakes.' He looked at Larne's crippled hand, then back at his face. 'You've got it all right here. You're careful; that's the best way. I'll not be coming every day, just now and then, that's all, no trouble. Okay? Let's get the guns.'

He got out of the van and Larne led the way to the box. Behind him Hagen kept talking – just talk – as if he was trying to bind them together now, or lead Larne to some subtle point. When they got to the box Hagen tapped it lightly with his toe. 'What do you think about this lot? Have you looked at them?'

Larne said 'They're okay,' and bent down to hold one end. 'Got it?'

'Yeah.'

They lifted and moved the box and when they had it in the back of the van Larne finally put more than two words together.

'Two things,' he said. 'If you want to leave stuff, or pick it

35

up, don't do it in dribs and drabs. You don't want to get your face or the van known around here, so do it all at one time. If you want something while the old man might be around, ring me. He's not involved, and I don't want him to be.'

Hagen brushed his hands clean and leaned on the van's rear door. 'Okay, but you don't—'

Larne gestured flatly. 'No, I'm not telling you how, just setting it out so you know the best way. It goes smoother if you know.'

'Okay,' Hagen said, bowing to that. 'What's the other thing?'

'Danny Mallon.'

'What about him?'

'Have you seen him?'

He shook his head and closed the back doors. 'I told you, he hasn't been around for a while.' He faced back to Larne. 'Why?'

'You ought to sort out who picks up what or you'll both be coming in for the same thing.'

'I'll see to it. Anything else?'

'Just let me know when someone's out to hit a few targets. If I know I can get things clear in case the coppers come round.'

'Will they?'

'They might.'

Hagen moved round to the side of the van. 'I'll see you're warned. Thanks, Joe. I'll see you again.' He held out his hand to shake and after a second Larne did. As Hagen got into the van he went to open the gate.

It already seemed light, at four in the morning. Where Larne sat he caught faint movements of cool air reaching down from the top frame of the bedroom window. Below and off to the right, at an angle, there was a small allotment patch and a sloping playing field, lined at the edge by street lights; a line of regular orange, spaced by their haloes. There was a light mist over the grass but it hid nothing. The glass of the allotment sheds was grey and the concrete posts of the surrounding fence were pale white. He could see in almost as much detail as in daylight: see enough to snipe. There were no bird sounds yet, but when an occasional car passed down the slope of the road under the lights its sound was magnified and forewarning without focus. He would watch it, follow its course like a glide, and when it was gone he went back to waiting.

But Danny Mallon didn't come, or use the phone, either that night or during the following two days of the weekend.

FIVE

On the Monday morning Larne got up late. It was no more than fifteen minutes, but the sounds and movements outside were out of step with routine. He seemed slightly more tired than usual, and it showed most around his eyes and in small movements which could be easily missed. He shaved and dressed as the hydraulic whine of a dustcart moved along the street, and as he went downstairs the letter-box flap rattled.

The letter-box was in the front door and Larne saw the package on the carpet as he went into the room. It was an almost square manila envelope but its contents were bulky and distorted it, and by the way one edge was crumpled it had only just fit through the box.

Larne eyed it, then seemed deliberately to ignore it. He went to the window, passing in front of the sofa, and pulled back the curtains. He paused there for several seconds, then finally went to the front door.

Looking at the package he squatted down and turned his head to read the address. It was written in black biro in capital letters whose individual strokes didn't always meet up. His name was spelled out as MR J LARN and although the house number and road were correct there was no post code. On the corner of the envelope there were two stamps, one of them overlapping a piece of sellotape which seemed to go round underneath and secure the flap. The postmark was dated two days before: Saturday.

Larne drew a breath and stayed on his haunches, assessing the thing. It absorbed him for some time before he reached out with both hands and grasped it gently at either end with the tips of his fingers. He lifted it carefully off the carpet, straightening at the same time and keeping it level. He carried it the same way, almost at arms' length into the back room and set it down in the middle of a drop-leaf formica table by the wall. Then he stood back.

The package wasn't heavy – about half a pound – and from

the way the envelope was creased whatever was inside seemed to be about the size of a paperback book, perhaps half an inch thick. No one sent books to Larne, or even letters apart from bills.

He moved away, pulled back the curtains in that room and then in the kitchen, as if doing that helped him, by distraction, to bring an old catechism to mind. The dustbin men had come round to the back of the houses to collect the rubbish and Larne stared at the orange-overalled man who took his black plastic sack and left the dustbin lid crooked. Larne didn't move from the window until the men had gone and the lorry had drawn down the street.

He kept a few tools and odd pieces of semi-useful junk in a drawer beside the sink and after digging around for a moment he brought out a roll of black insulating tape and a Stanley knife. He took them into the other room and used the knife to cut four six-inch strips of tape from the roll. He turned the envelope so that its flap lay closest to the wall and anchored it securely to the table top with the tape, careful at the same time not to press too hard on the envelope.

With that done he searched out a darning kit from a cupboard and removed a curved needle and a reel of strong brown cotton. He threaded the needle, pulled two feet of thread through its eye, and left the reel attached; then he drew up a chair, sat down and started to work across the table.

His breathing was shallow but his hand was steady as he pushed the point of the needle through the crease on one long side of the envelope. After a moment's juggling for position the needle's point emerged half an inch from the entry point and he drew it clear, followed by an arm's span of cotton. He repeated the operation an eighth of an inch along from the last hole and then again and again.

Ten minutes later the cotton wove in and out down the envelope's side and across the bottom. Larne unthreaded the needle and tied the loose end to the main thread, forming a large loop which he left slack. Finally he took a new reel and stuck its end on to the envelope's stitched corner with tape.

The concentration had cramped him. He sat back and rested his eyes and left hand from the strain. The envelope sat there, inert, barely touched except by the needle, and for a second Larne's face was sour as he looked at it. He stood up and took the spool from the taped-down thread and unwound it as far as the front room, leaving it trailing.

He returned to the table and picked up the reel of stronger cotton and this time he unwound it to an armchair in the corner of the room. He turned the chair so that its back was between him and the table, like a shield, and knelt down behind it.

He reeled in the slack, watching until the thread lifted off the carpet, and then drew back his head. Another foot of thread came and then there was resistance. The loop at the end strained against the thick paper of the envelope and for a moment it looked as if the thread would break before the paper tore, but it didn't. The cotton cut into the crease and Larne kept up the pressure. Section by section it slit the side of the envelope and then the bottom until finally it fell free. There was no explosion.

Larne waited for almost a minute before he stood up, and when he did he saw that the top and bottom of the envelope had separated slightly along the cut, but only by a quarter of an inch. He didn't go near the table. Instead he walked softly round the edge of the room to the door and followed the second thread into the front room. Again he took up the slack and then stood back and raised the corner of the envelope from the point where it was stuck down, but again nothing happened.

Larne tied off the thread on the door handle, still keeping it tight, and checked his watch. It was twenty-past eight and he looked pensive for a moment before he stepped round the door. He kept away from the thread and approached the table, bent down and from a distance looked at what the corner revealed. He took his time, his expression intent, but finally, inside himself, he seemed to relax. He stepped forward and pulled the envelope free of the tape, as if casting off his previous caution all in one movement, and then he let the thing lie.

In the kitchen he switched on the kettle and while it boiled he rolled a cigarette. He made a cup of coffee and took it back to the table and sat down. He eyed the envelope with the cigarette in his mouth, then picked up the package and shook out its contents.

There were three things: an untidy wad of used bank notes, twenties and fifties held together by a rubber band; a polythene bag wrapped round itself several times and sealed with sellotape so that it was opaque, and a slip of folded white paper. He pulled the paper towards him, unfolded it and held it down with splayed fingers. There were two lines of writing in the same black biro as the address on the envelope.

Dear Joe. Please hold this stuff for me. I'll pick it up when I can. I'll phone you. Thanks. D. Mallon.

Larne took the cigarette out of his mouth and drank some coffee, a little at first and then more when he found it wasn't too hot. He re-read the note at the same time, looking thoughtful, then rested the cigarette over the edge of the table and counted the wad of money. There was one thousand four hundred and fifty pounds.

He dropped the notes on the table and picked up the polythene bag. It measured about four inches by three and when he pressed it between his fingers it gave softly. He didn't open it. For a moment he stared at all the things on the table almost blindly, then he stirred.

It was half past eight and he put all Mallon's things — including the note — in a plastic bread-wrapper from the kitchen which he sealed with insulating tape. He screwed up the envelope and pushed it into his back pocket and after that, he put on his jacket, collected his tobacco, sandwich box and Mallon's things and went out.

He walked fast but without notable wariness, following his usual route for the length of four streets. Then, however, he made a detour which kept him moving in the same direction but held him away from the main road instead of taking him to it. It seemed like a simple variation made by chance inclination.

The Victorian houses in that area were better bred than the smooth red brick terraces and semis he'd come from. There was more stone, though most of it had turned black, and the gardens were often secluded with just a glimpse over a wall of well-established trees and shrubs. He turned a corner and turned again, into a short, almost square alley with a couple of stone gate posts at its end. Through the gate posts there was a solid square church to his left. It was small and had no entrance porch. Instead there was a heavy side door of varnished white oak, tightly shut, with a broken iron ring on the outside. The windows were high and Larne looked up at them briefly before scanning the rest of the ground.

The churchyard was on a slope, an enclosed throughway to the main road at the bottom. The grass was short, quite recently cut, and intermittently set with flat gravestones. Other age-green stones had been moved to line the walls of the place and Larne left the loose tarmac path and walked over the grass towards them. Trees overhung the wall from the far side and cut out the light and around the bottoms of the stones there were fringes of long grass and weeds that lawnmowers couldn't trim. He stopped there and took out the bread-wrapper with Mallon's things inside it.

He glanced round again, but he was alone and not over-looked. The sound of the road below was muffled by distance. He stepped sideways, put a foot in the weeds and bent down, thrusting the package in between a gravestone and the wall, pushing it well down amongst dead leaves and stalks.

When it was done he rose smoothly, paused as if fixing the gravestone in his mind, then strode on down the slope, returning to the path and going out through rusty iron gates at the bottom. He didn't look back and ten yards along the road he remembered to drop Mallon's screwed-up envelope in the gutter.

A few minutes before noon Wally brought the tow truck into the yard, braking it hard and banging the door as he got out. Larne was working further up the yard and Wally's head jerked round till he saw him.

'You 'avin' your dinner 'ere or what?' he demanded.

Larne straightened up from an engine. 'Yeah.'

'Well come an' 'ave it.' His raised voice dropped to a litany of swearing that Larne could see but not hear, then he turned his back and stamped off to the office. Larne watched him with mild curiosity and after a moment he followed the old man.

A strong gusting wind had grown up during the morning. It was warm but it made the grit fly in sharp clouds and when Larne went into the office he shut the door against it. Wally was in his chair, scowling.

'You know the bleedin' phone's broke?' he said to Larne.

'No, I haven't used it.'

'Well it is. I've 'ad bloody Slaney on to me. Rings me up 'an says he can't get through so he's callin' me at home. Then I try to ring you an' I can't get no reply neither.'

Larne picked up the phone and held it to his ear. 'It sounds all right. What did Slaney want?'

'Says you 'aven't collected that bleedin' Mini yet an' he wants the space. Jesus Christ, 'ow much space does a fuckin' Mini take up, that's what I want to know.'

'What did you tell him?'

'You're fetchin' it after dinner. An' I told 'im; if he can't keep a bloody car for a couple of days without ringin' me at 'ome he can keep *all* his bleedin' rubbish. I don't want it. Fuck 'im!'

'I'll go now. I told him I'd have it out of his way by Wednesday.'

'Sit down. Let 'im stew. I ain't 'avin' that bleedin' lark from 'im. 'ave your dinner.'

Larne looked round. 'What about you?'

'Came without it 'cause of bloody Slaney. Make a cuppa tea, you can bring somethin' back.'

'Want my paper?'

'Yeah, pass it 'ere. It'll gimme somethin' to do.'

Larne handed it over and made tea while Wally subsided with rumbling irritation, reading and snapping the paper to the background sound of the radio. When Larne gave him his tea he said, 'Cheers, kid.'

Without the newspaper, Larne's attention seemed to drift while he ate. His eyes stayed on particular things for a while, then moved on. Part of the time he looked out of the window, at the railway bank where the wind was pushing the dry weed stalks around, but whatever his thoughts were they didn't provoke any expression. He ate his sandwiches as a matter of routine and drank his tea the same way. Then, when he'd finished, he rolled a cigarette and at the same time seemed to put his thoughts away. He lit up as the radio news began. The second report was about an explosion.

'A man was killed by an explosion early this morning outside a house in Greenwich. The explosion occurred as the man, so far unnamed, was getting into a van which had been parked in the street for some time. He died instantly. Police believe that the blast was caused by about ten pounds of explosives and are working on a theory that the man may have been killed while transporting a bomb. No one else was seriously hurt in the explosion, but at least three people from nearby houses received hospital treatment for shock and injuries caused by flying glass.'

Wally lowered the paper and looked at Larne for a moment. Larne knocked ash off his cigarette.

'There's a bit in 'ere about that,' Wally said. 'You seen it?'

'No.' Larne shook his head.

Wally turned pages, then folded the newspaper and held it out, marking the place with a broken thumbnail. Larne took it. The piece was in a corner, only an inch long, and gave fewer details than the radio had. He gave the paper back.

'Anythin' for you?' Wally asked, but his voice left the question open.

After a moment Larne made a brief, negative gesture with his hand. 'No.' He stood up. 'I'll go to Slaney's. What do you want for your dinner?'

Wally's eyes stayed on him for a second longer, then he moved the paper and picked up his tea. 'Pie an' chips. Fish if they ain't got pie. An' gimme a bell, see if the bloody phone's workin' now.'

'Okay.'

He went out of the office and the mongrel was lying by the door. It stood up as he passed, stretched and followed him out of the shed to the tow truck. Larne only looked back at it as he opened the cab door and after a moment he clicked his tongue. The dog came round his legs and jumped up into the truck. It sat down on the passenger seat as Larne climbed in and started the engine.

Wally had left the truck with just enough room to make a left-handed U-turn and Larne hauled the wheel round, holding the truck on the clutch. He cleared the wall of the office by a foot but as he came out of the circle a car turned into the yard from the road.

It came in smoothly, central through the gate; a fawn-coloured Granada with two men in the front. Larne kept the truck moving but followed a line to one side of the car so it would have room to leave his way clear. For a moment it looked as if it would, but instead it braked to a halt and the driver switched off the engine.

Larne dipped the clutch and moved his head in a brief stare which tightened his jaw. He let in the clutch sharply, stalling the truck. The two men were getting out of the car, but Larne didn't look. He pushed his door open and got down in one step and walked back to the shed with hard strides. He left the door wide for the dog, and as he entered the office he left that door open too.

Wally looked up. 'Coppers,' Larne said. 'Coming in.'

' 'ow many?'

'Two. Plain clothes.'

'What . . .'

Larne shook his head, an instruction, and sat down by the desk. His face was clouded, like a man weighing a new situation but not rushing to conclusions. He scratched an itch on his arm by kneading the skin with his fingers a couple of times.

There was a movement outside and a light perfunctory tap on the wood by the door and the two men came far enough into the office to stand side by side. The one closest to Larne was the eldest and tallest; over six feet with a rough, bony face which was pock-marked and sore from shaving. His hair was straight and slightly greasy and he wore a corduroy jacket and a loose-knitted tie. 'I'm looking for Joseph Larne,' he said.

Larne leaned back in his chair slightly. It creaked. 'I'm Larne.'

The man turned towards him, although his eyes had never been very far away. They were soft, as if he'd never had any interest in hardness. 'Detective Inspector Thomas,' he said, and his voice had the same softness as his eyes, with a slight trace of a Welsh accent. 'This is DS Woods.'

Woods was in his late twenties and his face had nothing to offer; a face that relied on the words that came from it to relay feelings. He had a light-coloured moustache and the clothes he wore were well-fitting and casually neat.

'I'd like to ask you some questions, if that's all right, Mr Larne,' Thomas went on. 'Nothing much.'

'Let's see some bloody identification first.' Wally pushed himself out of his chair. 'We got work to do.'

Thomas turned to face Wally with a bow of his head as if the old man had raised a fair point. He reached into his pocket and said, 'Are you the owner, Mr—'

'Osbourne. Yeah. I'm the owner. Let's see your card.'

Thomas held it out and Wally took it, squinted at it, then offered it to Larne, but Larne gestured it away without looking. He was watching Thomas and Woods, waiting.

'Is it all right if we have a look round the yard?' Thomas asked, putting the card away.

'What for this time? We 'ad your lot in a coupla weeks ago. Whatcha want now?' Wally's hawk-face was tilted back aggressively, like a dagger ready to plunge into Thomas's chest.

'It's just routine,' Thomas said without changing his tone. 'We do have the right to inspect premises used for scrap-metal dealing.'

'Think I don't know that? Jesus Christ! Go on then, poke your bleedin' noses in. You won't find nothin'.'

'Thank you. And would you mind waiting outside while I talk to Mr Larne?'

'Mind! Fuck me, make yourself a cuppa tea an' all. Put your bloody feet up.' He glanced at Larne.

Larne said, 'Okay, Wally.'

With a snort of annoyance Wally pushed between Thomas and Woods and went out. A few seconds later he passed by the window, head down and shoulders hunched, pacing up the yard. Woods closed the office door.

The room was half empty now and Thomas ran his eyes over it before moving further in, close to Wally's chair. Larne was still waiting, watching his movements passively. Thomas turned and spoke as if starting again.

'Do you know why we're here, Mr Larne?'

Larne seemed to think about the question, then said 'No.'

'We're from C13. That's the Anti-Terrorist Squad, Scotland Yard. Did you hear about the man killed by a bomb last night?'

'It was on the news just now, I heard it then.'

'The man's name was Mallon. Do you know him?'

'Do you think I do?'

Thomas scratched his neck, eyed Wally's chair and sat down. He didn't cross his legs. By the door Woods leaned back gently on the wall. 'Where were you going just now?' he asked.

'To pick up a car.'

'Where from?'

'A garage in West Wickham.'

'Mallon was a carrier,' Thomas said. 'But he wasn't carrying anything last night. The bomb was under the seat in his van. He was murdered. Do you know who did it, or why?'

Larne searched out his tobacco, glanced down as he took the lid off the tin, then looked back at Thomas. 'No, I don't know,' he said.

'But you knew Mallon.'

Larne breathed out softly. 'If you can prove it.' He began to roll a cigarette.

'You were a carrier a few years ago. I think you knew Mallon. You could have been his banker, holding the stuff he moved. I'll know if we find anything in the yard.'

Putting the cigarette to his mouth, Larne lit it, drew and said, 'If you find anything you'll have put it there yourself. If you thought I was holding you'd have brought more than one man.'

Woods shifted. 'You're on file, Larne. It won't go away. Does your boss know?'

'Ask him.'

'Where were you last night, Mr Larne?' Thomas asked.

'At home.'

'Alone?'

A touch of humour crossed Larne's face, briefly. 'Yes.'

'Would you have any objection to a search of your house?'

'Not if you've got a warrant.'

Thomas scratched his forehead, just above his nose, with a fingernail. 'I'd like you to come to the local station. Is that all right?'

'I can't tell you anything.'

'I'd like a statement.'

'I just made it.'

As if thinking about that Thomas was still for a while, his soft easy-going look, incompatible with the sharp angular shape of his frame. Then he looked over at Woods and said, 'Have a look round outside.'

Woods dipped his head and went out.

'You saw Mallon at least once, in March,' Thomas said then. 'I know that, that's why we're here. The Prevention of Terrorism Act, section one: suspicion of belonging to a proscribed organisation. Danny Mallon was a Provo carrier and so were you, so I might make the charge stick. On the other hand, if you knew who killed him, or why, there'd be some profit in it for you.'

'I've told you, I don't know.' Larne's voice was flat.

'You could find out.'

Larne said nothing and Thomas let the words hang for a moment. 'What would happen if we did a proper search of this place?' he said.

'Nothing.'

'Because you've got your stuff tucked away somewhere else?' But Thomas's face slipped away from the question almost as he said it. He looked thoughtful. 'You wouldn't be interested in working with us?'

Larne frowned and it narrowed his eyes. 'Do you know anyone who would?'

'One or two.'

'If you're coming to me you're scraping the barrel. You're doing the rounds on the off chance. Your man said there's a file on me, but it's been dead for years.'

With a 'maybe' gesture Thomas said, 'You've been careful, that's all. But you saw Mallon in March, and that makes you a suspect. It means you haven't been sitting in the shade doing nothing.'

His eyes stayed with Larne, but then he let them stray round the walls of the place, moving over the gaskets and old, glossy nude calendars, considering. Outside the Alsatian barked.

'In for life, don't they say?' Thomas said, his voice mild. 'When you're in you're in for life. No one walks out. Isn't that right?'

Larne watched him.

'So what've you been doing, Mr Larne? Sleeping it off till they think we've forgotten you? But when you're on file you're on file for life too. Did you know that? Computers. Mallon was carrying, like you used to, and you were an associate of his. If I take you in we could hold you for a week, just on that. Search your house, talk to the neighbours, take you in again every time there's a bomb scare. Do you want all that?'

Larne drew on his cigarette but it had gone out. He tapped the dead ash off it and raised his lighter. 'What's the choice?' he said.

'Tell what you know, off the record.' Thomas's voice was still mild and unhurried. 'No evidence, just the information. You won't be bothered again.'

'Off the record or on it, I don't know anything.'

For a moment there was silence, then Thomas seemed to

make a decision, or lose the thread of his interest. He stood up in a quick unfolding movement. 'Thanks for your time, Mr Larne.'

Larne opened his hand and let it rest on his leg. Thomas watched the gesture as if it had said something but without a reply, he walked out of the office as quietly as his whole manner had been.

For a while Larne waited, hardly stirring, as though Thomas's presence still lingered, subduing the atmosphere. Then after a couple of minutes the police car started up and whined in reverse, out of the yard.

Wally didn't come back and eventually Larne got up and went out.

The old man was leaning on the edge of a water tank with a rust-eaten hole in its side. He had a ragged cigarette in his mouth and the breeze from behind him moved dirt by his feet. He was looking at nothing in particular.

When Larne was a few feet away the old man jerked his head. 'Pissed off,' he said.

'Yeah, I heard the car. Did they tell you?'

'Didn't tell me nothin', 'an I didn't ask.'

'I knew Mallon,' Larne said. 'The man who was killed by the bomb.'

'I don't care a fuck.'

'They could come back.'

Wally took the cigarette out of his mouth and spat lightly from the tip of his tongue, getting rid of a piece of tobacco. 'I don't care a fuck, kid,' he said again. 'You could shove a bomb up the queen's arse and wipe the shit on her dress for me. I ain't askin'. I know you an' I don't know them.

Larne nodded. 'The yard's clean,' he said.

'This bleedin' yard's never been clean,' Wally said with a grunt. 'Fuck it.'

Shadow

SIX

The rain fell in heavy straight lines, backed by a semi-darkness that mixed grey with black and a peculiar, sickly thunderstorm yellow. The window was open and Larne switched the television off. As he did so the hiss and collecting-to-run-away sound of the water was closer and clearer.

He stood still for a while, watching the street in its half light. It was half past seven and the rain had established its channels and gathered in spreading reservoirs by the kerbs and over drains so that the lines of their surfaces made it impossible to remember how deep the holes had been. In the street nothing moved but the rain, and in one or two windows there were dull lights showing. Larne still kept looking.

His own house was unlit. He preferred to watch television with only the light from the screen, and now that it was gone the electric illumination seemed to have been replaced in another, more subtle form.

The news had shown a follow-up report to an item it had carried the previous day, and that was mainly why Larne had watched. Nine terrorist suspects had been held after early morning raids on houses in London. Now, forty-eight hours later, the suspects were still unnamed, still helping with enquiries and although Larne felt a passing curiosity about them – who they were – he was more occupied with the fact that the arrests had been made the day after Danny Mallon was killed. But even then his thoughts still fell short of active theorising.

Above the house, in the distance, a light roll of thunder moved away. The weather forecast had predicted thunderstorms for most of the evening, and although the air was still warm it was cooler and fresher than for weeks. Larne came away from the window.

From a hook at the bottom of the stairs he took down a dark green kagoul and pulled it on over his head. He went to the back door and locked it, then put on his boots, which were still a little muddy from the scrap-yard. Finally, as he went to the front door, he put a dark knitted hat on his head. The kagoul had a hood, but he disliked the way it blinkered his vision and magnified the sound of the rain, so it stayed folded into the collar. He stepped out into the street, and as he turned to lock the door he felt caution rise smoothly and softly, like an engaging of gear, and as he started to walk away in the rain it was fully there.

He walked quickly, and although the rain had slackened since the first cloudburst three hours before it still fell heavily enough to bounce on the pavement. His jeans were soaked from the thighs down by the time he reached the end of the street.

Beyond that, in the through roads, the vehicles that passed him had their headlights on and misted-up windscreens under the beat of their wipers. The faces of the drivers were pale blurs, peering against the short visibility and the dazzle of other cars' lights. He walked in the closeness of the rain, and rather than bothering him he seemed to absorb it.

It took him five minutes to reach the road that led to the church, and then for the first time he looked round. He'd passed two or three people hurrying through the wetness in different directions, but now there was no one in sight and he moved through the church gate without looking back. There was a light behind one of the east-facing windows, making the red and green of the stained glass visible and the door he passed was slightly ajar. A drainpipe spattered water into a grate beside it. He judged the light and the door for a moment, then crossed to his right over the sodden grass to the gravestone-lined wall.

Under the shelter of the overhanging trees it became suddenly quieter. The sound of the rain on the nylon of his coat was replaced by the slower drip of water through the trees' branches and the low, distant rustle of the rain beyond the canopy. It was darker there, too, and as Larne squatted down by the gravestone he was nearly invisible.

His sleeve slid against the stone as he reached in behind it, and at almost the same moment someone started to play the church organ. Larne's hand stopped and he glanced at the building, then searched again, still watching the church. The earth and the weeds had stayed dry and he felt the plastic of the package. He caught hold of it, moved it closer, then picked it up. He straightened, ignoring the wet denim clinging to his legs, looked the package over, then zipped it up in the front pocket of his coat.

For a moment he stood still, half-listening to the organ music in the church. It wasn't a hymn and no one was singing. He didn't know whether protestant churches held evening services – perhaps not if the congregation wasn't large enough. He had Danny Mallon's package by his chest and he wondered if they'd held his funeral yet. He wondered about Danny Mallon too, and then he stepped out of cover.

A hundred yards along the main road from the church there was a telephone box against a tall stone wall that sloped back slightly. The light in the box shone dimly and with the door closed and his back to the road, masking his movements, Larne took out the package. He held it down on the metal shelf of the booth with his right hand and used the thumb and first finger of his left to ease off the strips of insulating tape that bound the polythene. With it open he reached into the bag, felt the wad of notes but left it alone and took out the second bundle wrapped in plastic.

He re-wrapped the money and pushed it into the back pocket of his jeans, then with care he set about opening the soft opaque sachet that Mallon had sealed. He stopped twice to wipe his fingers dry and when the thing was unfolded he was left with a compressed square of white powder in the bottom corner of a polythene bag. He eyed it for a second, then wiped the tip of a finger round the top of the bag, collecting faint traces of the white dust which he raised to his tongue. A second later he spat on the floor and folded the bag as it had been, without disturbing the powder.

With the bag back in the pocket of his coat Larne picked up the phone and punched out a number. It rang three times at the other end before it was answered and then a woman's voice said, 'Yeah?'

'Is Jack Bell there?' Larne said, turning to look out at the road.

'Who wants him?'

'Joe Larne. Is he there?'

'Hang on, I'll get him.'

From the sound it seemed that she'd dropped the receiver

on a hard surface. Larne heard her calling and after a while the receiver clattered again and Jack Bell said, 'Joe. How you doing?'

Larne took his eyes off the road and turned back into the booth. 'I'm all right,' he said. 'This is business. I want an agent. You?'

Bell's voice dropped a little. 'Okay. You selling?'

'Yes.'

'How much?'

'About half a pound. Heroin.'

Larne caught the sound of an intake of breath and Bell was silent for a moment. Then his voice came back, tight, sharp and low. 'Why don't you take out a bloody advert. This is the phone.'

Larne said nothing, waiting, looking at a card for a mini-cab service that was wedged under the plastic cover of the dialling codes information.

'All right,' Bell said in the end. 'When?'

'Tonight. I'll meet you.'

'Tomorrow's better. The banks are closed.'

'Tonight.'

'Okay, don't push it. Use the Duke; I'll find you.'

Larne nodded. 'Okay,' he said and hung up.

He made another, shorter call to the mini-cab number and then stood waiting in the phone box till the cab stopped outside. He got into the back and the driver craned his neck.

'You look as if you should've called me before you set out, mate. Whereabouts in Morden d'you want?'

'The tube station.'

'You goin' up town? I'll take you if you want.'

'No thanks.'

The driver shrugged and turned back to the wheel. 'All right by me. There's plenty of work this weather.'

It was nearly dark now, an hour or so early, and it was almost unnatural after the light evening skies of the previous month; a sudden foreshortening instead of the gradual twilight transition. The darkness seemed harder, less accommodating, and the rain didn't soften it. Larne wound his window down a couple of inches to draw out his cigarette smoke and as the car sped along the main road across Mitcham Common he thought he heard two rolls of thunder. He looked out of the window, listening to the sound of water on the road, watching the lights of cars through the oily glaze of rain on the glass. Once or twice, distracted, he glanced at the driver, but for most of the journey he was pensive, considering.

In Morden he paid off the driver opposite the station and crossed the road quickly, pausing in the entrance to shake rain from his coat and search out some change. With his head lowered he watched the black on wet road for a moment and then went inside.

He bought a ticket for North Acton and stood under cover on the open platform with a dozen other people, and out of an old habit that came back to him he gave them each a label. Woman, overweight, lank hair. Man, pinstripe suit and overcoat. Young man, black; white training shoes. The labels didn't mean much, but they picked out easily recognisable features that would stand out if he saw them again. It was a routine of being on the run and he slipped into it easily.

When the train came Larne got into the same compartment as the negro with white training shoes. Morden was the start of the line and the train was empty. Even before it went underground the darkness outside blacked the windows and made reflections of the bright interior, as sharp as a mirror with only colour depth missing.

The negro sat ten feet from Larne and as the train moved out he looked across, taking in the clawed shape of Larne's hand, then he deliberately fixed his eyes on the window opposite him and lit a cigarette. He flicked the dead match at the window and blew smoke in a grey shaft at the No Smoking sign.

At Tooting Broadway the negro got off and his place was taken by a middle-aged couple and a girl in her twenties who got on just before the doors closed. She wore a plaid shirt and a man's nylon jacket. The middle-aged couple got out at Balham but the girl stayed and Larne's eyes moved past her a couple of times.

Through Clapham South no one got on or off and the girl stared straight ahead. Then at Clapham Common she got up as the train slowed, and slid through the doors as soon as they opened. Larne waited, watching the doors and the tiles of the station outside, then he also rose. As he got both feet on the platform the doors closed.

In the moment before the train started to move Larne looked down its length, then across at the exits. He saw the girl from the carriage fall into step behind other backs and then turn out of sight. The train's hum rose, pulled on to a clatter as it re-entered the tunnel and left Larne alone on the platform. He sat down on a bench and rolled a cigarette.

He let one train come and go without moving, but got on the second. And by then his actions were a shade more relaxed, slightly less studied. He stayed on the Northern Line to Stockwell, then changed to the Victoria. Closer to the city centre the number of people around him grew, but by that time he knew he wasn't being followed. He moved with the crowd at Victoria station and got on the District Line to Hammersmith, where he made a final switch to the Metropolitan. He came out on the street in Shepherd's Bush and the rain had faded away to a drizzle. He breathed in some of the dampness as if it was new and looked at his watch. He crossed over the road.

SEVEN

The pub called the Duke was a ten-minute walk from the tube station at Larne's steady pace; away from the plate-glass shop lights and late night chemist signs around Shepherd's Bush Green. It stood in a side street off a main road, and down the side there was an alley the width of a car that led to a yard at the back. Larne looked down it as he passed, but there was no light beyond the first few feet and the space at the rear was invisible. He went into the bar without pausing outside.

From the street the place looked as if its rooms might be small and cramped, but inside the tall double doors the pub was like a trick box. Instead of small pockets of space the whole building seemed to open out and the fifteen-foot-high ceiling gave an impression of a hollow shell too large for the things in it. Dark wood panelling reached half-way up the walls to white plaster and in an off-centre line there were pillars of wood with circular shelves round them at chest height. The floor was covered by a faded and worn carpet and the bar stretched almost the length of the room on the right, backed by mirrors and shelves. Larne passed half a dozen occupied tables as he went to the bar counter and the barman nodded at him as if he wasn't completely unknown, but when he asked for a pint of bitter the man made no further attempt at familiarity.

Larne rested lightly on the edge of a stool while the barman pulled the beer and he looked the room over. The juke box was loud beside a piano, and there seemed to be more noise for the number of people than in other pubs; as if they were trying to drown out the space. He didn't see the face he wanted, but at the rear of the room there was a small area partitioned off into two boxes by more wood panelling and pieces of leaded glass. He paid for the drink and went back there.

It was only concession the place made to privacy, but even then, without doors or a ceiling, the alcoves were only slightly more private than the passage to the toilets beside them. The first one Larne looked into was crowded by seven or eight people playing dominoes and cards, but in the other, only one table was taken by a couple chewing at each other's mouths with their eyes closed. They didn't notice Larne as he sat down, and after he'd watched them for a moment he lost interest and waited.

For some reason he thought about waiting, too – like going over a skill he'd learned – and that in turn made him think about Danny Mallon. He wasn't sure why. Mallon had been on his mind anyway and maybe that was the reason: Mallon was the reason for what he was doing. But something about the act of waiting connected with Mallon in a different way. He thought back to the last time he'd seen the man and the connection seemed to grow stronger. In the café Larne had sensed that Mallon was waiting; not waiting for him, not even waiting exactly, more *expecting*. What?

Or was it just that Mallon had been tired and on edge because he still had six rifles in the back of his van? He'd been waiting for Larne, and Larne knew that sometimes, suddenly, you could wait too long in only five minutes, so you started to get itchy, no matter how good you were. Larne knew that, and when he thought it the thought had a sharp edge and he didn't explore it. He drank some of his beer, rolled a cigarette, kept waiting. A while later Jack Bell found him.

Bell was a slim man with a quiet face of clean lines but deep eyes that were used to looking hard to read, especially while he listened to business. He wore an ox-blood leather jacket over a shirt and a loose tie and settled himself almost unnoticeably on the stool opposite Larne. He set a half-pint glass on the table and when he looked up his face was friendly and casual. 'Been here long, Joe?' he asked.

'A few minutes,' Larne said. His eyes watched Bell for a moment, then glanced at the couple in the back corner.

Bell looked the same way, then turned back smiling with a touch of wryness. 'Give 'em a knife and fork.' He took a sip of beer to punctuate the comment. 'I might have a buyer,' he said. 'Where's the stuff?'

'Here.'

Bell thought about that. 'You said half a pound, right? Is it cut?'

'I don't know. I don't think so. You'll have to check it – weight and purity.'

'They'll do that all right.' He got out a cigarette. 'Not your trade, though, Joe. I heard about Danny. You filling in for him?'

'Not really.'

Bell nodded, as if he knew the truth and knew Larne didn't want to say any more. 'If it is half a pound, pure, it'll be worth about eleven, maybe twelve. I get five per cent as usual. Okay?'

'Okay.'

'You waiting for the cash or do I drop it?'

'I'll come with you,' Larne said.

For a second Bell frowned, then turned it into a squint at his lighter as he struck it to his cigarette. He blew smoke and said evenly, 'You think I'd skip on your lot? Not likely, not for half a pound.'

'No,' Larne said. 'But this is private.'

Bell straightened, putting distance between him and Larne. His eyes were steady and his face was still, as if a thin film had evaporated from it. His fingers stayed light on his glass, ready to leave it. 'Where's the stuff from, Joe?' he said.

'Private,' Larne repeated softly. 'But it's mine.'

Bell leaned forward again. 'Is it? Listen, if that stuff's been skimmed I don't want to know; specially if it's been skimmed from the Provos. No way. A gram here, a gram there, into a plastic bag and nobody notices, not until you've got half a pound to sell, private. Understand?'

There was quiet for a moment, only padded out by the background noises, then Larne said, 'All right.'

'All right what?' Bell's voice was still tight from the last time.

'Let it be,' Larne said. 'I'll use someone else. You don't want it.'

'Not if it's skimmed I don't, no. Is it?'

'It's not my trade.'

'So it isn't?'

'Not by me. Someone left it for me, that's all I know.'

Bell let out his breath audibly. 'You could've said so. All right, it's private and it's yours. That's all *I* know. We'd better move.'

He stood up, glanced out of the alcove into the pub, then turned back. Larne was standing. 'It's parked round the back,' Bell said. Larne nodded.

Bell went out first, down the passage to the toilets and a rear fire exit door. Larne went more slowly, on a curving route around tables to the door he'd come in. Outside he walked along the pavement to the end of the alley and crossed it as a car started up. It came forward, its lights washed the alley brick, bright, then dimmed as they mixed with the street lights. When Bell stopped beside him Larne opened the door and got in.

They pulled out of the alley, turned left, and at the end of the road turned left again into a light flow of traffic. Larne seemed to take no direct interest in the way they were going, or even in Bell until the man said, 'I'll make a call in a couple of minutes, then we drive around for a bit. I've warned them already so they'll be ready to move. They like to work out of the back of a VW camper so we've got to give them time to set out.' He looked at Larne. 'Where's the stuff?'

Larne patted his pocket. 'In here.'

'Next to your heart,' Bell said and laughed.

They stopped on a corner close to a phone box a minute or so later and Bell left the car engine running while he went to make the call. As if on purpose, he stood facing the road while he talked and Larne could see his lips moving. The call took less than a minute and when Bell came back he put the car in gear and eased out from the kerb before he spoke.

'It's on. Fifteen minutes, by the Union Canal past the Scrubs. I know the place.'

'Good,' Larne said.

The light rain had turned to nothing by the time Bell eventually stopped cruising and began to head towards North Acton. The windscreen wipers dragged on the glass and he switched them off, as if the noise irritated him. There'd been no talk between the two men for a while, and no sense of either one building up to conversation in the dash light; no waiting for a movement or event to trigger off comment. When Bell did speak, then, it sounded spontaneous.

'What happened to Danny?' he said. 'Do you know?'

Moving his eyes on the windscreen, watching the road, Larne thought for a few seconds. 'No,' he said, but the word was open-ended.

'I told you,' Bell said, 'I wouldn't mess about with your lot.'

In the closed semi-light Larne breathed a frown and shifted a fraction. 'Do you know that for sure?' he said, but the question wasn't quite clear or natural. 'You know it was them?'

Bell said, 'Not for sure, not if you don't. He was all right with me anyway.'

They followed a road and then the sidings and sheds around Willesden Junction were beside them; steel in the darkness, odd track lights and a pale moon with a yellow halo through thinning grey cloud.

'Did these buyers know Mallon?' Larne asked softly.

Bell shrugged, his voice natural, matter of fact. 'Not through me. When he had a load he dropped it with me and picked up the cash later on. Except last time, he just dropped it then. That was a couple of weeks ago, no three. Something about the money going straight over the water.'

'Who carried it?' Larne said. He was still looking out through the windscreen, not even glancing at Bell for the answer, but this time Bell seemed to detect the fact that the asking was unnatural to Larne. When he answered his voice had a faintly false, faintly guarded side to it.

'A young bloke – Hagen. You know him?'

'No,' Larne said. Bell lit a cigarette.

They turned south and then followed a road round, away from the houses and into the background dark of railway, canal and factory hinterland. They came to a place where the derelict and empty stood beside the new; industrial units, where lonely lamp posts lit patches of cleared ground and tall bushy weeds that showed briefly in the headlights. It was a place to get lost in and lurch on the uneven ground, and in the distance there was the floodlit shape of a warehouse or plant; a landmark that stayed when the carriage lights of trains had gone past. Bell knew the place and where he was going, and so, in a way, did Larne. It seemed that at night all open and stumbling-dark places like this were the same, became part of a whole, and because he knew others he knew this one and could find corners and holes away from the lights in the distance. It was how he lived.

Bell slowed the car where the tarmac petered out to yellow foundation stone and then became a double-rutted track which showed in the dipped headlights for ten yards or so. The car stopped just short of the track and Larne looked at Bell.

'You still want to be there?' Bell said. 'If I take it they don't know where it's from.'

After a moment Larne said: 'What difference does it make?'

Bell seemed to have an answer; he drew breath to make it, then instead he let the breath out. 'All right,' he said.

He let the car move forward in first, hardly touching the accelerator, so it rolled almost reluctantly over the ground. After twenty yards he turned to the left, came round in a wide circle and stopped, killed the lights. The engine ticked over and Bell seemed to be scanning the darkness. Nothing showed. He switched off the engine.

'They'll be here,' he said, still watching. 'Sometimes they're waiting, sometimes they come in after you're there. Got the stuff?'

Larne unzipped his pocket and took out the package. Bell took it, weighed it in his hand, then rested it in his lap. 'You're going to let me fix the price?'

'That's why I wanted an agent.'

'This is Danny Mallon's isn't it?'

For a few seconds Larne said nothing, as if still listening to the question. When he nodded he did it just once. 'It was,' he said.

'Then it's skimmed. Ten to one. And if he was skimming I'll give twenty to one that's what got him killed. No one likes a carrier who thieves, specially if they can't get back what he took.'

Quietly Larne said, 'So?'

Bell pulled a last drag from his cigarette and mashed it out in the ashtray. He shifted in his seat to face Larne. 'You should be worried. *I* should be worried. Mallon's dead but his stuff's not been forgotten.'

'How many trips would it take to skim half a pound?'

'Depends how much he took, how greedy he was. He took enough to get noticed, that's bloody obvious.'

In the direction they'd come from there were two dimmed headlights and the low sound of a rear-engined van, moving then stopped. Bell looked and turned back to Larne.

'I can tell them it's off.'

'It isn't,' Larne said. 'You don't know it was Mallon's and I'll make your cut ten per cent.'

Bell slid his hand on the steering wheel, round to the cross bar, then to his lap. He picked up the package and held it out to Larne.

'Okay,' he said. 'But that doesn't buy quiet if they come

64

asking, just quiet till they do, and then I thought you were selling for them.'

He let Larne take the package and reached to the lights, flashing them once.

The van moved forward again, came round in an arc as Bell had done and rolled to a stop five yards from the car. Bell opened his door so the interior light came on. He held it that way for a couple of seconds, then said: 'Okay, come on.'

They got out of the car and Larne matched Bell's pace but kept a yard to the left of him. When they were two or three steps from the van a side door rolled back and a torch shone. The two men stopped and the torch picked out Larne, making him look away to one side. When it snapped off there was a word from the van and its cabin light came on, showing the side door and the windows covered by thin cloth curtains.

A man stepped down from the door, glanced around and then looked at Larne and Bell. The yellow interior light showed only a quarter of his face and the blue shoulder of a denim jacket. Behind him in the van someone else moved, cast a shadow, and his voice said: 'Okay, Jackie, get in.'

Bell moved again, past the watchman, and climbed into the van, bending his neck. Larne came to the door but he stopped by its ledge and just looked in.

There were two men there besides Bell; the one who'd cast the shadow and another sitting on an orange and yellow patterned bench seat in the rear corner beside a fold-away formica table. There wasn't much room in the van and Bell had already taken a seat diagonally across from the man at the back. The other man half stood and half crouched behind the front seats, waiting for Larne. 'Get in, Joe,' Bell said.

Larne cast a glance at the step and got in, leaving the watchman alone outside. Bell moved along his seat but Larne ignored him and sat instead on a single seat facing the door.

There was silence for a minute before Bell made a move. 'Joe's just here to okay the price. He's with the Irish.'

'Irish?' The man in the front half of the van moved forward, slid the door closed and then sat in the place Bell had moved from. 'Kilburn or Killarney?'

He was about half-way through his thirties with brown hair, a straight mouth and blue, slightly sad eyes that in some way seemed remote from the rest of him. He wore a loose, navy-blue sweater with the sleeves pushed back to his forearms, showing the edge of an undecipherable tattoo. He moved lightly, as if he was used to the small space of the van.

'Neither,' Larne said.

The man smiled. 'Makes no difference to me. I'm not racist.'

At the back of the van the other man stood up and opened a cupboard above the back window. He could have been a year or two younger than the other but because he wore a short beard it was difficult to tell. His face was less open than the man beside Bell and his eyes were darker and less expressive. He took down a set of scientific weighing scales with a single pan and a calibrated needle and closed the cupboard again. 'How much do you want for the stuff?' he asked without looking at either Bell or Larne.

'Do the tests,' Bell said. 'We'll work it out. Joe.'

Larne took the package from his pocket and half rose to drop it on the table. It lay for a while as the chemist adjusted three screw-pin legs on the scales against a small spirit-level bubble. When he'd finished Bell pushed the package towards him. He eyed it, picked it up and put it in the pan of the scales.

'This polythene's crap,' he said, watching the needle settle. 'Use cling film – the dogs can't smell through it.' He lifted his sight to Bell. 'Two thirty-three point seven.'

Bell nodded and the chemist took the drugs off the scales and reached for a plastic tape cassette case with a handle on top. He brought it off the rear window ledge to the table and opened the lid back on three small glass bottles and some other pieces of laboratory glassware and plastic.

'Tool kit,' his partner said. Bell continued to watch the chemist as he set up the test but Larne looked at the man who'd spoken. In a way he seemed as separate as Larne from the details of grading the drugs.

'You seen this before?' the man asked.

'Once or twice.'

The man put a cigarette in his lips and offered the pack to Larne. Larne shook his head.

'Irish,' the man said, lighting up. 'I saw the news. You need the cash to pay for a brief?' There was a faint grin round the ends of his mouth.

'The news didn't say they were Irish,' Larne said.

'No, but you hear.'

Larne glanced back at the table – a pocket of quiet, mechanical movements; almost bored. The chemist had opened the polythene bag and tapped two small piles of the whitish grey powder into dimple-like wells in a plastic tray. Then, with a glass eye-dropper, he dripped colourless liquid on to each pile of heroin. He waited a moment and stirred each mixture with different ends of a steel spatula. Larne watched, waiting for the colour to appear, and outside the sound of a train going past was cushioned and ignored by the yellow-white light and small space of the van.

One well in the tray turned first – a faint transparent blue like ink in water – and the other wasn't much slower. Together their colour deepened, grew denser and evened out as the heroin dissolved. Finally, in silence, the reaction finished and the two wells were a dark blue.

The chemist looked up, briefly at Bell and then at his partner. 'Ninety per cent,' he said and laid an open hand on the table.

His partner looked mildly surprised, but it seemed like a token expression, designed to fill a gap because his eyes were thoughtful. He blew smoke between his teeth and said, 'Seven grand.'

Bell snorted. 'You really want an answer on that?'

The man grinned again. 'Eight then.' He looked at Larne. 'All right with you, Joe?'

'I'll say when it is,' Larne said, ignoring the man's smile.

'Eleven,' Bell said. 'You'll be cutting it tonight and they'll be shooting it tomorrow. I know you, England my son. You're looking at two hundred grand clear if you're still using that Scotch merchant to flog it.'

'Robson went home,' the chemist said. 'Back to the haggis.'

'Yeah? Well even so, you're still being tight over a lousy eleven grand. I can take it away.'

'You'd be back,' the man called England said. 'Ten and a half.'

Larne raised his head slightly. 'Did you ever meet Danny Mallon?' he asked England.

For a moment England did nothing, then he frowned, glanced at Bell and then back at Larne. 'The one with the bomb? Your Mallon?'

'Not mine.'

'Still Provo. No, I never met him. Why?'

'D'you know anyone who did?'

'No,' England said. His voice was flat and the silence after the word waited for Larne.

Larne was looking at Bell now, studying him as if he was more interested in the man's face than in England's reply. But Bell was tight-lipped, suspicious, and if Larne saw anything beyond that he gave no sign. When he turned back to England he nodded and said: 'Okay, ten and a half.'

England slid out of his seat and bent down at a cupboard behind the driver's seat. At the same time Bell also moved. His expression was dead and his eyes stayed off Larne.

Turning, England held out six flat wads of notes to Larne which he didn't count, hardly examined, before he put them away in his pocket. England reached out and pushed back the door. Larne ducked his head and got out.

The watchman had heard the door move and came round the rear end of the van. Behind him Larne heard a brief murmur of voices – Bell's and England's – then Bell got out of the van. England, in silhouette, said, 'Any time, Joe.'

Larne didn't reply. As he and Bell walked back to the car the van door slid shut, a front door opened and closed and the engine revved into life. As Larne got into the car the van was moving away, showing only rear lights. He closed his door and the sound stopped.

Bell took his place behind the wheel but made no move to start the car. He stared at the windscreen for a while, then turned to Larne.

'Is that what you came for?' he said tightly. 'To ask him about Mallon? You really put it out in the fuckin' open, didn't you? It was bloody obvious you were flogging his smack – bloody obvious I knew about it too. You owe me a grand fifty and I'm gonna keep it in my pocket till your lot come round, and then I'm gonna give it them. And anything else they want. Understand?'

'All right, Jack,' Larne said.

'And I'll take the cash now.'

In silence Larne took one of the wads of money from his pocket, thumbed back the fifty-pound notes, counting. He pulled half the notes free of their band. 'Who was Robson?' he said.

Bell considered. 'A seller,' he said then. 'Part of England's team.'

'What about you saying they'd clear two hundred grand on that stuff?'

'They might have, with Robson. They cut it from pure down to street strength and sell it direct; no middlemen taking a cut. Robson was the front, selling to the street pushers. He was supposed to take the fall if the pushers talked.'

'What is street strength – five per cent pure?'

'Less.' He reached out and took the money from Larne. 'But if you're thinking about getting into the market you want to look what happened to Mallon. Don't stir up trouble; no one wants it.'

Larne put the rest of the money back in his pocket. 'Danny Mallon might have been skimming, but that's not why he was killed.'

Bell started the car. 'Yeah? Well if they ask me I'll tell them that's what you think. Get out of my life, Irishman.'

EIGHT

As Bell's car pulled away Larne started towards the tube station entrance on the corner of Shepherd's Bush Common, but five yards from it he stopped and turned away. He wasn't sure why; perhaps because he didn't really know why he'd been going there in the first place. It had been automatic, part of the sequence he'd mapped out earlier on: meet Bell, sell the drugs, go home. But for some reason he didn't feel ready to go underground, to finish the sequence and go home. So instead, on impulse, he turned away.

It was gone ten now and the streets were still wet. They caught patches and washes of light from the traffic and windows like positive shadows. The people he passed carried umbrellas, wore raincoats and evening faces and their heels clicked by in a steady rise and fall.

He walked more slowly than most, but the minor, transitory objectives of the next corner, the next kerb to stop at, kept his footsteps from loitering. Dot and carry, from one unplanned point to another, he made his passage.

He had no reason not to go home, he *expected* to go home, but still he didn't. It wasn't even the money, which he knew would be claimed if Bell washed his hands and told McGiven's people about it. He didn't see that as a reason to stay away from home. If he'd been asked for the money then he would have handed it over. In a way that was what he wanted, what it seemed he'd been waiting for from the moment he'd arranged to meet Bell. He had mapped out the sequence of events to end at the meeting with the buyers. He'd expected something to happen then; expected events to mirror his desire for an event and produce it, but they hadn't. And that was why the automatic function of going home afterwards had failed, because the sequence itself had stopped when nothing had happened. You couldn't end something if it wasn't complete.

But that seemed unrealistic. Bell and England had only been there because he was, for no other reason than that it was

70

their business, like lawyers, doctors and plumbers, called out only when you needed them. To expect them to do anything more didn't make sense. Why should they? He had provoked Bell, made the man take a stand, but Bell was the wrong man and it had gained him nothing; unless he *wanted* him to go to McGiven. But even then, why? Larne wanted a reaction, something tangible, but couldn't think why, except that now he had started this thing it needed concluding. And that in itself made no sense.

He walked for some time and at random. He was somewhere in Notting Hill but he didn't know the area well. It didn't bother him, but when he saw the light of a café window he crossed towards it. The place was just as random as the streets, and they led him nowhere.

The café was called the Black and White Spot and there was a quartered circle painted on the window in alternate black and white. As he opened the door a light push of air carried a couple of rain specks against his face.

Inside the place looked as if it might be ready to close. It was halved by an aisle of black and white tiles, with a counter on the left running back to a partitioned-off kitchen. There were two lines of tables and although those by the wall were only large enough for two people, a strip of mirror tiles beside them gave a momentary impression that they were larger.

An old black man in a brown coat sat at the back with a table to himself and in front of him a loose, stubble-faced man also alone. Two young blacks were near the centre and three white girls sat at the table nearest the window. One of them had a white apron on over jeans and as Larne closed the door and moved to the counter she stood up and went through a small gate to the other side.

'Coffee or tea?' she said as Larne stopped by the stainless steel top of the expresso machine.

'Black coffee,' he said.

She made it and he paid and after a glance at the tables he took one of the small ones by the mirrored wall. He poured sugar into the coffee and looked round again as he stirred it. There was no music, although a juke box selector was fixed to the wall by the door; there was no life, except in the expresso machine. The lifelessness seemed natural and Larne rolled a cigarette and sat as he had in the pub, not waiting now but still looking absorbed and inward in the way of a man used to solitude. He didn't stare at the distance because people who stared stood out. He knew the trick of moving his gaze even when his thoughts didn't follow it, and at the same time being ready for something to trigger sight back into focus.

A while later something did. One of the girls at the window table stood up and went out. The girl who'd made his coffee was still behind the counter, wiping things down with a cloth, and the other sat alone behind the random litter of cups and an ashtray, her back to the street. She did nothing, and Larne's gaze moved away, back to its slow wandering.

Then the girl got up with a decided movement, as if she'd made up her mind to leave too. She had a bag on a thin strap over her shoulder, but instead of opening the door she put a couple of coins in the juke box selector and pushed a series of buttons as though she knew them from habit. The music that came out was beaten, catchy but not loud. She moved towards Larne.

He was already looking up when she stopped by the rounded corner of his table.

'Want to dance?' the girl said.

Larne frowned slightly. 'No.'

'Can I sit down?'

'Why?' He looked at his cigarette, tapped ash off it and the girl sat down anyway, putting her bag on the table.

'Waiting for someone?'

Larne laughed a little. 'Not you. What do you want?'

'Nothing,' the girl said lightly.

He frowned again and looked at her. She was older than the others she'd been with, perhaps twenty-five, twenty-six. Her hair was short, dark reddish brown, razor cut around her face. Her eyes were dark, too, high-lighted only by her eye shadow. Her mouth hovered somewhere between a smile and nothing. She wore a faded blue sleeveless jacket with zips on the pockets and she looked straight at him as he looked at her. When he'd seen enough he picked up his cup and sipped coffee.

'You're Irish aren't you?' the girl said.

Larne nodded but didn't reply.

'I went to Ireland once. Dublin, for a week. Are you from the north or south?'

Larne drew on his cigarette and watched her. The girl let him do it for perhaps ten seconds and then seemed amused.

'Okay,' she said. 'I'll go away if you want. I was only asking.'

'For what?'

'Nothing. I felt like it, asking. I'm not on the game or anything like that.'

'No?'

She laughed. 'Did you think I was?'

'Maybe,' Larne shrugged. He wasn't really interested.

'Maybe I should be then,' the girl said, still smiling. Her eyes wandered, as if she was exploring the idea, and then came across Larne's left hand, crooked on the table. She looked up and saw he was watching her, but instead of shying away as most people did she looked at it again.

'What did you do to your hand?'

Larne breathed out slowly and for a moment his attention was focused like the girl's on his hand, as if it was a dead object, no part of him. Then he moved the bent fingers, as if proving it wasn't. 'Nothing,' he said.

There was silence again for a time and Larne was still, then he reached across the table and picked up her bag and brought it towards him. She half moved to stop him but didn't.

He put his cigarette aside and opened the bag. Inside there was a purse, a flower-patterned makeup bag, keys and a packet of cigarettes. He took out the purse and opened the wallet side. There was a cheque book, cheque card and a picture of the girl on the grass in a park. He closed the purse and put it back and the girl drew her bag back. 'Find it?' she asked.

'Find what?'

'What you were looking for.'

Larne finished the last of his coffee. 'I was just looking.' He collected his tobacco tin and lighter in front of him and glanced round the café like a preparation to leave.

'Going home?' the girl asked.

He looked back at her for a second. 'Are there any hotels round here?'

She considered, then reached the cigarettes from her bag and lit one. 'What sort, cheap or expensive?'

'Neither.'

'I know one or two. Do you want me to show you?'

The question seemed to hang for a long time, and in the end Larne said simply, 'No.'

She drew on her cigarette. He put his tobacco and lighter in his pocket and stood up.

'Decided where you're going?' the girl asked, her head raised.

'Good night,' Larne said.

He moved away from the table to the door. The girl didn't turn and when he stepped out into the street it was raining again. He walked to Holland Park Avenue before he found a taxi.

NINE

The taxi went east, crossing the river at Westminster Bridge, and although Larne looked at the window he didn't seem to see past the reflection of his face. Outside was nowhere and the lights that might have given it substance were past and gone too quickly. Inside the cab's air was stale from the day and the seats were dry and dirty from too much cigarette ash.

He got out on Deptford High Street and began walking again. It was eleven o'clock and because the dark and wetness continued they made it seem, in some way, that he'd been moving all evening; that movement, instead of being just the links in a chain, was in fact his purpose. The stops he'd made shrank in time and became short pauses, and seeing them like that didn't seem strange.

It took him ten minutes to reach the road he was looking for and the rain damped him like a heavy mist. There was no warmth left in the air and his legs were wet and cold. He walked with both hands in his coat pockets, which made his shoulders hunch slightly and kept his head down.

The road was on a slight rise, and at the bottom he read its name on a new sign fastened to a wall. In front the houses lined up in tall pairs, semi-detached and prewar, dark behind and between the spaced street lights. No one moved on the road and only a few of the houses showed lights. It was quiet and the cars parked by the pavement held the rain in large speckles on their roofs and bonnets and water trickled night quietly in the gutter.

Larne followed the house numbers as he walked up the street, but at least half his attention seemed focused on the dark places he passed. And when he was nearing the house he wanted his eyes moved to the houses across the street and stayed on them for several seconds.

The house number was eighteen and it was higher than its neighbour, fronted by a low wall and iron gate with a patch of rough, banked grass behind them. The front door was above a couple of steps and on the left of it the ground-floor window was curtained, though a faint light escaped, as if from the back of the room. Larne glanced at the two upstairs floors but all their windows were dark. He walked past the house and turned in at a narrow dividing passage where the front wall made a corner. When the darkness had hidden him he stopped for a couple of seconds to look back.

The rear end of the passage was blocked by a wooden gate with the latch on the outside and a spring-loaded hinge. He opened it quietly and slowed its return so it didn't slam. Beyond it there was a garden, the width of the house with a wooden fence to his right. A paved path turned along the back of the house and white light from a kitchen window was cast a short distance on to the stone and the wet grass of a lawn. Larne stopped again to look down the passage, then walked softly along to the back door.

He knocked twice, watching the door's square pane of frosted glass and after a moment of silence a dog barked inside. The noise didn't last and Larne waited nearly a minute before he saw movement.

Her figure was indistinct and dark through the glass and when she stopped by the door she seemed to stand sideways, as if to minimise her presence.

'Who is it?' she said. Her voice was clear but held down and she didn't open the door.

'My name's Joe Larne,' he said, quiet now. 'I knew Danny. Can I talk to you?'

'What about?'

'He left something with me.'

There was a moment of silence, waiting, then she turned a key and slid back a chain. When she opened the door Larne didn't move.

She was in her middle twenties, about five and a half feet tall and slim. Her hair drew attention first; dark and hanging down in long narrow spirals well past her shoulders, held back by the band of a folded blue scarf. She wore well-faded jeans under a black cotton blouse that reached to her thighs. It had belled sleeves and an open neck, and against it and the colour of her hair she looked pale and drawn. She gave out a sense of impalpable weariness, perhaps just from the way she stood, because when Larne looked at her blue eyes they were clear and observant. Her face was slim and angular and her mouth was formed into a straight line.

Larne gave her a while to look at him and then he said, 'Did Danny tell you he knew me?'

'He might have,' she said and frowned slightly, shifting her eyes to his hands. Larne moved his left into the light by a couple of inches, turned it slowly and then let it fall back.

'He mentioned your name,' the girl said. 'Joe, not your last name.'

'And my hand.'

She nodded and took a step back. 'Come in.'

He went in softly, past her, and stood near the centre of the floor while she closed and relocked the door. Without turning towards him she also leaned over a fitted, wood-finished sink unit and drew down a roller blind on the window.

'I think Danny liked you,' she said, coming to face him, and then – as if the two were connected – 'You look wet. Do you want a drink?'

Larne nodded. 'Thanks.'

She moved past him to switch on the kettle and put coffee in two mugs, and whether purposely or not, she kept her face turned away from him. Larne made no effort to change that. Instead he looked round the neat kitchen taking in the way it was fitted, the way it was kept, with glass jars and a trailing green plant by the door; a calendar and mirror side by side next to the door and a child's toy on top of the gas boiler. The room looked as if it had been cleaned too many times recently.

The kettle boiled quickly and Larne watched the girl's back as she poured water and added milk to the mugs. She put them both on a tray with a sugar bowl and finally turned around.

'You live in Croydon, don't you?' she said.

'Yes.'

She made no reply to that but moved towards the door and Larne stepped back for her, then followed.

The living room ran from the front of the house to the back, high ceilinged and with a rectangular arch near the centre. The carpet in the rear half seemed more worn than that in the front and had a pine dining table close to the window, bare except for a cardboard box of toys. The only light in both sides of the room came from a wall lamp angled into a corner. In the other side there was a sofa facing the orange-blue glow of a gas fire and two armchairs with a footstool that didn't match. In the alcove next to the chimney breast there were book shelves and a hi-fi, and a television in the corner of the bay window. There were plants too, hung like the one in the kitchen, and in the dim light the place seemed lived in and close, with a sense of things tidied away temporarily, until the people who lived there inevitably came and moved them again.

Mallon's wife put the tray on the footstool and straightened. She moved a hand at a chair by the fire. 'Sit down,' she said, as if Larne was too formal.

'Do you mind if I take off my coat?'

She shook her head and said 'Go ahead' in the same easy voice.

She sat down on the sofa while Larne pulled the kagoul over his head and laid it on the floor. He still looked mildly uneasy, and he seemed aware of it too, but he took the chair and sat without crossing his legs, at an angle to let her see his face. The gas fire hissed and began to warm the calves of his legs.

'Danny didn't tell me your name,' Larne said after a while when the girl made no move to speak.

She drew a breath through her nose, like a recovery. 'June,' she said.

'I didn't know you'd got a kid either.'

'Two. They're in bed.'

That reminded her of something and she got up again and opened a door into the hall. A moment later a part-collie dog with a long muzzle came in, stopping after a couple of steps when it saw Larne. June Mallon said: 'Sit, Flynn,' and it sat, but kept watching Larne.

'Would you like a whiskey in the coffee?' she asked, standing by the tray, and when he said yes she was already moving to get it from a high shelf.

She poured it into both mugs and brought his over to him and then took her place on the sofa again. Her legs curved sideways and she rested an elbow on the arm of the seat, as if half drawn up ready to sleep. There was silence again. Larne sipped his drink and let the mug rest on his leg.

'The funeral was yesterday,' June Mallon said. 'I wanted it quick.'

'It's best,' Larne said.

'Would you have come if you'd known?' Her clear eyes were

watching him but their interest was dulled, as if she already knew what he'd say.

'I don't think so.'

'The police?'

He nodded. 'They came round after the bomb. I told them I didn't know him.'

'You came here, though.'

'They're not watching now, I checked.'

He put his mug aside and reached over the arm of the chair to get his tobacco. 'Do you mind if I smoke?'

'No. Do you want one of these?' She gestured at a pack by her arm.

'No thanks; I prefer these. I've got the taste now.'

'You were in prison?'

'You don't have to have been in jail to roll your own.' He smiled and then let it fade. 'But I have.'

'What was it for?'

'Illegal possession of ammunition and belonging to a proscribed organisation.'

He rolled his cigarette as he said it and she didn't interrupt him, but when he'd smoothed out he looked up. 'Do you know what Danny was doing?' he asked.

She thought about that for a long time and Larne waited. She was quiet past the time when it seemed that she could answer and into a silence that felt as if it needed something new and outside to end it. Then she said: 'Some things, yes,' and raised her cup to her mouth. Her eyes watched the wall as she drank.

'There was a phone call,' she said and put the cup down. 'Ten minutes after he was killed, before the police came to tell me. A man asked if I was Mrs Mallon, and then he said "Don't talk Mrs Mallon, or it'll be worse for your kids." I was awake when the police came because he'd woken me up.'

Larne's expression darkened for a moment. 'Did the police tell you anything about Danny?' he said. 'What they thought he was doing or why he was killed?'

'No,' she said and got up. The dog also stirred, following her with its eyes. She took a couple of steps, then seemed to have forgotten why she was standing and sat down in the other armchair. 'They said they didn't know anything for sure. They asked about his work and I said he was a builder and sometimes drove lorries for Gillespie's.' She looked directly at him. 'I knew enough not to know any more. Is that what you came for?'

Larne put his unlit cigarette on the arm of the chair and picked up his coat again. He took out the separate bundles of notes and held them. He also took out the note Mallon had written.

'Danny sent me some things,' he said. 'There was fourteen hundred pounds and two hundred grams of heroin. I got them on Monday. I sold the drugs tonight, so there's another nine thousand.'

He rose, crossed to her and gave her the note. When she took it he put the money on a low table beside her chair and went back. This time he sat as if he was soon going to leave.

She read the note twice and Larne lit his cigarette. 'You didn't come to check up then,' she said.

'No.'

'Who does the money belong to?'

Larne made a small shrug. 'It was Danny's, so I brought it to you.'

'Where did he get it, the drugs I mean?'

'He was a carrier,' Larne said quite softly. 'He transported things. Did you know that?'

She gave a short, humourless laugh. 'Builders don't drive lorries across the Channel. He always said he was filling in for drivers off sick, and he got paid. I told you, I knew enough not to know, so I didn't ask questions. He was born here but his father was Irish. I knew.'

Larne heard her out with a nod and it seemed as if all this was only being said to reveal as definite things they already knew.

'I used an agent to sell the drugs. He guessed they'd come from Danny. He thinks they were skimmed from loads Danny had carried – stolen. The buyers don't know anything much, but if the other man talks someone will come round to see me.'

For the first time June Mallon looked worried and she drew her lower lip over her teeth and stared hard at the floor. 'You don't steal from the IRA,' she said quietly, then looked at Larne. 'Is that what he did?'

'I don't know.'

'But you think so.'

'I don't know,' Larne said, and his voice had a hard edge. 'I only met him when he left things with me.'

'What about the money then? If they think it's theirs they'll want it back. Won't they? So why give it to me?'

Larne turned his cigarette in his fingers. 'They'll come to me if they want it,' he said. 'Then it'll be my business.'

'Why should it be? I don't want it. Give it back if they want it.'

Larne shook his head. 'Someone may come here, asking about it, or about Danny. It's your choice; you don't have to tell them I came, but you can.'

'What about you?'

'They owe me,' he said and put his cigarette out.

'Aren't you part of them?'

Larne thought for a while. 'I used to carry,' he said. Then: 'Did Danny have a cache anywhere? A hiding place?'

'I don't know.' She made a distant gesture. 'There's a lock-up garage on John Street. He kept tools and things in it.'

'Do the police know?'

She let out a tired sounding sigh. 'They didn't ask.'

She got up and walked past Larne to the kitchen. When she came back she gave him a key. It had a piece of wire attached to it in a bent loop. 'The number's on it. I think he had a locker at Gillespie's too, but I haven't got a key.'

Larne nodded and put the key in his pocket. He stood up.

'Are you going there?' she said.

'Tomorrow.'

'If you find anything you want, keep it.'

'I'll let you know.'

She shook her head forcibly. 'I don't want to know. Not even who killed him. I want it finished.'

Larne watched her face for a moment, then bent and picked up his coat. She moved towards the kitchen and he followed. He pulled the coat on and said: 'Keep the money. You're entitled.'

'I'll see.'

He went to the door and opened it. 'Thanks for coming,' she said, but her eyes were tired and less clear now.

Larne didn't say anything. He closed the door and walked down the dark side of the house to the street.

TEN

Wally grunted sourly when Larne told him he'd have to open the yard, but he didn't ask why. His only comment was: 'It's Friday. What about your wages then?'

'I'll pick them up,' Larne said.

There was a pause. 'You need anythin' else?'

'No I'll see you later.'

'All right, kid,' but he was already muttering darkly to himself as he hung up.

Larne waited for about an hour after the call, then he caught a bus into Croydon.

The streets were still damp from the rain during the night and the sun was white through a thin wash of cloud, as if it was still gathering strength. He walked for a while, moving easily with the knots of shoppers stocking up for the weekend, and he didn't look back very often. Finally he went to his bank and queued until he could draw a new cheque book, three hundred pounds and a balance slip told him that he had one hundred and fifty pounds left. With that he walked south.

The car rental place was in a semi-basement, under the concrete lintels and sheer wall of windowless brick which made up the rear of a badly designed office building on the edge of town. Around the corner twenty yards away there was a glass and white netted frontage of social services and income tax offices, but on the one-way street that Larne came along the only entrance to them was marked by a sign for a health and fitness centre. The red and blue design of the sign stood out sharply against the flaked wood of the door and the scuffed concrete stairs of the entrance.

It was quarter to ten and the street was lined with abandoned cars, nose to tail between yellow lines. With the sound of traffic on the main road distanced by the building it was quiet.

Ten yards past the fitness centre Larne glanced at the long sign that said Hains Rental and Sale over the entrance to a garage. Below it the roll door was up and the interior of the place was dark. Someone's whistling echoed cavernously and without pitch. The concrete ramp down from the road to the half-basement didn't catch the sun and its surface was still wet, with a long thin puddle at the bottom where it levelled out. The sun also hadn't caught the two cars and two vans parked sideways on the ramp to the left either, and they sat looking grimy and rotten, as if they hadn't been moved for some time. Larne pushed a hand in his pocket and went down the slope.

It was quite steep and at the bottom the entrance was taller than it seemed from the pavement. Inside it was also less dark.

The garage was about twenty yards long, with pillar supports making bays on either side. At the far end there was a steel mesh of bars with gates in it that gave out on to the main road. The light there was a soft grey, like the light at the end of a tunnel, but it didn't filter back very far and the air was dank and smelled of petrol and exhaust from the semi-visible vehicles tucked back behind pillars.

Larne stopped to look round just under the entrance, but the whistling had stopped and nobody moved, so he turned to the only source of direct light in the place.

The office was a hut slotted into a recess beside the entrance, made of creosoted wood with a large window framed in white. It was a couple of feet above the floor and Larne took the steps up to the door and went in without knocking.

A counter split the office unevenly, its top littered with leaflets giving details of hire rates and insurance, and there were shiny trade posters of new cars and vans tacked to the walls. As Larne closed the door a moon-faced girl with dull brown eyes and severely plucked eyebrows looked up from a form she'd been filling out on the counter. She wore an off-white twin set at least ten years too old for her and said 'Can I help you?' without seeming to move her mouth.

'I need a van,' Larne said.

'What size?'

'Thirteen hundredweight.' His eyes moved past the girl to the rear of the hut where a man at a desk was working on a calculator. The girl waited passively and when he came back to her he said, 'I'll see Mr Hains.'

She turned her whole body. 'Mr Hains—'

Hains looked up from the desk at Larne and after a second

he nodded in recognition. He was in his forties and well built in the way of a retired middle-weight boxer. His hair was brushed back and going thin at the sides and when he stood up and came closer Larne could see the scar tissue over his eyes from fights in the sixties. He wore a blue suit with a loose tie and held out a dark-haired hand to Larne. 'If you'd like to look at the vans we can go outside,' he said.

Larne nodded. 'Okay.'

Hains came round the counter and opened the door for Larne, then shut it after them with a definite click. Larne didn't look back. He let the motion of descending the steps carry him a couple of paces away from the shed, then waited for Hains facing the length of the garage.

'It's been what, a couple of years?' Hains said, standing with his hands in his pockets at an angle to Larne. His voice was flat and didn't offer much. 'I thought you'd retired.'

Larne continued to look down the garage. 'From what?' Then he turned to Hains. 'A thirteen-hundredweight van for two or three days: plain.'

'Will I get it back, though?'

Larne's expression didn't change. 'What's your problem?'

Hains looked black for a moment, as if Larne should know better. 'I don't need your business.'

'Why's that?'

'You know why. No one wants to know your lot. Nine people picked up and in with the law for three days. How long before they start dropping names out?' He made a sour noise. 'You couldn't get a budgie to talk to you.'

Larne cast a short, speculative glance round the garage. 'You're talking,' he said.

'Not any more, I've got work to do.' He took a last, disdainful look at Larne and began to move away.

Larne said: 'I'll have a look at the vans outside.'

Hains turned back angrily. 'I told you. You aren't looking at anything. Get lost before I drop your name out myself. You get nothing from me. I wouldn't even give you my air.'

'You sound like someone's been here already.'

'No one's been because I don't give them reason, and that's how it's staying. You want a van, go somewhere else.'

'They'll have a reason if I give them one,' Larne said. He was standing square on to Hains, one hand still in his pocket, but the easiness had gone out of his voice. 'People like you stay

84

clean because others stay quiet; so long as you're useful. You'd better be useful. I need a van, off the record – not hired, not bought and not stolen.'

'To do what?'

'My business, but nothing to come back to you, if I get it.'

He watched Hains and the man's expression didn't lighten, but it didn't refuse either. Then Hains turned sharply on his heel and went back to the office. He came out again with some keys in his hand and started towards the ramp, not waiting for Larne.

The two vans were side by side and without any reference to Larne Hains opened the door of a dark green Bedford closest to the garage and got in. After a moment of sorting out the ignition key he pushed it into the lock and twisted it. The starter motor turned over with an off-centre sound, then stopped. Hains tried it again. On the third attempt it seemed to work free, become faster and the engine caught. He pushed the accelerator down, held it and then let it up slowly. The engine ticked over quickly, fed by the choke.

Hains got out of the van, letting the door swing closed. 'That settle it?' he demanded.

'It'll do,' Larne said. He took out his wallet and started to count money.

'I don't want your fuckin' money,' Hains said. 'Just don't come back – you or anyone else. The Irish aren't the only people with muscle. Ring up when you've finished and I'll have it fetched. If I see you again I'll have you put down.'

Larne took that in, but as coolly as Hains sounded hard, as if he was studying the extent of the other man's reaction. But Hains wasn't there to be studied and when Larne said nothing he stepped away, disassociating himself by the movement. He went past Larne into the garage.

.rne drove the van easily at first, getting used to the handling and brakes. The steering felt light compared with the weight of the tow truck and the speedometer needle flickered more readily as he changed gear. He got used to the rattle of the back doors and the thin vibration under the rubber floor mats and ignored the settled dust and distinctive enclosed smell of a vehicle left standing for weeks. He filled the tank at a service station and it was quarter past ten when he turned into the scrap-yard gate.

He didn't stop by the office but took the van up to the top of the yard, the tyres printing shallow tracks in the thin surface mud caused by yesterday's rain. When he stopped he let the engine tick over for a moment, listening to its sound, then he switched it off and walked back to the office.

Wally had come out and watched him like some ill-omened bird with a cigarette protruding under his moustache.

'Got your own fuckin' transport now then,' he said sardonically. 'What's up, you tired of walkin'?'

'Something like that,' Larne nodded. 'Are my tools in the shed?'

'Where you left 'em.' He followed Larne inside to the office, trailing light footprints. 'You 'ad a phone call.'

'Who from?'

'Didn't say. Asked if you was 'ere an' I said no.'

'What time?'

' 'bout 'alf an hour ago. You want a cuppa or are you rushin' off out again?'

'I'll have one.'

Larne sat at the desk and looked through some papers from one of the drawers while Wally made tea. After a minute or so he found the log book of a van that had come in to be scrapped six months before. The details were the same make and size as the one he'd got from Hains but four years older. He got up and went into the shed where a collection of old number plates had been dumped by a wall and picked through them until he found the two from the scrapped van. When he came back to the office Wally was moving away from the desk and the log book.

Larne put the number plates down by his tool box and retook his seat. There was a brown envelope on the desk next to his tea.

'Your money's there,' Wally said with a nod at the packet.

Larne picked up the log book and raised his eyebrows at the old man. 'Did you read this?'

'Should've been cancelled,' he said. Then: 'Plates don't mean nothin'. What about tax? You ain't got the right disc.'

'I won't need it. The plates are only a precaution.'

'When you comin' back?'

'I'm not going far.' Larne sipped his tea.

'Bank holiday on Monday. Place'll be closed.'

'Okay.'

Wally didn't say any more. Larne drank his tea and put the wage packet in his pocket, then he stood up. 'I'll borrow the A to Z from the truck. Okay?'

'Help yourself, I ain't goin' nowhere new. Gimme a bell when you're comin' back.'

Larne nodded and took the plates and the tools to the van.

The roads north towards Deptford weren't particularly busy and Larne made good time. But unlike the journey to Shepherd's Bush the previous night he wasn't expecting anything, and although he paid attention to the vehicles around him it was a quieter, more abstract caution, perhaps as a result of a change since last night. He didn't feel tied to expectation any more. The loose-ended feeling when nothing had happened last night had somehow been its own end. He didn't know why he felt that, but it seemed as if the sense that something *should* have happened had been replaced by a knowledge that something would. It turned expectancy into a prepared waiting.

John Street was a quarter of a mile from Mallon's house; a narrow, badly made up road on a slight rise between terraced houses. It seemed to be a dead end and Larne drove up it slowly, without much room to get past the two or three parked cars drawn in to the side. A soft-drinks van rattled over a sunken tarmac patch and pulled in to one side to let him pass.

Five yards from what seemed like the end of the road he saw that it made a sharp right angle turn by a high wall on the left, and when he followed it round the road seemed to have cast off the narrow line of the street and opened out into its own private space. He pushed the clutch down, held the van on the brake and looked around.

There was no other way out and that fact occupied his attention more than any other features of the place. In front and to the right there was a grey square of tarmac, framed by a low wall and sections of wooden fences shielding the gardens of houses beyond. In the corners of the square there were crescents of long grass and weeds edged by loose gravel that turning cars had pushed outwards. On his left there was a wall with a twelve-foot gap in the middle, making the entrance to a separate courtyard in front of garages.

Larne let the van move forward again and took it round, clockwise on the turning circle, still moving slowly. When he was half way round a group of nine- or ten-year-old boys dashed out from the garages towards the street, yelling and armed with toy guns, dressed up for war games. Larne watched them go, then took the van over twin ruts into the garage square. The surface was rough, covered in cinder and red shale with short weeds showing through green, as if risen with the night's rain. He stopped the van, took the keys and got out.

There were two sorts of garages; the ones on the left and in front were old red brick with double wooden doors and roofs of corrugated asbestos grown over with moss. The others were newer and their pre-cast concrete walls and steel lift-up doors were still fairly clean, except for a couple of spray-painted football slogans in large angular letters.

Larne took the key that June Mallon had given him and checked its number against those painted or nailed on the garage doors. It matched the nine of an old garage set at an angle in the left hand corner of the square, and when he got closer he saw that the lock was internal, not a padlock like most of the others.

The key made a dry sound when he turned it in the lock and he had to tug at the brown bakelite handle to open the door. Inside there was light from a small grey window at the far end of the garage and he closed the door behind him. As a second thought, he dropped the bolt at the bottom to keep it that way.

The light from the window was as grey as the glass and he stood still for a minute, looking round. Two-thirds of the floor space was empty; a concrete base, thickly oil stained in one place and covered with dust. There were roof joists just above his head, holding up a ladder and a store of timber like a false ceiling. At the far end three old kitchen units had been put together in an L-shape and mounted with a vice to make a bench top and cupboards.

Larne took it all in and then seemed to make up his mind. Starting on the left wall he moved slowly along, shifting propped tools and off-cuts of wood and pipe to look inside and behind them. He didn't move anything more than he had to to examine it, and the up and down sound of children playing outside didn't disturb him.

It took him two or three minutes to reach the cupboards below the window. Its glass was cracked in one corner and hung with the dry shells of flies in cobwebs. He squatted down to look through the contents of the shelves. How much of the stuff was Mallon's and how much had been there for years was difficult to tell but Larne looked at it all, opening old paint tins and shaking apparently empty oil cans. His hands got dirty and found nothing apart from the junk, but he didn't pause until he'd worked his way back up the other wall of the garage to the place where he'd started.

The only things he hadn't searched by then were two hundredweight-bags of cement, a bag of red sand and the roof.

He rolled a cigarette, lit it and took out a jack knife. He used it to cut flaps in the top sides of the cement bags and then got a shovel and probed the grey dust in lines from one end to the other. There was nothing but cement in the bags, but he repeated the probing in the sand after he'd tipped it out in a pile.

The sand yielded nothing either, and as he looked at the roof the sound of a car outside took his attention. It seemed to stop on the turning circle, then backed up a short way before the engine was cut. Larne moved to the doors and pushed one outwards by an inch until there was a gap he could see through.

The car was out of sight behind the wall around the garages, but the sound of two doors closing came soon after the engine died and then a man showed. He was about five feet ten, quite heavily built with short reddish hair and a heavy moustache. He had light-tinted sunglasses on his face and wore a summer jacket with cuffs turned back. For a moment Larne had a good view of him as he looked round at the garages and then the man looked back at the car and said something indistinguishable. A second or two later David Hagen came into sight.

Larne watched the two men looking round, and when they started inwards he eased his hand off the door and bent to the bolt at the bottom. He straightened up and his movements seemed to be timed, then he pushed the door lightly.

It swung outwards through half its arc and caught on the ground. As it shuddered Larne walked out.

Hagen and the other man had both stopped, tense, but the

attitude lasted longest in the older man, while Hagen seemed to shed it as soon as Larne came into the light. When Larne stopped Hagen dipped his head, like either a greeting or an acknowledgement. 'Joe,' he said.

Larne nodded back, without sign of surprise that Hagen was there.

'You know him?' Hagen's partner said. He'd eased when Hagen had spoken but still wasn't quite sure. It only seemed a little incongruous that as the older and possibly stronger of the two he appeared to be waiting for Hagen's lead. Seen like this Hagen showed a quiet form of assurance and power.

'Yeah,' Hagen said. 'He's all right, aren't you Joe. How long've you been here?'

'About fifteen minutes.'

'Find anything?'

'Not yet.'

Hagen came forward again, passing alongside Larne's van. 'This yours?' he asked.

'Borrowed,' Larne said.

'This morning? I tried to phone you but the old man said you weren't there.' He glanced at the garage. 'Do you want to finish looking?'

Larne shook his head. 'I've finished.'

'A double check wouldn't hurt, though,' Hagen said, turning to the other man. 'Have a look, Gerry.'

When the man moved so did Larne, partly out of his way and partly towards the van. 'Why did you want me this morning?' he said to Hagen.

The young man looked briefly thoughtful in a questioning sort of way, then pushed his light blond hair back with spread fingers. 'Don't you know?' Then, as if dismissing the question: 'Want a drink? There's a pub round the corner.'

'What about your man?'

'He'll meet us. Hold on.'

He went into the garage and spoke to the other man and Larne got into the van. He had it started by the time Hagen came back, and when the younger man was settled beside him he backed out of the courtyard and started down the street.

The pub was about quarter of a mile from the garages, set back on a corner with a main road. It had tall white-painted walls and Larne parked the van on a band of tarmac between it and the pavement.

They got out and Hagen led the way to the door a pace in front of Larne, then halted on red and white tiles in the entrance. 'Tap room or lounge?' he asked Larne.

'Please yourself, you're buying.'

They went into the lounge and while Hagen bought the drinks Larne took a seat with his back to a window, in sight of the door but not the bar. It was only just after opening time and there was no one else in the room. There was a vague smell of cleaning polish in the air and the large plastic ashtrays on the tables were empty. Taped music suddenly started playing quietly through a couple of speakers but Larne took as little notice of it as he did of the room; this early in the day the pub was still dormant and characterless.

Hagen brought two pints to the table and sat down facing Larne. 'That's the second one I've bought you,' he said and took some out of his own. 'Last time you said you wouldn't take another.'

'You were careless,' Larne said.

'Aren't you?'

Larne thought for a moment. He didn't ignore the question, but he put it to one side. 'Who's your man?' he said.

'His name's Gerry Naulty. He's helping.'

'To do what?'

'Odd jobs. You've seen the news. They've charged all nine – conspiracy to cause explosions, and they got John Keeble for murder. There isn't much left. Everyone's digging holes, getting out of sight. Me and Gerry are tidying things up. We're both clean.'

Larne drank, then rolled a cigarette. 'What did you want to talk about this morning?' he said.

'How much stock have you got? McGiven wants to know.'

'Eleven shorts and some ammunition.'

'Safe?'

'Safe enough.'

'And you're staying where you are?'

'I've got nothing to move for.'

'You were moving last night,' Hagen said and his eyes were level on Larne's. 'What's your interest in Mallon?'

Larne lit his cigarette. 'Does McGiven want to know that too?'

'Not just him. They want to know where you got the drugs from.'

Larne drew smoke. 'From Mallon, by post.'

'Why?'

'You'd have to ask him that.'

'You were a friend of his.'

'I knew him.'

'You went to his house last night, his wife told us.'

With a barely perceptible acknowledging movement Larne said: 'When were you there?'

'An hour ago.' Hagen lit his own cigarette and glanced over his shoulder at the rest of the room. He looked dissatisfied with it and when he turned back his voice mirrored his look. 'You're poking around,' he said. 'What were you looking for in the garage?'

'I was just looking.'

'All right. McGiven wants the money you got for the drugs, and after that you're to leave things alone. That's the message.'

Larne picked up his glass. 'Don't threaten me,' he said tonelessly.

'*You* were careless,' Hagen said sharply, and the indictment hung for a moment, almost as if it reflected back on himself in some way. 'Go and see McGiven,' he said.

'Did he say he wanted to see me?'

Hagen shook his head: 'No.' Then: 'What're you playing at?'

Strangely the question seemed to amuse Larne in some private way. His face lightened and there was a faint smile round the corners of his eyes. He let it fade slowly, as if it had answered the question. 'Danny Mallon told me you were good with a rifle,' he said. 'Like your brother.'

'He got himself caught.'

'So have a lot of people.' He raised his glass and finished his beer. 'I'll be going. Thanks for the drink.'

'Are you taking the van back?'

'I will later.'

'Where're you going now then?'

Larne stood up. 'I don't know yet. I'll see you around.'

ELEVEN

The broad line of the dual carriageway east seemed cut to match the fenced off flat tracts of land to its right; the docks and coal depots, oil-storage tanks and warehouses on the north side of the river. The road passed these open, often empty acres as London petered out, as if the four lanes of traffic wanted to by-pass the rough edges as quickly as possible, not go near them. There was something both disturbing and fascinating about the way so much land could seem to hold as little and as much at the same time, sketched by roads drawn to die in dead ends, and chain-link fences protecting what no one would want. The view of the ground changed: sometimes it was cut off by an enclave of housing, mistakenly separated from its kind to the north; sometimes the reach of the land came right up to the road, as if threatening it, but the main quality of the area, felt even when it couldn't be seen, was of power and reality – that it offered a true picture of life in its size and its naked industrial dirt, steel and cinders. The power station, factories and sewage farm didn't need anything else for completion.

Larne drove towards Dagenham but turned off the dual carriageway before he got there, into an area that skirted the industrial flat lands with a mixture of houses and dirty pot-holed roads that seemed to turn deeper into the place with no desire to lead anywhere.

Eventually there was a break in the houses that exposed them to the space beyond. The van wheels banged over a rut and Larne slowed and came to the open steel-gated entrance of a yard with high walls topped by broken glass and rusting barbed wire. He turned in.

The yard was in the same state as the road, its surface hammered and broken by the weight of lorries and trailers, blackened and greasy with oil and exhaust fumes. Like an island there was a two-storey building at its centre, built of smooth surfaced red brick with iron stairs leading up to the first floor on the outside. Between the windows of the two floors there were weather-worn letters painted in white on the brick and facing the gates: GILLESPIE HAULAGE (UK) LTD.

There were half a dozen cars parked along the side of the building, but Larne took the van left and stopped clear of the gates by the inside of the perimeter wall. He got out, closed the door, and looked round without hurry.

There was no sign of life in the yard. At the back, beyond the offices, there were five container trailers spaced out and parked without tractor units to move them. To the right there were two flat-bed trailers, empty and abandoned, nose to tail. The only place where someone might be working, out of sight, was an open-fronted shed where a Leyland tractor unit was parked, cab tipped to give access to the engine.

Larne lit the end of a cigarette which had gone out, puffed it a couple of times and then moved towards the shed at a stroll. He gave the front of the truck a measured look as he rounded it and stopped beside the raised back edge of its cab. At the rear of the shed a man in blue overalls was working at a bench with his back turned.

'Good day, George,' Larne said.

The man called George turned round, still holding a piece of metal. He was Jamaican, a few years older than Larne, with strands of grey in the hair that showed beneath a red baseball cap. The skin of his face was vaguely purple, pitted, and above rounded cheeks his eyes had an almost marble-white look. They creased up slightly in a grin as they saw Larne.

'Joe Irish,' George said. 'How're you, man?'

'Okay, how're you?'

'Bloody busy.' He came forward with a cylinder valve in his hand. 'Ever seen a cow with six wheels? You're right next to it.'

'What's the matter with it?' Larne looked in at the smooth steel and exposed wells of the cylinder block.

'Blows gaskets every two minutes. It's a warped cylinder head, I *think*. It's bein' checked now. Take the damn thing for scrap if it's not.' He laughed. Then: 'You lookin' for the boss?'

Larne made a half nod. 'Passing through. How's the business?'

'Seems to be gettin' enough. Got nine trucks out now.' He angled his head at Larne. 'Wantin' a job?'

With a last draw on his cigarette Larne dropped it and trod it out. 'Is there one going?'

George shrugged. 'Maybe. You heard about Danny Mallon, yeah?'

'I heard,' Larne said. 'What happened here?'

'Lots of police.' He turned and went back to the bench and Larne followed on. George plugged in a kettle and leaned on the bench beside it.

'Monday,' he said. 'They were here all day.'

'Doing what?'

'Asking questions, searching stuff. They didn't bother me much but they had Gillespie in the office two or three times.'

'D'you know why?'

George blew down his nose. 'I've been working here ten years, man. Another ten an' I'm going back to Jamaica while I can enjoy it. You know what I mean?'

'How many times did Mallon go out in the last couple of months?'

'Hard to say.' He tugged at his ear, reckoning up. 'About four. One trip in June I remember because he had a truck I was supposed to service and he came back late.'

'Where was that to?'

'No, I don't remember.'

'What about the others?'

'One first week this month – Amsterdam, then one about a week after that, somewhere in Belgium.' He moved to switch off the kettle. 'You know Gillespie can tell you better. D'you want tea?'

'No thanks.' Larne put a hand in his pocket and watched the man's back for a moment. 'The police didn't take Gillespie in at all?'

'Not that I saw.' He stirred a tea bag round in a mug.

'Okay. Thanks George. I'll see you around.'

'Leavin'?' George turned.

'Yeah.'

'Okay. Watch how you're goin', man. We'll have a drink next time.'

Larne went out of the shed and walked back towards the van. He didn't look at the offices, but when he was about five yards from the van a man came out on to the iron steps and watched him for a moment, then whistled sharply. Larne stopped and turned, looking up. The man beckoned him in.

Larne seemed to weigh it, but he walked back towards the offices and the man came down the steps. He was in his fifties with thick wavy hair, a mixture of dark brown and yellow, oiled back from a lined forehead. His face could have been sharp once, but that had dulled, except round his eyes. They had a business directness – observant and used to authority – and when he spoke there was a faint southern Irish accent.

'Were you looking for me, Joe?'

'Not really,' Larne said.

'What do you want here then?'

Larne's voice was easy. 'Just passing.'

The man rested a smooth hand on the rail of the steps and glanced round the yard. 'McGiven didn't send you?'

'I haven't seen him in six months.'

The tone and the look of the man's face changed slightly, became more insistent. 'You'd better say what you want, Joe. If you're not from McGiven what are you doing?'

'I was on my way out.'

'You're a liar. What's going on? McGiven knows no one's to come here till I say so. There's been enough trouble.'

Larne's gaze froze a little, and so did his voice. 'If you've finished I'll be going.'

'You'll tell me.' He caught hold of Larne's arm as he started to turn.

'Take your hand off, Gillespie. I don't work here.'

There was a moment of stillness, then Gillespie withdrew his hand and Larne moved away. Gillespie watched him for a couple of paces before turning and going back up the steps at a trot.

When Larne reached the van Gillespie was already inside the building, but the mechanic was standing by the cab of the truck looking his way. Larne tipped his head and got into the van.

It was mid-afternoon when Larne got back to Croydon, but he stopped half a mile from home to buy fish and chips. He ate them parked by the kerb, abstractedly watching the movements around him, absorbed in a blank sort of way. It was almost as if the stop was designed to finalise something from that morning; as though he'd come across things he'd already half expected and now he was judging how they would affect him. When he drove away the matter seemed settled.

He parked the van two streets from his own, out of sight of the route someone would take to get to his house. He walked the final two hundred yards and the streets were almost empty except for two or three women with young children and shopping and a small group of teenagers lounging at the end of a road. He let himself in through the front door and locked it behind him.

There was a card on the floor to say that someone had been to read the gas meter and would call again tomorrow. Larne picked it up, read it and dropped it on the living-room table as he passed. He took off his coat and looked round the room, as if looking for changes, but it lasted just a few seconds and then he let himself out of the back door.

Past the protruding block of the kitchen the back yard of the house had a high wall to the right but shared open space across the rear of two others to the left, separated only by a variety of low wooden fences and scrubby privet hedges. Patches of grass and narrow borders were enclosed by paths of tarmac or flagstones which led twenty feet to the coal sheds and dividing wall at the bottom. Beyond them the houses of the next street backed up close.

Larne's garden was neat but bare. He kept the square rug of grass clipped and weeded the edges but he hadn't replaced the plants that had died since he'd come there. The sun caught the earth at an angle, moving round, over the houses to the street. Next door yellow sheets hung heavily on a washing line, dripping water on to the light grey soil, already dried out since last night. Three doors along a teenage girl in a bikini and sunglasses was stretched out on a sun bed, that strange, spare-fleshed mixture of adult and child. She seemed to be asleep.

Larne went down the path to the coal shed and opened the stiff door. Inside it was dirty and dark, empty except for the rusted frame of a pram at the back. He reached up to the ledge where the gapped tiles met the wall and took down a pound-hammer and a broad-bladed cold chisel, both roughly coated with rust.

Carrying the tools back towards the house he stepped over a border on to the grass. At the top edge of it a rectangular drain cover was inset across the edge of the grass and the soil, and after a glance at the way his neighbour's washing shielded him from view he squatted down.

The depressions below the cover's lifting bars were half filled with caked dirt, but he cleared one of them out enough to get his fingers under the bar and then lifted. The lid came up as if sealed, peeling away dirt round its edges. Larne raised it clear and let it fall back on the grass. The hole it exposed was the same shape as the cover, brick lined and three feet deep. At the bottom two pipes fed into a damp concrete gutter which disappeared away from the house.

Larne lowered himself into the hole, placing his feet on either side of the drain, and with his left hand curled round the chisel he lined the blade up along the cement holding the middle brick of the top layer. There wasn't much space between himself and the brickwork, but he swung the hammer and began splitting the mortar. The thuds of the work seemed to carry a long way in the quiet, house-backed afternoon, but only at first. He didn't make any attempt to be surreptitious and he didn't look round.

The mortar split fairly neatly, not damaging the bricks, and it took him less than five minutes to loosen half a dozen. He didn't remove them till he'd finished hammering, but then he laid them out in order on the grass.

He glanced up, but as far as he could see he'd aroused no interest and he looked back at the gap he'd created. Instead of a flat wall of earth behind the place where the bricks had been there was an angled hole like the top of a larger space below. Its rim was just below the sunken rim of the drain cover and was about a foot wide.

Larne bent over and put his arm in and down, caught hold of something and pulled it out. It emerged as a piece of packaged canvas, black and oily-looking, like a tool roll. It was about two feet long, nine or ten inches wide and flattened. The canvas was hard like old leather.

He lowered the bundle inside the drain, resting across the bottom, and began to replace the bricks. In a few places, where the mortar had chipped and fallen away, there was a gap left, but by the time all the bricks were back the lining could pass at a glance as simply decaying. He climbed out of the drain, taking the package with him, and lowered the cover. He put the hammer and chisel away and went into the house, locking the back door behind him.

Upstairs there were two bedrooms; his own at the back, and

one at the front with bare floorboards and a dry, closed-off air. There was nothing in it except a wardrobe and an old bed and bare mattress which had been in the house when he'd arrived. The curtains were always half drawn. He took a look at the street below, then moved to the bed.

The crossed strings which held the package closed were stiff like the canvas, but Larne wasn't hurrying. He worked the knots loose with his nails and when that was done he opened the canvas, working the folds until they stayed flat. Inside the package there was plastic-wrapped metal.

At first sight, even when he'd removed the polythene, the weapon didn't look very much like a gun. It was an Ingram M11, less than ten inches long with the stock folded, and the only curves were those of the trigger guard and grip. The rest was a box of rectangular stamped steel and only a short barrel protruding from the box gave the object a meaning in its strange combination of ugliness and functionalism.

Larne worked the bolt on top of the machine pistol's action, but the gun was empty and he began to strip it down, his hands working as if they knew the natural law of how all components worked together, whatever they were a part of.

The gun had been in the ground for nearly three years, but the coating of oil that left his hands slick had kept off the rust, and when he had it in pieces on the mattress he took a cleaning kit from the package and tended each part like a restorer; methodically and with a thoroughness that seemed to combine both preparation and the passing of time. But unlike others he'd seen preparing a weapon for use, there was none of the ritual – like enjoyment – about how he worked. Like a summation, his preparation had an intense pragmatism, and beyond that seemed devoid of either feeling or responsibility, as if it was simply the end of a logical chain of events.

When he'd finished he reassembled the gun and let it lie while he fed thirty-two bullets from a box of a hundred into each of two magazines. He slid one magazine home into the base of the gun's grip and put the other beside the six-inch tube of a silencer which could be screwed to a thread on the gun's barrel.

Finally he stood up and took a thin wad of ten-pound notes from the canvas, then rewrapped all the surplus items and put the package in the bottom of the wardrobe. He took the Ingram, magazine and silencer downstairs with the money.

TWELVE

The telephone broke the near silence of the house, sudden over the muted sound of the television. Larne got up from the armchair and went to answer it. The house was dark and the curtains were open. Outside the sun had set twenty minutes ago.

As he picked up the phone there was the urgent sound of a call box wanting money, but no money was put in. The sound lasted five seconds and then the caller hung up.

Larne did the same. He went back to the front room, unlocked the door and turned off the television before going back to his chair. Propped beside it, upside down, was the Ingram.

Fifteen minutes later the sound and lights of a car stopping close to the front window made Larne move again.

He reached for the Ingram and stood up, holding it loosely in his right hand. He took a step forward to look at the car outside; white and the same model he'd seen Hagen with earlier that day. Someone, alone, moved to get out and Larne went to stand by the door at the bottom of the stairs. As he did so he transferred the gun to his left hand, forming his crooked fingers round the grip and the trigger.

He didn't hear the car door close, but after a moment there was a knock on the front door.

'It's open,' Larne said.

The handle turned and the door came inwards. A man's figure came with it, the face only vaguely discernible. The action was smooth but not fast, perhaps a little cautious. A step into the room he said, 'Larne? It's Naulty.'

Larne watched his hands, one on the door, the other by his side. 'Shut the door.'

As Naulty turned to do that Larne switched the light on. Naulty turned back. He was dressed the same way he had been that morning but without sunglasses to hide his brown eyes. In the artificial light his hair seemed a darker red and his

almost bullish features also looked pink, as if he'd been in the
sun slightly too long. His eyes picked up the Ingram, half way
raised in Larne's hand, and they stayed on it, weighing it up
for a moment.

'McGiven sent me,' he said.

'What for?'

'To pick you up. He wants to see you.' His eyes went back
to the gun. 'You won't need that.'

'Are you carrying?'

'No, why should I?' He held his hands away from his body
in an open gesture.

Larne took it up. He moved forward and Naulty turned
himself to be patted down. Larne did it without fuss and
moved back when he'd finished. 'Why didn't McGiven call
me?' he said.

'We're going to pick up Dave Hagen.' He lowered his hands.
'Are you coming?'

Larne stepped away from the man, then turned as if he'd
made up his mind. He rested the Ingram on the back of the
sofa and got his leather jacket from its hook. Naulty watched
him button the jacket, but when Larne went to pick up the
Ingram again Naulty said, 'I told you, you don't need that.'
There was nothing in his voice, just statement.

Shifting the safety Larne put the gun in his side pocket.
'Maybe,' he said.

After a second Naulty shrugged. He opened the door and
stepped out. Larne switched off the light and followed.

They drove north and Naulty kept quiet. He was an edgy
driver with no sympathy for the car and no feeling for the
traffic. Twice he cut through lights already on amber, but
Larne said nothing. They crossed the Thames at Rotherhithe
and headed east, into the industrial dockland beyond Poplar.
A few minutes later Naulty slowed and turned into the
entrance of an industrial trading estate close to the river. In
the darkness the buildings were identical; tall sided, fairly
new, occasionally lit on a corner by a hooded light. Larne
didn't ask questions and Naulty offered no explanation of
where they were going.

They followed the avenues of the place for a short time and
eventually the headlights showed a cul-de-sac cut across by a

fence. Parked in front of the end building, backed up to it, was a white Transit van with a hire firm's name on its side. Naulty pulled the wheel round and stopped the car next to it. He turned off the lights and the engine and opened his door. When Larne didn't move he said, 'Hagen's inside.'

For another second Larne stayed still, then he also opened his door and got out.

The unit was the last of a row. It had a large roller door on the right and an ordinary one by a window on the left. The ground rose to the main door in a ramp and above ten or twelve feet of light brick wall the top part of the building was made of broadly corrugated steel with a flat roof. Most of the other units had a name or a sign, but this one was blank and the window was boarded up on the inside.

Naulty didn't wait for Larne. He went to the side door and knocked lightly. Larne watched from six feet away, unobtrusive.

There was a brief pause, then Naulty said his name and the door opened inwards, shedding light. He stepped over its threshold and held it, glancing back at Larne. Larne went in.

The interior was half lit and half not; strip lights hanging in pairs from steel rafters. The first sense was of an absolute emptiness that threw back the slightest sounds from the naked brick walls and white-grey concrete floor, harsh and without anything to break it.

Hagen had opened the door and he stood to one side of it now, letting Naulty take over as guard, waiting for Larne to join him. Larne looked around the space, at a spot by the far wall on the edge of the light, and then his attention focused on Hagen.

'Okay, Joe?' Hagen said.

Larne made a slight nod. 'What's going on?'

Hagen drew on a cigarette. 'Questions,' he said and moved towards the rear wall, expecting Larne to follow.

He did, but as they got closer his face became set, almost imperceptibly dropping all trace of the thoughts behind it, his eyes moving steadily, without expression.

Two men were standing there, neither lightweights, although one was shorter and more obviously powerful than the other. He was balding on top, stripped to his shirt sleeves and had heavy boots on his feet. The second man had on an open jacket and his long hair had fallen across his eyes. He

102

flicked it back with a jerk of his head as he put a gold wristwatch back on his arm. Between them on a tubular steel chair was a third man and they stood slightly back from him as Hagen and Larne came closer.

The seated man's face was hidden. His head hung down, half-turned sideways, and his shoulders were slumped forward. He was held to the chair by nylon washing line tied round his stomach. He wore a T-shirt, but it had been ripped in two down the front and below it he was naked, his trousers and underpants in a bundle round his ankles. His chest, T-shirt and legs were caked in blood and around and over himself and the chair there was vomit and a yellow patch of urine. The air stank of it, and of sweat, made more sickly by an aftershave scent from one of the others. Larne saw the rising blackness of bruises on the man's skin, and on his arms the red blistered flesh of cigarette burns. A yard from the chair there were two truck batteries, jump leads and a bucket of water. No one spoke as Larne took it in.

'Who is he?' he said.

'He was a friend of Danny Mallon's, that's why he's here.' Hagen's voice was simple.

Larne shifted his eyes to him. 'Naulty said we were to see McGiven.'

'He'll call. Shouldn't be long.'

'Has be been here?'

Hagen nodded, pulling on his cigarette. 'A while ago.'

Larne studied the younger man's face for a moment, then turned away and began to walk back across the empty concrete floor. He'd gone six steps before Hagen called after him.

'You've got to wait, Joe.'

Larne stopped, turned slowly. 'Have you finished?'

'With him?' Hagen's hand gestured at the man on the chair. 'Just about.'

'Call McGiven.'

'I told you, he'll call us.'

'Call him,' Larne said softly.

For a moment Hagen did nothing, then he shrugged. 'All right, Joe.'

He came back towards the door and Larne moved with him. On the floor beneath the boarded up window was a phone. Hagen picked it up and dialled a number. Larne stood a few feet away, eyes hooded, not looking at anything.

When the phone was answered Hagen said: 'Hello. Yeah, it's me. —Yeah, I know. —It's okay, he's here. —No, no. Okay, about twenty minutes. Yeah, okay.'

He hung up and put the phone back on the floor. When he straightened he was looking at Larne. 'We're going. All right?'

Larne raised his eyes but didn't say anything.

'Want to finish it?' Hagen said.

Still Larne said nothing, and then, as if tired of his silence, Hagen tugged back his jacket and there was a revolver in his hand. He hefted it, moving his fingers round the grip, then strode hard to the far wall. He barely seemed to halt by the chair, but he put the muzzle of the revolver close to the man's head and pulled the trigger.

The sound of the shot expanded like gas to the walls and the roof, hitting them, being cast back instilled with their hardness. The man's body jerked sideways and he toppled the chair to the floor, lay twitching slightly, but already Hagen was coming back.

Larne looked at Naulty. The man had winced at the impact of the shot, but now his gaze was neutral and he appeared almost oblivious. Across the floor the two other men bent to the body. Larne opened the door.

'Make it deep,' Hagen said to Naulty. 'And lock up.'

Outside Hagen followed Larne to the car without speaking, but as he opened the driver's door he said flatly, 'I do my job, Joe.'

They climbed the stairs in the middle of the tenement block and emerged on the second-floor landing, jutting like a shelf over the forecourt below. Hagen turned left and they passed three or four doors next to windows, most of them with curtains drawn, and sometimes faint, disjointed sounds beyond. In the darkness the balcony felt like an isolated catwalk, exposed above half-hidden movements and noises, random lights and emptiness, all distant below. And Hagen was distant. He didn't refer to Larne, but not as if Larne wasn't there. Instead it was almost as though Hagen had adopted Larne's silence, had lost the need to fill spaces with comment or glances.

He stopped by a door, knocked and stood without moving. A few seconds passed until a man's voice inside asked who it was. Hagen said his name and there was the sound of a chain coming off the door, then it opened.

The man inside was short. He wore a green nylon knit shirt with its flimsy collar open around a scrawny neck and somehow incongruous gold chain. His face was shrunken, unhealthy and his hair was speckled with dandruff. His hand on the door was claw-like and old.

'All right there, Davey?' he said. His accent was south Irish and sounded as if he used it a lot.

Hagen nodded. 'Where is he?'

'In the front room. Go on through, son.'

He kept hold of the door till Larne had gone past him, then closed it and put the chain back.

Larne followed Hagen down the hallway. They passed a side door into a kitchen where the light was on over a table and crockery; untidy, and beneath that somehow bare looking and bleak, as if it would be left that way. Two more doors were closed on the passage, but at the end the one to the sitting room stood a foot open.

Hagen went in and the room beyond was dim, lit by the light of a colour television and a standard lamp in the corner. The light caught only what faced it; the back of a settee; a low glass table scattered with magazines and newspapers; the brown side of a beer bottle; the plastic lid of a cheap record player. The colour of the yellow geometric wallpaper ceased to mean anything beyond the radius of the lamp and the air was stuffy and too old.

Hagen moved his hand to the light switch.

'Leave it alone.'

Hagen's hand fell away.

'Did you do it?'

Hagen took another step into the room. McGiven stirred in his armchair, turning his head and looking up sourly. 'Did you finish it?'

'It's done,' Hagen said flatly. 'No trouble.'

McGiven turned his head back. 'Wait for Naulty. In the kitchen.'

For a couple of seconds Hagen continued to look down at McGiven, then he moved back and went past Larne to the passage.

'Come in, Joe,' McGiven said. 'Shut the door.'

He seemed to be watching the television, but as Larne

closed the door he picked up a remote control and turned its volume to practically nothing. 'Bloody rubbish on TV these days. Just crap. D'you ever watch the cops and robbers, Joe? You should. They always get their man, even in this country. Z Cars, Sweeney, all that. It's the soap opera with uniforms. Doesn't matter what they've got – drug addicts, glue sniffers, armed robbers – it all comes right in the end. And if people see enough of it on the TV that's how they start thinking. Doesn't matter, it'll be right in the end.'

Larne stood by the arm of the settee, the third point of a triangle between McGiven, the television and himself. The light from the screen reflected as small squares in McGiven's eyes below a rough fringe of hair. He had long sideburns and his face was like Larne's in some ways; heavy and without any fine lines. But it was younger – five or six years – and it had a dark quality, like a mood, constantly hovering close to its surface, threatening, even when its expression or McGiven's words were light.

He looked up at Larne. 'Aren't you going to sit down?'

Larne seemed to consider, then he moved in front of the settee. He put his hand in his pocket and took out the Ingram and as he sat down he placed it beside him on the seat.

Something made McGiven laugh, lightly, and it carried into his voice. 'How long've you been carrying that around?'

'Not long.'

'A squirt gun is it? What's that, twelve hundred rounds a minute? Just squirt them out.'

He leaned forward, showing the straps of a shoulder holster over his shirt. He reached under his arm and took out a pistol, holding it so that Larne could see it against the flat of his hand. Its muzzle was swollen by the tube of a silencer. 'Have you ever seen this one here, Joe? They call it the hush puppy. The yanks had it made for Vietnam; killing guard dogs round enemy camps. The hush puppy.'

He laughed again and put the gun back in its holster, then he got up, quite quickly as if he'd been meaning to do it for a long time.

Behind his chair there was a shelf with bottles and glasses laid out on it. He reached in and lifted a bottle of whiskey and two tumblers, brought them back and put them on the table while he retook his seat. He poured and passed Larne a glass.

'Who was the man?' Larne asked.

'Did you know him?' McGiven sat back, straighter than he had been.

'I didn't see his face.'

'It wouldn't have done you much good if you had. Who finished it – the Boy Wonder?'

'Hagen,' Larne said. 'Who was he?'

McGiven's eyes glanced at him, as if annoyed that the question hadn't been dropped. He raised his glass and drank from it. 'John Gilmore,' he said. 'He grassed Danny Mallon.' His gaze went to the television screen and stayed for a while.

'Did he tell you that?' Larne said.

'Aye, he talked.' McGiven's voice was empty.

'Why did you want me there?'

McGiven took his attention away from the television. 'Are you going soft, Joe? Didn't you like it?' He reached forward and tipped whiskey into his glass. 'Where's the money you got?'

'Put away.'

'It's not yours, though.' He drank. 'Jack Bell called me last night. You shouldn't have told him it was Danny's stuff you were selling. He got the jitters. I want it back.'

'It's gone,' Larne said.

'Get it back!' McGiven's voice rose, but Larne didn't move.

'It was his cache,' he said.

'He'd been skimming it off.'

'Gilmore didn't grass Danny Mallon,' Larne said. 'He did it on his own and he was going on the run. He sent me his cache to look after and then you put a bomb under him. Who was it – Hagen?'

'The Boy Wonder,' McGiven said scornfully. 'You know who he is? Paul Hagen's brother. You remember Paul Hagen. You should.' He finished his drink, tossing it off angrily, the black mood on his face now.

'What's he doing here?' Larne asked.

The hardness didn't leave the other man's voice. 'Taking after his brother.'

'Paul Hagen was INLA.'

'Aye, and maybe the Boy Wonder's on rent. Don't ask me. Since your pal Danny brought the police down the rest's gone to hell in a barrow. You think I'm in here for the good of my health? I've not set foot past the door since Tuesday except for tonight. But our friend Hagen is running around. Ask *him* what he's doing.'

McGiven leaned back with the whiskey bottle in his hand. He clinked its neck against the rim of his glass, pouring lazily, as if he was spent, or meant getting drunk. Larne was quiet for a while, as though he didn't want to stir the other man again. Eventually, though, he took a ready-rolled cigarette from his tin and lit it. He let the smoke drift and said: 'Why did you want to see me tonight?'

Only McGiven's eyes moved, under half-closed lids. 'You've been poking around. You saw Gillespie and you were searching that garage of Mallon's.' He said it quietly and he was watching Larne.

'Are you warning me off?'

'I want to know what you were doing.'

'And seeing Gilmore, that was to encourage me?'

'He had it coming. He earned it.'

'Not because you lost those nine men.'

'*We*.' McGiven sat up again, turning to face Larne. 'We. We're all part of it. You're making waves, casting shadows. There's fuck all left, but there'll be less if you keep on prying around. What were you after, tell me that. Did you have something going with Mallon, is that it?'

Larne shook his head. 'I saw him once in two or three months. He left six rifles with me. That's all.'

'So why did he send you his cache to look after? Why did you visit his wife?'

Again Larne shook his head, denying a reason. 'I don't know.'

'You don't think he grassed? He was seen doing it. I *know* that.'

Larne thought about that, and when he spoke it was as if he was putting it together for the first time. 'He could have been forced to. The last time I saw him he was nervous. If he'd been caught with a load the police could have put pressure on to make him talk, letting him move around for a while so they could pick up other names.'

'So why didn't they come to you? They came to everyone else.'

'They came to me. He'd warned me to clean out the yard.'

'Told you and nobody else!' McGiven's voice was sharp.

'And if he had, what would you have done?'

'I'd have shot the miserable whoreson, and he knew it.'

'If you'd given him chance he might have come. He was going to pick up the rifles he'd left.'

'To buy himself out?' The anger had risen in him again. 'I'd still call him a treacherous bastard. He was scum, and now he's dead scum.' He pulled one hand into a tight fist.

In that moment the door opened and Hagen came in. McGiven glanced up. 'What d'you want?'

Hagen looked a little disparaging but he kept his voice toneless. 'Got a drink?'

'You know where it is.'

Hagen moved behind McGiven and poured himself a drink, taking his time.

McGiven waited and when Hagen finished he brought the drink round, but instead of leaving the room he passed in front of McGiven towards the other armchair. As he did he noticed the Ingram beside Larne and gave him a faint, almost cynical smile out of sight of McGiven. He sat down and looked content, as if waiting for someone to start talking again.

In the end it was McGiven. He put back his whiskey, poured another and then put the bottle aside. He said: 'How much stock have you got, Joe?'

'I told him this morning,' – a small gesture at Hagen – 'eleven pistols and some ammunition.'

'Nothing else?'

'No.'

'Where are they?'

'Buried.'

'Dig them up.'

Larne tapped his cigarette over an ashtray, watching his hand. 'What for?'

'Never mind. I want them.'

For a moment Larne didn't reply, and then Hagen saved him the need. 'We want plastic, not pistols.'

'No one asked you.'

'Tell me we don't. You can't go near Keeble's stuff, or the others'. If they've talked the cops'll be waiting; maybe even if they haven't.'

'We'll get word now they've been charged.'

'And walk into a set up.' Hagen made a noise of disgust. 'We need fresh stuff.'

'Do you think so, Joe?' McGiven looked squarely at Larne.

'If you can get it. What's your hurry?'

McGiven's mouth tightened. 'I'm not letting the bastards make mileage out of catching our people. Fuck that. We'll hit back and hit now.' He looked at Hagen. 'And if it's fresh plastic you want you can have it. I made a deal today. You go north and pick it up tomorrow; both of you.'

There was silence, then Hagen gave a slow acquiescent nod, but Larne said, 'You don't need me.'

'The stuff's coming from Curwin. You know him, he doesn't.'

'No,' Larne said. 'I've finished carrying.'

'You'll do as I tell you. If you're working you can't be nosing around making trouble, and *you've* got the money to pay Curwin.'

'The money's gone.'

'Your problem.' McGiven pointed a finger at him. 'Get it back, get some more or get the plastic without it. Maybe you can sell your cache like you did Danny Mallon's. You're going to do something, though; you've been pushing it and it won't go much further.'

'Are you saying *I* owe *you*?' Larne asked, his voice quiet.

Briefly McGiven's insistence wavered. He looked hesitant, unsure. Then he pulled himself together. 'Do it,' he said. 'I told Curwin two and a half grand for five hundred pounds. That's about five times what it's worth, but I want it. Call him when you get up there. He'll arrange the meeting.' He stood up. 'Sort it out between you what time you start tomorrow. Naulty will drive you home when he gets back.' And with that he moved around the settee and left the room.

When he'd gone Larne stirred. 'Is there a phone here?'

Hagen nodded to the darkened side of the room. 'Over there. Who're you calling?'

'A taxi. Naulty could take his time.'

He got up and made the call, arranging for the cab to pick him two streets away in ten minutes. When he hung up he came back into the light but didn't sit down.

Hagen watched him, and as Larne picked up his tobacco tin he said 'What about tomorrow?'

'What about it?' Larne said.

Hagen's gaze was direct. 'Are you coming?'

'You heard your man.'

'What about the money? Have you got it?'

110

Larne's answer was simple. He picked up the Ingram and said, 'No.'

'You'd better bring that then. I'll pick you up about ten.'

Larne manoeuvred the gun into his pocket. 'Call first.'

Hagen nodded. Larne turned to go, but then Hagen said, 'Wait a minute, Joe.'

He stood up and came a step closer to Larne. He seemed not quite sure how to phrase what he was going to say, but when he did his voice was a shade lower than it had been.

'I've heard some talk,' he said. 'They say you had a cache hidden away when the police took you – a big cache. Is it true?'

Larne's eyes were slow, almost distant. 'What would you want to know for?'

'Someone told me it was good stuff; a half-inch machine gun and rifles. If it's still there—'

With a short laugh Larne said: 'It's explosives he wants.'

'*Explosions*,' Hagen said. 'And no money to pay for them. Why d'you think he wants Mallon's money? He's got to get back in the good books or he's had it, and the only way he'll do that is with bombs. He's got to make up for nine men and he's running scared of what they'll do if he doesn't.'

'You think a machine gun would help him?'

'Not him, he's had it. But if we got those guns across the water, something to shoot down their helicopters . . .'

Larne shook his head.

'It could buy you out, Joe.'

'And you in? You shouldn't listen to stories.'

'Are you telling me you don't have the stuff?'

'I'm not telling you anything. I'll see you tomorrow.'

He moved to the door and went along the hall. The small man in the green nylon shirt glanced up from a newspaper spread on the table and rose to let him out. He relocked the door and chained it when Larne had gone.

THIRTEEN

The next morning Larne packed. He got up at his usual time, but then he ate breakfast, which wasn't routine. He used up most of the perishable food in his fridge; an open tin of baked beans, three eggs, and the last four slices of a loaf. He put a lettuce and a small block of cheese in the waste bin and then emptied the bin outside. After he'd put milk in his coffee he poured the rest down the sink. He ate and washed up and then he packed.

In the street there was more activity than during the week. People went to and came from Saturday shopping and more cars lined the pavements. The weather was warm and high white cloud coloured the sky. A couple of times Larne glanced out at the road, but only in a casual way as he passed a window. He seemed passive and most of his attention was focused on things he would need to take. There wasn't a lot; just a few spare clothes packed tightly into a medium-sized holdall with a handle and shoulder strap. He was already wearing clean jeans and a shirt and a light canvas windcheater that he rarely put on was laid out ready to go.

He finished what he was doing just as the phone rang, as if he'd known when it would. He answered it and Hagen's voice said, 'Ready?'

'How long?'

'Fifteen minutes.'

'I'll be on London Road.'

He hung up and went to lock the front door. Finally he put the Ingram in the top of the holdall and zipped it up. He put on his jacket and went out of the back door, emerging on to the street from the side passage.

As he walked he felt no particular strangeness at leaving. The idea of it had been with him yesterday evening, and earlier, when he'd dug out the gun. Even before that some sense of impermanence had always lived with him; the knowledge that at some time something could force the action

112

without warning. Leaving at that moment was caused both by himself and by others, but from now on he knew it became simply himself. He didn't think about going back.

On London Road he began to walk north, facing the on-coming traffic which was mostly buses and cars. He walked by the edge of the kerb but passed on the inside of lamp posts and signs. As a normal precaution he looked back every so often and kept his pace steady, though slightly faster than the strings and knots of people shopping along the road. And because he was facing the traffic it would be difficult for anyone to follow him by car. He wasn't sure who he thought might try, or even if anyone would, but that made no difference. He had taken the aspect of a carrier again and that removed the need to reason out caution.

Five or six minutes later a dark red Capri slowed into the kerb. It was eight years old and its paint and black vinyl roof were matt and dusty with age. In places it was specked by dried bird droppings, as if it had stood outside for some time. The windscreen had been cleaned in double arcs by the wipers and behind it was Hagen. He looked up at Larne, then leaned over to open the passenger door. Larne got in and twisted round to push his bag into the back. As he closed the door Hagen moved off.

For a few moments the younger man concentrated on the traffic, then he glanced across at Larne. 'What's the bag for, Joe? It won't be a long trip.'

'Maybe.'

'Did you get the money?'

Larne shook his head and turned his eyes to the road. 'No,' he said.

Hagen seemed to have planned the route he wanted to follow. He turned west and then north on the Mitcham road, and from there up through Wandsworth, crossing the river at Putney Bridge. The traffic was steady but not very fast moving until they reached Hendon and slipped on to the M1. Then there was more space as the six lanes slid past house backs and through concrete-walled cuts. Most of the other traffic was going south, in towards the city, with coaches hauling past cars and passengers just beginning to look up. Hagen pushed their speed to seventy-five and his face was quiet, settled into a mask for the driving, expressionlessly guiding the wheel through his hands. He looked almost bored.

It was Larne who made the first move to talk, when the road finally moved out into open country. He'd glanced at their speed a couple of times, but after the initial push at the beginning of the motorway Hagen had come back to the limit. Larne took a ready-rolled cigarette from his tin and as he lit it he said, 'Where's the car from?'

Hagen seemed to think for a moment. 'From a fella I know. I got it this morning.' He paused again. 'It's not hot if that's what you're thinking.'

'No.'

'I wondered if you'd be there this morning. You were right, it's not a two-man job, not if it's straight.'

'Have *you* got the money?'

'Me?' Hagen laughed. 'Not two and a half grand.'

'Then it's not straight.'

'Did you bring your gun.'

'I've got it.'

Larne smoked for a while and they passed a slip road on to the carriageway. Hagen moved from the middle to the outside lane to give room to a car and then decided to stay where he was. There was farmland beside them and several fields showed the signs of harvesting; cut hay left to dry and the shaved tracks of combined harvesters in concentric squares.

'What about Curwin?' Hagen said. 'Will he think it's straight?'

'He should. It has been before.'

'When?'

'A few years.'

'What's his connection with the plastic? Does he buy it or steal it?'

'Didn't McGiven tell you?' Larne drew on his cigarette.

'He gave me the name and a number to call. He wouldn't have done that if he didn't need the stuff in a hurry. I told you last night, he's running scared. He's not talking to anyone. He thinks if he keeps what he's got to himself then they can't pull him out. He's wrong, though. He's only got scraps.' He let the last sentence hang for a second, then glanced at Larne. 'So what about Curwin?'

Larne shrugged. 'He's a connection. He works from Manchester, sometimes Leeds. I never asked where his stuff comes

114

from. It'll be demolition and quarries for sure, though.'

'Who'll choose the place?'

'Probably him. We'll call when we're closer.'

'And then?'

'And then *what*?' Larne's gaze was outside and his voice was flat, uncompromising and suddenly uninterested. Like an abrupt wave he didn't want to talk any more; as if being there, beside Hagen and moving, had just become real and didn't please him.

Hagen seemed to sense it. He negated his question with a sharp move of his hand. 'Never mind.'

It became warmer and brighter as they drove, and the sky lost its high overcast look to large banks of cloud. The tarmac and hard shoulder had a greasy summer sheen, unwashed and unclean in an uncomfortable heat that only emphasised the dirt. The road seemed populated by drivers in shirt sleeves, uncertain at the wheel, with children and luggage in the back and plastic-flapping roof racks. And as they passed through the shires the lanes only became more congested by these families who wanted to move before the bank holiday.

In one place two cars had collided and one had been forced up the bank, leaving a scar and coming to rest pointing down, its side caved in. A patrol car was there in front of an ambulance and as they passed Larne saw the people for a moment, frozen in position, as if they had nothing to do.

These were the victims but Larne felt nothing for them, didn't even think about them in passing. The crash was a part of the landscape, as remote from feeling and as unremarkable as the contours and towns in the distance, too far away for life to be seen.

And in a way, the idea of landscape was a part of Larne, a part of his sight. He didn't remember it as always that way, but for long enough now to know that it wouldn't change. It was too deep and too basic, however it had come about; this knowledge, like an unvarying base line, that landscapes were inhabited by people, were moved on, but *only* moved *on*. They were ground and everything else passed over. And like that, Larne didn't really think about people, except as moving, transitory surface features. Inside himself he knew his landscape was empty, or at least could be scraped clean and left empty. When his mind drifted with nothing to hold it, so too did his vision of people. They became only faint ghost illusions. The crashed cars they had passed were empty and dead.

In the end it was Hagen who broke the long silence of Larne's eyes on the road and the land beyond it. His voice sounded new. It was gone noon and they had been following the M6 for more than an hour, through Birmingham and past Stafford. A blue sign marked services in less than a mile and Hagen said: 'We'd better call Curwin.'

Larne nodded, as if waking up. 'Pull in at the services.'

'I was going to.'

They moved in to the slip road, slowing. The engine note changed and eased off and Hagen let the car drift round a high-kerbed bend, following the signs. On a large tarmac apron divided by lamp posts he rolled the Capri in to a halt between white lines. A hundred yards away the cafeteria building was almost lost behind ranks of parked cars, their roofs catching the sun. On a patch of grass to one side there was an inflated castle painted yellow and red and grubby from children. Above it all a limp flag hung from a pole.

Hagen switched off the engine and undid his seat belt, then just sat for a moment, relaxing his legs. Finally he turned just his head towards Larne. 'Do you want to call Curwin?'

Larne eased his own legs. 'No, you do it. If McGiven's arranged it he'll be waiting. I'm only here for the ride.'

'You sure about that?' Then he ran a hand through his hair and sat upright. 'What about the place?'

'Not in the city. We want it quiet.'

'Okay. Do you want something to eat or drink while I'm there?'

'A sandwich. Here.' He reached in his pocket but Hagen shook his head and opened the door.

'It's on me,' he said. 'I'll not be long.'

He got out and pushed the door to behind him. Larne watched him for the first five or six yards, walking stiffly to ease his legs, then he also got out of the car, but left the door wide.

The air smelled of lingering fumes, without a breeze to stir them, and in the background there was the continuous passing sound of traffic. The motorway was beyond a wooden fence and a strip of yellow-green grass and Larne looked at it for a while before turning back to the car.

Hagen was out of sight now and Larne knelt across the seat and took the keys from the ignition. He went to the boot, unlocked it and raised the lid. Inside it was empty, with a few bits of mud and rust over the floor covering, the curves of the wheel arches scratched and dusty. He appraised it for a moment, then peeled back the mat to look at the spare tyre well. The tyre was there, along with an old jack and wheel brace, but nothing else. He replaced the mat and closed the lid.

As he put the keys back in the ignition another car came in and drew up opposite the Capri. A few seconds later it spilled a family of five looking sticky and worn, but Larne took little notice. He opened the glove compartment and checked the shelf under the dash, then lifted both seats. He found only an old can of de-icer, a duster and pieces of grit. Apparently satisfied he sat down and waited.

Hagen took nearly a quarter of an hour to come back. When he did he looked hot, with flushed circles under his eyes. He still had on his jacket though and it was fastened to stop its billowing and showing the gun Larne knew he was wearing. He sat down behind the wheel, cast a glance at the children milling around the opposite car and passed Larne a wrapped sandwich and a can of orange. 'It's packed in there. Queues to the bloody doors.'

'Did you get through?'

'Yeah.' Hagen put his own food and drink on the dashboard and unfolded a new map. 'It's a place called Rainsow, about twenty miles out from the city, so he said.' He searched the map, following road lines with his finger.

'He suggested it?'

'Yeah. What's he like – jumpy?'

'Not particularly.'

'Maybe I'm wrong then. He wants us there first. It's a small reservoir. He'll come about two, see if it's clear and stop if it is. There.' He pointed to a small patch of blue close to the unshaded line of a minor road. It was on the descent of the moors and thin stream lines curved away from it along the contours of a valley.

Larne held out his hand and Hagen gave him the map and turned his attention to his food. He unwrapped a meat pie as Larne traced a route from the reservoir back to the motorway.

117

'You'll need your gun out, Joe.' Hagen said. 'We can't do it without.'

Larne nodded, still looking at the map. 'I told you I'd got it.'

'I heard you, but you've still got that bag back there too.'

'So?' Larne looked up.

Hagen bit into his pie and ate as he talked. 'It makes a difference. If you're thinking about not going back maybe you wouldn't be too worried if this job didn't go right.'

'You'll get the stuff.'

'So you're not going back?'

'I didn't say that.'

'Did you think about what I told you last night? We can drop this if you get that machine gun.'

'It's not the same thing. If the Army Council want bombs they want bombs. A machine gun makes different targets.' Larne opened his can and took a drink.

'The Council's not in it,' Hagen said. 'I thought you knew that. McGiven's out on his own. He's more scared of the Council than he is of the police. No one's told him they want bombs, he's gambling. He thinks if he makes up for losing those cells the Council will forget it. I don't care if they do or not, but if we take a machine gun back over there the Council can do what it wants with McGiven and we're in for a reward. I told you, that gun could buy you out if that's what you want; you'd be clear.'

Larne was quiet for a moment, aware of Hagen's eyes watching him. 'I'm clear now,' he said.

'Yeah? So why are you here?' He went back to his eating, but he hadn't forgotten the subject.

'Why would you help McGiven if you're ready to leave him in the lurch?'

Hagen shrugged. 'I don't have to, but if there's nothing else going . . .' He rewrapped the remains of his pie and put it away. 'McGiven's digging; he'll either get deeper into the shit, or else he'll get out. It doesn't make any difference to me. One way or another he won't last long anyway. He's cracking up, and that's another good reason for him to stay clear of the Council.'

'And did the Council have any say when Danny Mallon was killed?' Larne's voice was flat.

Hagen stiffened, almost completely still, like a missed beat, then he came back to movement in a reach for a cigarette. 'I don't know.'

Larne waited, then seemed to let it drop. 'He knew better,' he said.

'If—'

'No, it's dead.'

Hagen lit his cigarette. 'It is for me,' he said. 'Listen, you please yourself what you do, Joe. If you want to get out I'll not stop you. Maybe it would be better for you if you didn't go back. McGiven's jumping at shadows, like Gilmore last night. He doesn't trust anyone who knew Mallon. He's getting paranoid, you saw him.'

'So he doesn't trust me?'

'No, you scare him, Joe. You wouldn't give him the money and you knew Mallon, but there's something else.' He paused, as if waiting for Larne to confirm or deny it, but Larne only opened his sandwiches.

'Enough to get Gilmore's treatment?' he asked.

'Gilmore was unlucky.'

'He was that.'

Hagen shook his head. 'No, he was stupid, and stupid people are unlucky, but that's not what I meant. If McGiven hadn't been there Gilmore would have been all right.'

'You'd have let him go?'

'Sure. I told you, he was just stupid. He hadn't done much.'

'And you'd have let him go, with a grudge and knowing names and faces.'

Hagen looked thoughtful, then made an open, admissive gesture and half smiled. 'Well, maybe not.'

'No, you're right,' Larne said, for the first time letting agreement sound in his words, as if there was an understanding between the two of them now.

Hagen took it in. 'You've got to take it all the way sometimes,' he said. 'Like today.'

Larne nodded.

'Do you want to finish eating before we go?'

'No, let's get it done.'

Hagen closed his door and started the engine.

FOURTEEN

They left the motorway a few miles further on and Larne followed the map, glancing up from time to time, checking landmarks. He didn't say much except to tell Hagen when to turn, but on Hagen's part there seemed to be an easier air. More than once he commented on something they passed and he appeared to accept an affiliation of some sort from Larne. Larne did nothing to counteract or deny that, but he also didn't confirm it. Hagen made the running, and because of that Larne seemed almost more passive, more separate than he had when there'd been silence between them.

The land rose and became blunted and open. For two or three miles they followed the crooked path of a main road laid bare across the treeless shape of the peak tops. There were drainage ditches beside it and occasional places where the side of a hill fell away close to the verge. Grey sheep wandered in strung-out groups between the wooden roadside markers and the light was bright and strong. A breeze swayed the coarse grass and sometimes entered the car through Hagen's open window.

The road wasn't empty. They passed an intermittent flow of cars containing three, four and five people, heads turned to the windows. On some of the roadside verges the same family cars were parked with the same sort of people eating picnics, staring at the traffic that passed as if they needed relief from the stillness of the landscape. 'We could do without them,' Hagen said.

He turned off the main road on to one without lines, a single track that was often crumbling and uneven at the edges. It ran along the ridge side of a hill, with sharp bends often forcing Hagen to slow, and high walls on the right. The only building Larne saw was an isolated, square stone house, small in the distance, then he indicated a turn and said, 'That one. Right.'

The car went uphill, then down on a curve with walls on both sides. Ten yards further on the wall on the left had a gap

120

that led on to an unmetalled path. 'Hold it here,' Larne said.

He looked at the map and then at where the road continued on, upwards, to the skyline a quarter of a mile away. 'Where is it?' Hagen said.

'In there.' Larne nodded at the gap in the wall, then pointed ahead. 'There's another road up there. That's the way they'll come; so they can see down. Go on.'

Hagen took the car in slowly, its tyres crunching over the loose stone track for ten or twelve feet before it gave out. The ground sloped downwards and he turned the car, then reversed so it was skewed at an angle on the slope, backed up to a wall. He pulled the hand brake on tight and stopped the engine.

The reservoir was small, held in a natural depression like a basin. On all sides the ground dipped smoothly in an uneven square, with walls on the shoulders and yellowing grass on the banks. Below the grass the sides of the reservoir were lined with flat irregular stones like a broken mosaic, their surfaces grey and dried out. It was impossible to tell how deep the reservoir was but it seemed more than half empty. The band of its stone lining was about fifteen feet wide and ringed like a tide line close to the water. At the top of the bank to the left there was a small, yellow brick hut with a green door; square and out of place.

Hagen looked at his watch and said: 'We've got an hour. What d'you want to do?'

Still looking at the reservoir Larne said: 'Just wait.'

Larne had got out of the car for a while and gone as far as the brick hut, walked round it and found nothing. In the grass by the car there was a used condom. Now he sat in the passenger seat and the open door was sometimes tugged when a breeze caught it. The brightness was deceptive; it was warm but the wind was cool.

A yard from the front of the car Hagen sat on the grass, leaning back on his hands with his legs out straight. He had on a pair of sunglasses and looked out across the reservoir, not restless but seemingly bored. He had taken off his jacket and shoulder holster and made a bundle of them to rest his head on. Periodically he changed between lying and sitting and he smoked a couple of times. The light skin of his arms didn't seem to take the sun very well and his fair hair was untidy now. Larne noticed all that for want of anything better to do.

There was a skylark in the air and Hagen coughed from smoking and then there was the sound of a van's engine.

Larne looked back towards the road and at the same time Hagen let the weight off his arms and lay on his back, as if to concentrate better on the sound. It got closer and Larne saw the red roof of a Transit above a wall, coming downhill. It disappeared for a moment, then there was the sound of it slowing and it made the turn into the reservoir's enclosure.

There were two men inside and as it stopped Larne rose slowly and stood beside the car. Hagen rolled on his side and watched, still looking bored.

The van stopped on the slope and the men got out, leisurely closing their doors. They came the short distance towards Larne.

One of them was tall, dark haired and had a sharp broken nose, caved in on the bridge. He took an open, almost disapproving notice of Hagen, who still hadn't moved.

The other man was shorter and slightly older than the first. He wore a lightweight sports jacket and an open-necked shirt and his expression was pleasant in a business-like way. His round face looked as if it had been in the sun and when he twitched back a forelock of hair his forehead was peeling pink. 'Larne . . .' he said, holding out a square hand.

Larne shook it with a nod.

'Been a bit since I've seen you,' Curwin said. 'This is Brian Whitehead.'

'Who's that?' Whitehead was still looking at Hagen.

'His name's Hagen,' Larne said. 'He called you.'

'How you doing?' There was an insolent note in Hagen's voice and the laziness of his attitude.

Curwin didn't react. 'I heard you'd had some trouble down south,' he said to Larne. 'I hope you're going to watch what happens to this stuff. I don't want it traced back.'

'It's not happened yet,' Larne said. 'Where's it from?'

'Different places.' Curwin smiled. 'You know. Five hundred pounds is a lot. I had to buy some in.' He looked at the Capri. 'Can you get it in there?'

'We'll manage.'

'And the cash?'

'In the car.'

Larne turned and leant into the Capri and at the same moment Hagen pushed himself up. 'Come on, let's get it moving,' he said. 'We've waited long enough.'

Whitehead's gaze turned towards him, about to say something, but Hagen wasn't looking. He dusted down his jeans with one hand and bent to scoop up his jacket with the other. His hand came up with a gun.

Larne was turning back now, but both Curwin and Whitehead were looking at Hagen and then Whitehead moved, dipping into his jacket pocket. Hagen fired.

The shot echoed round the banks of the reservoir, filling them out, and the bullet hit Whitehead's chest, pushing him back in a stagger. A hand waved behind him, as if seeking support, but support wasn't there. He gave a silent cough which spilled blood over his lip and put surprise in his eyes, then the strength in his legs seeped away. He sank dead.

Curwin's head moved suddenly to look at Larne but seeing the Ingram he held still. Then he stepped back. Larne didn't move.

Curwin took a second step. 'Jesus Christ. Fuckin' hell. *Larne!*' His voice was rapid, higher pitched. He cast a wide-eyed look at Hagen, then back. 'Take it,' he said. '*Take* it. Jesus. Don't.' He had begun to take a third step when Hagen fired again. The sound was the same as the first time, but Curwin fell straight away. He hit the ground on his side and for a moment his arm made a numbed swimming motion, then ceased.

All sounds had stopped. For a short while there was nothing, until the sound of Hagen drawing a short breath through his nose seemed to put an end to the idea of silence. He lowered the gun, moved to come forward, then remembered his jacket and bent to retrieve it.

Larne shifted quietly, just clear of the car door. 'Leave it,' he said. He had the Ingram pointed at Hagen.

Hagen's head rose but he didn't straighten. 'Don't joke, Joe,' he said, but the words knew it wasn't a joke.

'Let the gun drop. From there.'

The gun moved a fraction. 'What's the idea?'

'Do it. Don't talk.'

Instead Hagen let his jacket fall, then slowly stood up. Larne said nothing more. It rested on Hagen, and he did nothing except watch Larne for the space of three or four heart beats. Then he opened his fingers and let the gun fall.

'All right, Joe; your way.'

Larne's eyes stayed on him. 'Turn round and walk into the water. Up to your neck.'

Again, for the same length of time, Hagen was still. He seemed to be counting, but finally he took a pace back, which changed to a turn and he walked downhill towards the reservoir, arms swinging slightly.

Larne watched him until he'd covered ten or twelve feet, then he almost seemed to lose interest. He leant into the Capri, put its keys in his pocket and took out his holdall. He carried it across to the van and opened the driver's door. The keys were still in the ignition and he pushed the holdall across the seat and looked in the back. Four brown military ammunition cases there seemed to satisfy him and he moved away again.

With a glance at Hagen, now at the water's edge, he went to Whitehead's body and took the gun from its pocket. It was a small semi-automatic, made in Spain, and he kept it with him as he searched Curwin. The older man had no gun, so he put the pistol and the Ingram in his holdall and walked down the reservoir bank as far as Hagen's fallen revolver. It was the same one he'd given him three weeks before and he held it loosely for a moment, then looked at Hagen. He was standing up to his knees in the water, a yard from the edge, watching Larne.

'I said up to your neck,' Larne said.

Hagen didn't move. 'You'd better kill me, Joe,' he said. 'But you won't, and I'm not going to push you into it. You'll have enough trouble, later.'

'Move back,' Larne told him.

Hagen began to walk backwards, slowly, and the water swirled around him. When it touched his hands he sculled it lightly past him.

'You're not going to tell me why?' His voice sounded mildly discrediting. 'What'll you do with that much plastic?'

Larne didn't answer. He let him move another couple of feet, then said, 'Keep going. You can come out when I've gone.'

He half-turned away and Hagen called, 'Joe—' But either he changed his mind or never meant to say anything more.

Larne walked back up the bank. He started the van and

124

turned it. When he looked out of the window he saw that Hagen was standing still again, the water half way up his chest. Larne drove away.

Darkness

FIFTEEN

He waited, past the time around five o'clock when the traffic on the road increased for a while, going by with going-home speed. He sat in the parked van, hardly moving, until the sun was low and broken through the trees at the end of the lay-by and there was a low, premature darkness in the undergrowth of the wood beside him.

He had driven east from the reservoir, for a while with no destination in mind, just the desire to be down off the peaks, as if in some way he couldn't or wouldn't trust their openness. But for several miles, to escape them, he'd had to go up and he'd driven faster, perhaps only half-knowing he did it. Only when he started a long, hill-sided descent, curving with the road, did he appear to breathe out; not because fear or any other single emotion had constricted him before, more as if at that point a distance had been achieved, like a marker of some sort of freedom, the kind achieved only by a combination of distance and time.

And for a time he'd had an odd, acute feeling from out of the past. He called it carrier's squeeze because that was what it did. Being on the run was different; then you *knew*; you were wanted and there was nothing left to happen except be caught. It was solid and definite – clear cut. But when you carried you didn't know whether the precautions you took were needed, or working; whether you were watched or suspected, or if someone had fallen apart and the police would be waiting for you at the end of the run. Nothing showed, and in that vacuum the squeeze could start and gradually build up so that nothing looked safe and you waited to be caught, almost wanted to get it over. Your mind wouldn't leave that one thought alone, and so it got worse. And if you let it the squeeze broke you – all of a sudden or a piece at a time. He'd felt it and he'd seen it happen, always when someone couldn't forget any more.

But despite that there *was* a freedom in it, where no one

who hadn't experienced it could imagine it to exist. It was the freedom of opposition, somehow increased by it. In the past it had been the police and the army, arranged not so much as enemies but as competitors or barriers, but now he had cut out on his own side and he knew how his actions would be interpreted. Yet in spite of that, or maybe because of it, he didn't try to shake off the remembered feeling he had. It meant something to him.

After a while he got out of the van and walked round the near side, sheltered from the road. There was damp gravel and a few dying leaves by the bottom of a broken V in the drystone wall that separated the lay-by from the wood. He urinated into the overgrowing bushes there and then went to the back doors of the van, pulling on a pair of leather-palmed work gloves he'd found in the cab.

The door wasn't locked and he climbed in, letting it swing closed behind him. Bent over he looked at the four metal canisters there, then opened them up. Inside, the explosives were packed in equal amounts, rectangular blocks wrapped in wax paper. Besides that there was nothing to see. He looked for detonators but there were none, and he knew there was nothing in the front. He assumed that McGiven must have his own stock or source of supply, but it also crossed his mind that he might not have trusted Hagen with the means to use the explosive.

He closed the lids on the boxes and fastened them down, and as a final test he tried to lift one of them by its handle. It moved a couple of inches and he let it down gently.

Outside the van he went back to the place in the wall where the stones had fallen inwards. Beyond it the ground rose on an irregular slope. There was a swathe of bracken and brambles alongside the wall, but further up the ground was clear between the trunks of silver-birch trees. He leaned across the wall, looked along it in both directions and climbed over.

Around the gap the bracken was trodden down and there was a litter of wrappers and drinks cans. He moved to the right and after three or four paces there was an overgrown ditch on the inside of the wall, about two feet wide and one deep with black earth and dampness in its bottom. Undisturbed bracken hung over it on long brittle stems.

He made up his mind and went back to the van. After a glance at the road he started it up and edged forward to the end of the lay-by and then further, with the nearside wheels on the thin grass verge. After five yards he stopped and began to move the explosives.

He did it as quickly as he could manage, listening for traffic on the road. Twice he stopped and stood out of sight until a car had gone past. The boxes weighed over a hundredweight each and as he took the weight of the first the muscles in his arms and back cracked audibly. He swung it up to the top of the stone wall, let it rest, then tip forward under its own weight, crushing the undergrowth below. He repeated the action three times, dropping each box a little further along the ditch, and when the last one had gone he moved the van back to the lay-by and left it while he finished off.

He knew it was a second-rate way to cache the stuff, open to chance, and that nagged at him slightly. But it seemed vaguely appropriate too. He had known how it would be as far as the reservoir, but after that any plan he'd had was both solid and open to circumstance at the same time; a strange mixture of wanting to do something, but also of wanting events to shape themselves, as if he had an intuitive feeling that might break, disappear, if he tried to pin it down in too much detail. The only thing he did plan, then, was to get rid of Curwin's van, before the dead men were found and anyone had a chance to see and remember him at its wheel.

He wiped off the Ingram and spare ammunition and put them in one box, then moved each box down as far as it would go into the ditch, covering them with bracken and branches. Being away from the lay-by he didn't think anyone would find them by accident, at least for some time, and it wouldn't be long before he came back.

As he returned to the van he wondered briefly what Hagen had done, or was doing, and felt he was right to be ditching the van.

He drove as far as Wakefield, another thirty-five miles, using the motorway for the last ten. In the town he parked the van on a piece of cleared ground quite near the centre and got out. He'd worn the gloves since leaving the lay-by and wiped his prints from the switches and knobs as he drove. He took his bag and Whitehead's pistol but he left Hagen's revolver in the bin under the passenger seats. He'd no use for a gun that could be linked with three killings.

It was dark now and there had been a light rain which had dampened the pavements. He walked away from the van and the broken dark shapes of half-demolished walls towards a main road. He was a slightly hunched figure, although his pace was long and regular, and with his holdall he looked like a man used to travelling, with that look of detachment because he hadn't yet reached the place he was going. Still on the main road he asked a youth in a leather jacket the way to the railway station and followed his directions until he found the place, half shut down and withdrawn for the night. Inside only the ticket office was lit and a man in British Rail trousers was sweeping the rubber mat floor. He had the same look as everything else in the station; of stains and cigarette ash and litter forced into corners.

Larne studied the timetable on the wall for a while, looking at several destinations, but in the end he came back to one. By luck his timing was good and when he'd bought his ticket he only had ten minutes to wait. On the platform he drank thin coffee from a vending machine. There was a mild breeze down the length of the track and beside him there were four other people waiting. The train came on time.

It took about half an hour to Huddersfield and outside the station Larne took a black and white taxi with a fat woman at the wheel. He told her the name of a road through the window, then got in the back. The engine was running but she didn't move off. 'What number, love?'

'I don't know. The end of the road'll be all right.'

'Okay then.' She had a faintly hoarse voice with cracks of higher pitch. As she drove away from the station she said: 'You don't live round here then?'

'No, Birmingham.'

'Never been there. Don't like cities, me. Got enough trouble here.' And then, as if to prove the point, she spoke into the radio and told the despatcher where she was going.

The drive took five minutes and at the end of the road Larne paid her off and waited till she'd driven away.

The road was on a hill going up to a crest forty yards on and for that distance the houses were about fifty years old – semi-detached with brick built porches and protruding fronts. The gardens were well established and the rectangles of grass beside the pavement were newly cut. Over the brow of the hill, however, the houses were newer, squared off and of a different design. There was cedar boarding along their fronts and the gates to their driveways were mostly wrought-iron and flimsy. In one or two the curtains weren't drawn and Larne could see people inside watching television. By the kerb outside one there were four parked cars and the faint sound of music.

He followed the road as it started a descent, occasionally checking the numbers by doors or on gate posts when he could see in the light of a street lamp. They had changed too, from old fashioned cast-iron to angular alloy. At one point he crossed a side road to the right and had a view down through a whole estate of the same uniform design.

The place he wanted was a house on its own, the same style as the others but different. It stood slightly higher than the pavement and instead of a garden tarmac rose like a forecourt to the front of a shop, built like an extension – single storeyed and flat roofed. There was a large single window a couple of feet off the ground and a door above two flagged steps to the left. The window was lit and stuck with orange and green posters advertising prices on coffee and butter. Above it a long sign said G H & P J NEWHAM OFF LICENCE AND GENERAL STORE SILK CUT.

For a moment Larne looked pensive. He knew only the address, nothing else, but as a teenager came out of the shop with a clinking carrier bag he went forward.

The door rang a bell and when he stepped on to the green linoleum floor it felt springy. There was a faint smell of cardboard and soap in the air from the shelves round the walls and the fittings that divided the place into two aisles. The logic of how the goods were arranged wasn't immediately obvious but he noticed that the shop was slightly darker at the back and that there was a circular mirror in the corner of the ceiling.

He stood just inside the door for a couple of seconds, then moved to the right. There was a counter there, two-thirds the length of the shop, backed by cigarettes and bottled spirits, fronted by the light of two chill cabinets. Behind them there was a man in a hooped grey and green sweater with the sleeves pushed up. He was taller than Larne, about six feet two, and heavy looking in a slightly soft way. He had a thick brown moustache and looked shopkeeperly pleasant as Larne went up to the counter.

'Evening,' he said, his voice light.

Larne nodded. 'I'm looking for Pauline Larne,' he said.

'Pauline?' The man looked a little surprised, about to ask a question, then not. 'She's in the back,' he said. 'Hold on a minute.'

He moved a couple of steps along the counter and called her name: 'Pauline, someone to see you.'

He came back. 'Are you from Ireland then?'

Larne nodded again, holding a quietness about him. The man's face lightened. 'That's it then; you don't know we're married. George Newham.'

Before Larne could reply a woman came out from the back of the shop.

She wore a blue and white nurse's uniform, though without the belt and hat. She was an average height and slightly plump in a large boned way, and without makeup her face looked almost plain. Perhaps because of the uniform she also seemed to have a practical air, but when she saw Larne her step slowed and something like a shadow seemed to wash through her face.

Both men were looking at her and after a second she picked up her step and came to the counter, her low-heeled shoes making no sound on the floor. She stopped a yard from Larne and her eyes studied him hard. She said, 'Hello, Joe.'

'Pauline.'

She turned to her husband. 'Joe's my brother.'

Larne took little part in the surprise or conversation of the next few minutes. Most of it was directed at him by George Newham who didn't seem sure whether Larne's existence intrigued him more than the fact that his wife hadn't told him about it. But although Larne's answers were open they were also general and oblique, as if he knew they'd have to be made again later. He spoke sparingly, and there was the same reserve about Pauline. Her eyes flickered quickly to Larne's face with each new question or comment made by her husband and watched until Larne had replied. When a customer came in to be served she took the opportunity to lead Larne away into the rear of the shop.

They passed through the centre of a small store room

134

crammed with boxes and then into a living room which ran the length of the house to a curtained back window. On the right there was a door to the kitchen and hall. The television was on in front of green dralon furniture and against a wall there was a dining table set with three chairs.

Larne followed Pauline into the room and then halted. Without turning she went to the television and switched it off then sat down on the end of the sofa, her arm resting on the side, held ready. She stared at the wall for a moment and finally turned her eyes towards Larne. She said: 'Are you in trouble?'

He shook his head and put his bag down beside a dark-stained wall unit with a drinks cabinet in the centre. 'I thought I'd see you,' he said. 'I didn't know you were married.'

Pauline Newham searched for a packet of cigarettes, lit one and blew a strong plume of smoke. 'And George doesn't know about you,' she said. 'I'm not going back to lifting curtains again, looking out for the police. I don't want you stopping, Joe, whether you're in trouble or not.'

He moved to the side and sat on an upright chair by the table, angled sideways. 'I was just passing.'

'And that's why you came?'

'To see how you were.'

She eyed him for a while longer, then seemed to accept it, at least on the surface. She took another draw on her cigarette and stubbed it out. 'I'm all right,' she said.

Larne too appeared to loosen up a little. He allowed himself to look round in more detail, at the glass shelves, ornaments and books. 'It's a nice-looking house,' he said. 'I didn't know if I was right when I saw the shop. You're still nursing?'

She nodded. 'George runs the shop.'

'How long've you been married?'

'Nearly six years. Do you want a drink?'

She stood up without waiting for an answer and went to the cabinet. She poured whiskey for him and gin or vodka for herself, adding orange juice to it. At the same time she spoke, as if using the actions to cover her words. Some of the time she had her back to him.

'George had some redundancy money,' she said. 'So we bought the shop. We've got a boy: Paul. He's four.' She turned. 'You'd better stay tonight – if you want – but George doesn't need to know anything. All right?'

'I didn't come to make trouble.'

'I don't know why you did come,' she said and put his whiskey on the table. For the first time she noticed his hand, perhaps because it had held his bag before. He caught her gaze and moved it a fraction.

'Is that what happened?' she asked, quite flatly, but then as she continued to look her voice became a little more pained and her detachment seemed to waver. 'Oh, not the left, Joe.'

'It's not too bad,' he said.

'Can you use it?'

He nodded, but then she was angry. 'Stupid, just bloody stupid; all of you.' Her words ran out and she went to sit on the sofa again, hunched tight this time to hold something down.

Larne didn't say any more. He waited for her to say or ask something, almost as though his coming there had fulfilled whatever it was he'd wanted to achieve and the rest was a blank he hadn't foreseen or knew how to fill. He had a sensation of distance, of observing something he had caused but now wasn't a part of.

'Where do you live now?' she said, in the end.

'In Croydon, near London.'

'With a job?'

He nodded. 'In a scrap-yard, breaking up cars.'

She was quiet again for a time, and then: 'Nothing else?'

He didn't answer straight away, and then the moment was lost because George Newham had closed up the shop and come to ask his own questions.

Later Larne heard them talking; a low, undefinable sound occasionally mixed with the weighted creak of bedsprings from the room above. He lay on the sofa feeling heavy from the meal Pauline had cooked and the beer he had drunk afterwards. He didn't go to sleep until their voices ceased.

In the morning he heard them moving upstairs and got up. A small boy came down and peered at him while Pauline introduced him to his uncle. To Larne he looked unlike either of his parents, but he was polite.

Larne also noticed that Pauline watched her son in the same way she'd watched her husband through most of the previous evening, with an element of both protection and readiness, as if to stop them before they did something unknowingly. Her watch over George Newham had gone, though, and he himself seemed to have used up all his questions. At ten o'clock he opened the shop and a while later Pauline took her son to Mass.

Larne looked through the Sunday paper, alone at the table, but there was nothing of interest to him. After a time he went and used the telephone in the hall, occasionally making notes on a pad of paper beside it. When he'd finished he put the paper in his pocket and screwed up the two sheets below it into a small ball. He knew Pauline was waiting for him to leave – it had been clear since she got up. There was a fixed look behind whatever expression she'd made, to keep his part of the bargain. He'd come for his own reasons and she'd let him stay, for one night, as long as he went quickly and quietly the next day.

He went into the shop and stood by the counter for a while, talking with George to pass time. But the steady flow of Sunday morning customers for Oxo cubes and cigarettes seemed to occupy the man more than anything else. His conversation was still pleasant enough, but it was more reserved, in the way of novelty worn off, or something else. Larne didn't persist. When Pauline came back he said he was leaving.

There was no relief, just acceptance, and she offered to drive him to the station. He shook hands with George and they left from the back of the house.

'Will you go home now?' she asked as she drove.

'No, not yet for a while.'

'Where then?'

'I don't know.'

She watched the road for a time. 'I told George you'd been in prison. I had to, with you turning up and him not knowing I had a brother.'

'But you didn't tell him why I was there?'

'No.' She shook her head. 'He wouldn't understand.'

'It wouldn't have mattered. I don't mind.'

'No, but *I* do.' She glanced at him, then looked at the windscreen as if she wouldn't ever look away from it again. 'Do you know I was first out of bed this morning, just so I could look at the road to see if there was anyone there? That's what I mind, Joe – you coming here and making me do that, without thinking.'

She turned the car and stopped it outside the station building. She didn't look at him. He opened the door and got out with his bag. 'Thanks for the ride,' he said.

She nodded with half-closed eyes. 'Take care, Joe.'

He closed the door and she drove away.

SIXTEEN

By three o'clock he was in Hull; too early, even with the trains running to a Sunday timetable. The ferry to Rotterdam didn't sail until six, and even though the booking clerk had told him to arrive no later than five to confirm and collect his ticket that still left two dead hours.

The day, too, seemed dead in some way. It had been slightly overcast but bright when he'd left Huddersfield, but as he walked out of the station now the sky was just grey and there was no warmth in the air. A few people had emerged with him, but they soon scattered in different directions and only one took a taxi from the three waiting. He paused for a moment on the kerb of the empty road, then stepped out and began towards the town centre, walking with the pace of someone who knows they'll go round in a circle.

Quarter of a mile on, past the City Hall and art gallery and all the dark-glassed windows in between, he turned right and walked alongside Prince's Dock basin, then further out still, beside Humber Dock. He could feel the wind there, cold off the river, smelling of mudflat and tide. It moved the surface of the water in the basin, making it look darker, the colour between green and black that all trapped water has on days with no sun.

At the end of the dock he stopped and leant against a steel post with a length of chain attached to it. He rolled a cigarette and lit it. He didn't do much else. Once in a while people passed him, mostly couples, talking between themselves, strolling into the wind.

He thought about Holland and the soft route. The ferry took thirteen hours to Rotterdam, overnight, and by mid-morning tomorrow he'd be in The Hague. After that it would probably take another couple of days to get what he wanted. The detonators were no problem, but it would take time to have the timers made up. When he'd got them he'd come back the same way, because more often than not the customs checks on ferry passengers were not as strict as at airports, not totally free, but more certain. Larne distrusted airports and his experience of them was bad. They were too closed in and too heavily staffed and he could never understand why drugs carriers in particular seemed to insist on coming through Gatwick and Heathrow when, for the sake of a little extra planning there were a score of less risky and less obvious routes.

But sometimes it was force of habit. He knew how carriers got to think of one route as special or lucky, or soft. Sometimes it only had to pay off once and they'd use it permanently, getting careless by stages, establishing a pattern that was easy to spot. Habit could be made to work the other way, too, though. It could keep you careful by routine suspicion, but even that had its pitfalls. If you forgot, if you let habit take over completely, then there was nothing to tell you it hadn't always been so. What had started out as false became real, and you no longer had any way to distinguish the difference. It was like that in prison, in the scrap-yard, even for Pauline who'd gone to the window by instinct to look.

As he thought about it Larne understood what she'd meant. It was the effort, the push, to keep from submerging, to keep sight of the habit and see it as different – unnatural perhaps – not to go blind and retreat into what was around you, within arm's reach.

And beyond that? What did it do to others. Did it make any difference how you achieved an end as long as you did? He doubted it; no, he knew it did not. You came through or you didn't; as part of a larger organisation, as a process but not an end product. But he had changed that, the process had been broken, so what did that make him?

He walked back to the railway station and in the toilet there he transferred the pistol from his bag to the back of his jeans, inside the waistband and covered by his jumper. Then he got a taxi to the ferry terminal at King George Dock.

As he got out on to the tarmac apron and paid off the driver the wind felt stiffer and seemed to have caught the people there off guard. The ship was by the dock wall and cars were edging across the damp steel drawbridge into the open stern. Beyond the reception building the first passengers were making their way to the ship, and around him people who had just got off a bus turned up thin coat collars against the wind as they tried to keep luggage and offspring together. Larne watched their movement towards the lee of the buildings for a moment and then he followed their flow.

Inside the reception hall he had to wait in a queue at the bookings desk behind an obstinate man who tried to sort out the price of his ticket. Larne saw a nervous-looking woman with two children watching the man from three yards away. Twice she made as if to come up to the desk, but each time she faltered. In the end the man moved off, shaking his head, still bent over the slips of paper.

Larne's ticket, reserved over the phone that morning, was there and he let the bookings clerk explain things he already knew and then paid. Again he followed the flow of people, channelled by lines and signs towards customs. The faces around him didn't worry about checks as they would coming back; they were innocent, only bothered with luggage and tickets. Larne could feel the unnatural shape of the gun rubbing lightly against his spine, but even though the metal radiated a light, cold feeling that held the bottom of his stomach, nothing showed. The green lane was bare anyway; the long counters were empty and only one uniformed man stood by the exit, hardly watching.

As Larne stepped outside he wondered what it was like to travel clean.

SEVENTEEN

The crossing was calm but Larne didn't sleep very much; only in the really dead hours between two and five in the morning when people had drunk enough to quieten down in the seats around him. When he got off the ship in Europoort and caught the bus for Rotterdam Centraal he didn't feel rested. He'd thought it might be different this time, but it wasn't. It was more a mood than anything physical, and he had always had it before: he was at the sharp end, feeling the carriers' squeeze like a shadow, and a peculiar restlessness that kept him from decent sleep. He knew enough not to let it show, but being pleasant, reacting to other people was a conscious act then, and that too was wearing. Inside he was withdrawn and critical.

He ignored Rotterdam except as a transit point and got on a train to The Hague which arrived at ten thirty. From the station he took a tram which crossed the old, square-angular canal that was more like a moat round the city centre. He knew his way as far as he was going and got off the tram opposite a corner of the Knights' Hall and the Vijver pond. It was eleven o'clock by then and in the open spaces the tourists were out like the sun, wandering in patches, curious obstacles that refused to be hurried. It was mild and the air was only just losing its freshness.

He went north and then east into a pedestrian precinct, and there the people seemed denser, walking slowly to gaze. He matched the general pace along the straight of Hoogstraat, but he only looked in the shop windows in passing. The noise of feet and voices, like the people, seemed denser, but the fast Dutch meant little to him and he ignored it. Once he caught a phrase in English almost by his shoulder and it made him turn, but then he couldn't tell who it had come from. He didn't think much of himself for rising to its bait.

In the end he turned off the street to the left, on to a narrower one with a newspaper stall on the corner. He almost walked past it, then changed his mind. He scanned the wire-held racks for a moment and picked out a copy of the *Daily Telegraph*, the only English paper there. He paid a man in a flat cap and folded the paper to fit in his pocket.

The street ran east west and there was a café fifteen yards past the newsstand, on the right. An angle of sunlight cast down on the round tables by the edge of the pavement and made dark shade under a canopy over the shop's door and window. After a glance at another café a few yards along the opposite side of the road Larne went to the first.

A couple had just vacated a table and Larne took the man's place in a tubular-framed chair laced with plastic. The table hadn't been cleared, but after a couple of minutes, while he was still running a light gaze over the other people around him, a young waitress in jeans came out with a tray and a cloth. *'Dag mijnheer,'* she said and Larne nodded.

She cleared the used cups and ran the cloth over the table's plastic surface, and when that was done she seemed ready to take his order.

'Een kopp koffie, alstubleift.'

She nodded and wrote on a pad. *'Met room?'* She looked up. 'With cream?'

'A little, yes.'

'Anything else?'

'No thanks.'

She went back inside and as if he'd seen enough of the street and the meandering people he unfolded the newspaper and began to read it, folded in half against the edge of the table.

He read slowly, spending two or three minutes on each page, scanning the headlines, sometimes reading the first paragraph or two. When he turned a page his gaze would shift temporarily to the café across the street. He drank coffee at intervals and smoked a cigarette. After twenty minutes he caught the eye of the waitress.

'Ik betalen, alstublieft.'

'Your Dutch is not bad,' she said as she wrote out the bill. 'Are you a tourist?'

'Sort of.'

She nodded. 'Most people do not bother to learn Dutch for a holiday. French maybe, but not Dutch. I think it is a difficult language for strangers.'

'Like Gaelic.'

'Gaelic?'

'Irish – Ireland.'

'Ah.' She was quite pretty in a dark, heavy sort of way and she seemed to fix the new word in her mind, as if it was useful to a collection. 'Are you Irish?'

Larne nodded and waited to see if it drew a response, but it didn't. She handed him the bill and he gave her a note. 'I will get your change,' she said.

'No, that's all right.' He stood up with his bag. *'Tot ziens.'*

She smiled and emphasised her English. 'Goodbye.'

He looked in the window of a bakery next door until the waitress went inside and then he crossed the street towards the other café.

It was on the shaded side of the street, next to a boutique, and the pavement there was narrow and without tables. As if to emphasise the shadow, the surround of the café's old-fashioned windows and door was painted a shiny black and the lettering above was in gold. From the outside it gave the impression of a coffee shop rather than a café, to attract the tourists who didn't want to go native and sit in the road, but inside the façade gave up. The tables were covered in beaten sheet copper and the sepia prints on the walls were reproductions. The dark beams across the whitewashed ceiling looked as if they were plastic and the pile of the dark red carpet was lifeless and flat.

Larne went in and at the back there was an L-shaped counter with pastries and sandwiches behind its glass front. In a corner at the rear there was a door fixed with a No Smoking sign. The air smelled of cigarettes and ground coffee.

He glanced at the dozen customers and then back to the counter, but there was still no sign of a waitress. Then the rear door opened and a woman in her late twenties came through it carrying a large tin of coffee. She put it down out of sight as Larne went towards her.

She looked expectantly at him and he said, 'Do you speak English?'

'Yes sir. What would you like?'

'I'm looking for Pat Kavanagh. He used to work here.'

'No, I am sorry. He does not.'

'Did he leave a forwarding address?'

'I am sorry, I don't understand.'

'Do you know where he lives?'

'No. He has been gone for six months. I don't know.'

'What about the manager, would he know?'

'I don't think so. Is it important?'

'Yes, quite important.'

'You are a friend of his?'

'Yes. My name's Larne.'

She looked him over a little more, then: 'I will see if Mr Kester, the manager, knows his address. Please wait here.'

She went back through the door and half a minute later a boy in his teens came out to mind the counter. Larne moved out of the way and sat down when a man came to pay his bill.

Nearly ten minutes later the girl came back, but as Larne rose she came around the counter and he noticed the arms of a sweater draped over her shoulders and a leather bag in her hand. She slung the bag from its strap and said: 'I have the address. I can take you there.'

'There's no need, I can find it.'

'Perhaps not. Come.' She moved towards the door and Larne had no choice but to follow.

Outside she turned left with only a short pause to make sure he was with her, then she walked quickly with easy long strides. She stayed just a little in front of him, always leading, so he caught only a glimpse of her face beside dark blonde hair, straight except for a curl at the bottom where it swung against the wool of her sweater. Her arms were bare and light brown below sleeves of a pale green T-shirt and she was quite tall, despite the fact that she was wearing flat shoes.

They turned right after a dozen yards and then followed a seemingly erratic course through streets that were often narrow. Some were like back alleys, with few shops and cars parked with wheels on the pavement beside motorbikes and chained cycles. Then they passed under an arch and a few yards beyond it they entered a park through open iron gates. There were trees dotted around at random and the sun seemed brighter there. For the first time the girl slowed and her pace became less purposeful, as if she'd reached her destination. She moved towards a bench by a path and sat down, looked across the grass for a moment, then up at Larne.

'Sit down,' she said, half invitation, half command.

He did, with about two feet between them, and she watched until he was still. 'What's your first name, Mr Larne?'

He noticed that the awkwardness of her English had gone,

although there was still a slight accent, perhaps Dutch or German.

'Joe,' he said. 'What's yours?'

'Christina,' she said simply.

He studied her face for a moment. She had a high forehead and blue-greenish eyes lined lightly with mascara below well-shaped brows. Her mouth was broad. 'Where's Pat Kavanagh?' he said.

With a look at his hand she said: 'He's not in The Hague. I spoke to him on the telephone just now in the café. He knows you but he wants me to ask what you want.'

'You're a friend of his?'

'Sort of.' She gave a vague shrug. 'I can take you to him if I think it's all right. So, what do you want?'

Larne thought for a while, weighing it up, but in the end he didn't answer her question. 'Your English is pretty good,' he said. 'Better than it was. Why's that?'

Another shrug. 'I didn't know you.'

'Are you Dutch?'

'German.'

'Can I see your papers?'

'What for?'

'I don't know you. If you're not Dutch maybe you're not the police either.'

'You think I'm laying a trap for you?' She shook her head. 'Are you on the run from the police?'

'No.'

'And you want to see Pat about business?'

'If you'll tell me where he is.'

'Amsterdam,' she said. 'But it will be easier if I take you. You can trust me that far. If I was with the police or Pat didn't know me you would find out when we got there, wouldn't you?'

He thought and then nodded. 'Okay. What about your job?'

She got up, and like the rest of the time her gestures seemed to answer as much as her words. 'It's only temporary. I can please myself. Are you ready? We have to walk back some way, but then we can drive.'

Larne didn't have much idea of where they were as they walked. He knew they were heading roughly east, but that was all. The girl walked less remotely than before but still didn't say much until they crossed a main road towards the end of a broad tree-lined avenue. There, as a passing interest, she pointed to a church.

'That's the Loosterkerk. It's the oldest church in The Hague. Someone told me that on the first day I was here and it stuck in my brain. Now I've passed it on. Turn here.'

They took a side street and Larne had an idea they were following short cuts she knew quite well. 'How long have you lived here?' he said.

'Oh, about nine months.'

'And you don't like your job.'

'It's okay. When I took it I needed the money.'

'Is that where you met Pat?'

'No, I met him in a jazz bar near where I live. We had a mutual friend – a Frenchman.' She gave him a direct look. 'I know Pat is in the IRA. I know you are too, Mr Larne. Pat said you could be trusted so I trust you. I'm not er – talking *out of turn*, and neither was he when he told me. It's all trust, you see?'

'As long as you trust trust.'

She seemed amused at that. 'You aren't like a Communist then; you don't believe that trust is like money or food and as long as everyone is equal in it all will be well.'

'No, I'm not a Communist.'

'Well, no one is perfect.' She said it with a laugh.

'What's your surname?' he asked.

'Remer, Christina Remer. Do you know it?'

He shook his head. 'No.'

'I didn't think so.'

Her rooms were at the end of a scruffy alley, almost as wide as a courtyard, sided by brick walls with small, high rear windows. Two of the walls had been whitewashed but the paint was flaking and there were dustbins sitting crookedly in odd niches. Two cars and a collection of bicycles were parked around the edges of the brick cobbled cul de sac but there was no sign of their owners or where they had gone.

Christina Remer led the way up a single flight of steel steps like a fire escape to a door on the first floor. Next to it was the narrow protrusion of a black-tarred flat roof. There was a thin window beside the door with geraniums on the sill inside and a nylon washing line was coiled on a hook set in the mortar. She unlocked the door and opened it inwards, holding it briefly for Larne as she went through. 'Come in,' she said. 'I want a few things and then we'll go.'

The room was an odd shape, as if it was made up of scraps of space that nobody wanted. The floor was on two levels, different by eighteen inches, and in one place the ceiling sloped at an angle. There was a sink and a cooker in the far corner of the higher level and a bed and furniture on the lower one. Sticking out of an alcove there was a thin partition that might have hidden a bathroom. The place was pleasant enough, though a little airless; lived in but not overcrowded with belongings.

He watched her gather clothes from drawers and drop them in flat piles into a small, soft-sided suitcase. She was unself-conscious about knickers and bras, but it was obvious from the fact that she was packing clothes at all that she intended to be away for more than one day. He didn't say anything about that, but with her back to him she gave an unsolicited reply.

'You've only got to be away a short time and you don't know if a place will still be there when you get back.' She turned to open a wardrobe and take two shirts from their hangers. 'How long will you stay in Amsterdam?'

'If Pat's quick, not long.'

'He'll do what he can. I know him. How did you come over, by boat or by plane?'

'Boat.'

'Are you carrying a gun?' She said it as she opened a drawer and took out a pistol, a Walther. She worked the slide with a click and set the safety on the side. As she put it in her shoulder bag she looked at him for an answer.

Larne indicated his bag. 'In there.'

'All right,' she said. 'Let's go.'

Her car was one of those in the alley; a Citroen 2CV with specks of rust on its high wings. She told him matter of factly that it belonged to a friend who let her use it, and for the moment the friend was away on holiday. She drove it as freely as she tended to move, with a certain disregard for the mundane.

They caught a little of the midday traffic as they used the Utrechtsebaan motorway east out of the city, but then at the interwoven symmetry of a junction beyond Voorburg they turned north on the A4. A sign gave the distance to Amsterdam as sixty km.

'Do you know Amsterdam?' she asked over the strained noise of the Citroen's engine.

'Some of it, around the docks.'

'How long is it since you were there?'

'A few years.'

'You were a carrier then?'

He glanced away from the straight, bright lanes of the motorway. 'Pat told you a lot over the phone.'

'Only enough,' she said. 'I told you, it's trust.'

Larne didn't make an answer to that.

EIGHTEEN

The bar was on the eastern side of Amsterdam's Centrum, in from the curve of the Zeedijk but not far from its influence. It stood on a narrow street that wound between two parallel canals, cobbled and quiet in the daylight before the neon signs were switched on over side entrances and passages. It felt like a place waiting for darkness before starting business.

Christina Remer led him there from the other side of the Damrak, where she'd parked the car with others beside a canal lined with trees on one side and tall gabled houses on the other. He didn't ask why she'd parked that far – nearly half a mile – from where they were going. He was content to let her lead for the time being, but from the time they left the car she became distant again; particularly as they passed through the streets near the Dam. It was almost as if she despised the tourists and tourist shops, and that cut her off from everything else. Larne knew the sort of feeling, but he wondered about the way she let it show.

The crowds grew less as they got closer to the bar and Larne recognised the road by the Voorburgwal canal. When they entered the last street Christina slowed slightly and transferred her case from one hand to the other, using the movement to look back. They passed a couple of black youths in white and blue clothes and crossed over the cobbles behind them towards the bar.

It had an old, brown look from the outside, set with its door on a passage corner. The windows were large plate glass like a shop's, but they were hung with sagging white nets that rose above head height and stopped anyone seeing in. There were stickers on the door advertising beer brands and pool, and the glass and wood were dusty.

The girl pushed the door and went in and it was even dimmer than the street. The air didn't move and seemed the more still for the turned down volume of an old chrome juke box playing bland oompah music. Larne closed the door and turned slowly, letting his eyes grow used to the dimness.

There were bench seats, tables and stools round the edges of the room and the bar was in the centre; a horseshoe shape of dark wood. Glasses and bottles hung behind panels directly above the counter, giving it an enclosed look. Beyond the bar there was a square arch into another room that hadn't shown from the street and Larne noticed a door set in a wall above two steps, as if it led to rooms above.

The quiet, subdued air seemed to have infected the customers, too. An old man with a pregnant paunch and braces on his grey flannel trousers sat alone in a corner, and by the window a young couple were talking in murmurs over a Japanese camera and empty tonic bottles. A man in working clothes sat by the bar and in the back Larne thought he could detect two or three others, but not clearly.

Only the barman seemed untouched by the quiet. He was perched on a stool just inside the end of the bar, holding a cigarette near an ashtray. There was a glass of lager in front of him, half empty. He wore jeans and a denim shirt which showed the hairs on his chest and his eyes were active, as if they didn't know boredom. He was Pat Kavanagh.

The girl went close to the bar and smiled as he did. In English she said: 'Hello, Pat. I've brought a friend. Yes?'

She turned to Larne.

'Pat,' Larne said and shook Kavanagh's hand as he straightened off the stool.

'Long time, Joe. How's yourself? Fancy a beer?'

'Thanks.'

Christina slipped behind Larne and around the corner of the bar. She put her case down and as Kavanagh turned she said something in a low voice that Larne didn't catch. It sounded as if it could be in Dutch. Kavanagh nodded and then Christina made for the door. It rattled as she shut it behind her.

Kavanagh put a glass in front of Larne and freshened his own. 'We can talk over there,' he said. 'Leave your bag there.'

Larne moved to a table and sat sideways on to the door, letting Kavanagh slip past on to the bench seat backed to the wall.

'Good health,' Kavanagh said and tilted his glass. He had a square chin and there were faint crows' feet at the corners of his eyes. His dark hair was parted with commas across his forehead that he occasionally pushed back. His features weren't heavy, despite his dark colouring, but it was his hands that seemed to express most about him. They were long and lean with square nails and a practical look, as if they were kept ready for some intricate craft.

'You went to the café then,' he said.

Larne dipped his head mildly. 'The last time I'd heard that's where you were.'

'Yeah? Who was that from?'

'Danny Mallon I think.'

'Before Christmas, that'd be right. Danny's okay. I get the news when he's through here.'

Larne rolled a cigarette. 'Why did you leave The Hague? I thought you were settled.'

'Aye, too bloody settled. Too much international justice floating around.'

'You beat extradition.'

'Yeah, but who's to say they won't change their minds.' Kavanagh shook his head. 'Why make it easy? They let me stay because I hadn't done anything here, that's their law, but coppers are coppers. The Brits have got fourteen charges waiting as soon as I put a foot over there. Maybe they'll do the Dutch a favour one day, and as a pay-off the Dutch try to dig dirt on me here. If I'm not where they thought I was I'm one step ahead. Right?' He drank some more beer and the man by the bar caught his eye. 'Hold on. Got a customer.'

He got up and went to serve the man. While he was doing it the couple by the window went out, camera re-slung, guide-book in hand. Kavanagh collected their dead glasses, put them on the bar and came back to Larne.

'So what d'you think to the German – our Christina?'

'Who is she?' From the way he behaved Larne seemed to have come there for nothing more than to pass the time. He made no attempt yet to steer Kavanagh's chat.

'Another stray,' Kavanagh said. 'But not official.'

'On the run?'

'Well she's not going out of her way to attract attention; after that, I don't know. She's all right, though. Anyone who gets Klaus Bethmann knocking at the door has got as much to lose as you. Bethmann's white hot over here – specially with the Germans. They keep putting his picture in the paper but they haven't caught him yet.'

'Did you see him?'

'Sure. He had tinted glasses and about a week's worth of beard but I knew him. Two o'clock in the morning. I put my pants on and left, and all the time he says nothing. Still,' he gave a faint, one-sided smile. 'She's a bright girl, the German. Did she tell you she speaks half a dozen languages?'

'No.'

'Aye. English, French, Dutch, Italian, Russian and German. She told me once and then said it didn't make a scrap of difference. I have enough trouble with Dutch. Jesus, I don't think they understand it themselves sometimes.' He took a pull of his beer. 'So how long you over here for, Joe?'

Larne drew smoke. 'It's business. How do you stand?'

With a vague, open shrug Kavanagh said: 'I haven't got any stock, they know that – just contacts. You putting a run through?'

'No. There are problems, Pat. Did you see the police had taken nine people in London?'

'Who reads the papers?'

'And Danny Mallon's dead.'

The lightness slipped out of Kavanagh's voice. 'That's bad. He was okay. I liked him. How did it happen?'

'They say he grassed.'

'Did he?'

'I don't know.'

'Shit.' He lit a cigarette from a pack in his shirt pocket and blew a long draught of smoke.

There was quiet for a while and then Larne said: 'Can you still make the circuits?'

'No reason why not.' He drank beer. 'What sort?'

'Good timers and radio control. I need the detonators built in and tremblers on the clocks.

'No alarm clocks and wire then?'

'No.'

'Where would they use the radio control, in the North?'

'The mainland, why?'

'Ah, well they've got receivers in the North. When you check a radio circuit they pick up the signal frequency and broadcast it back a couple of seconds later. Up goes the bomb and you with it. Devious bastards, but you can beat them. You use two random code signals, different for the check and the detonation. It costs a bit more, though, and you've got to know how to build the thing in the first place.'

'How much do you need?'

'Detonators are cheap, but the rest . . . How many timers and how many radios?'

Larne thought for a moment. 'Seven timers, three radio controlled.'

'Okay. If you use the same transmitter without the random code it'll be about a hundred quid.' He grinned. 'All in, no labour. But don't take the radios over the water.'

'Do you want it now?'

'No, later'll do.'

'How long?'

'A couple of days. Wednesday. Have you got somewhere to stay?'

'Not yet.'

'Stay around till Christina gets back, she won't be long. I'll sort something out.' He got up with a nod, closing the deal, and took his beer back to the bar.

The girl came back about ten minutes later, ignoring Larne when she first walked in and talking to Kavanagh at the bar as he got her a drink. When their conversation ended she came over to Larne and sat down.

'You need somewhere to sleep,' she said. 'Do you like boats?'

'What about a hotel?'

'Maybe, if you want, but it's the holiday season. Anyway, the boat wouldn't cost you anything. It's divided in two. You can have one half for two nights, no problem.'

'Who has the other half?'

'Some people I know. They won't bother you.'

'All right,' Larne said.

'Good. I'll make a phone call.' She got up and when she returned to the table she was brisk and had her suitcase in her hand. 'It's okay. We can go now.'

She finished her drink standing up and as Larne rose Kavanagh raised a hand and nodded him out.

The boat was a twenty-minute walk from the bar. It was tied to the side of a canal, cushioned by half a dozen car tyres. On the bank beside it there was a break in the line of angled parked cars with their tyres to a low rail and across the road from them, there was an irregular skyline of narrow, five- and six-storey buildings without space in between. Most of the ground-floor rooms in the buildings were commercial offices and the space above them was either more offices or sometimes what looked like flats. The parked cars looked as if they were there till the end of the day and there were only a few people about.

'Quiet,' Christina said. 'Not quaint enough for the tourists.'

She stepped down on to the boat first, to a small area of deck at the stern. Apart from the curve of the hull the boat was ungainly, about thirty feet long and squared off, box-like, on top. The upper structure was tallest at the front, with round-cornered windows, but two-thirds of the way back it took a step down and the rear windows were at deck level. It was painted a mixture of red, white and green and there were pot plants on the cabin roof. Christina bent down to a niche under a bulwark and came up with a key to the padlock that sealed the hatch.

Larne followed her in, down almost vertical steps to the level of what might have been the engine space at one time. He had to bend his head slightly to avoid the roof. Immediately to the left of the steps was a cupboard-sized toilet and beyond that a sink and two-ringed camping stove. The window above the sink looked out on the canal side. Further along there was a studio couch covered in curtain print material, a fold-down table and a couple of cupboards, squeezed into the available space. At the far end of the cabin there was a mattress pushed sideways into a three-foot high space beneath the floor of the forward compartment. Altogether the cabin had about twelve feet that you could stand up in.

'It's small,' Christina said, putting her suitcase on the studio couch. 'But it's clean.'

She slid back a door under the sink and looked at two water containers and the cooker's gas cylinder. 'You'll need some food,' she said. 'Are you hungry now?'

'Not very,' Larne said. He was still in the same place he'd stopped when he first came down the steps. It was almost as if he was waiting, perhaps for some remark from the girl that was final. It didn't come, though.

'I'm going to see some people,' she said. 'I'll bring you some food.'

'What do you want?'

'Want?' She laughed as if she didn't understand. 'Nothing. Listen, I'll be two or three hours. Okay?'

Larne put his bag down and took fifty guilders from his wallet. He held it out to her. 'For the shopping.'

'Okay.'

He moved to one side and she went past him, climbed the steps and was gone.

For a minute he waited, then he moved along the cabin, poking around as if to familiarise himself with it. There wasn't much to look at and when he'd finished he went up to the deck to look at the canal and the road.

About ten yards along the bank there were two Volkswagen vans side by side and facing the water. He looked at them for longer than the other cars, but in the end there seemed to be little to do, about anything. He felt a certain resignation, or maybe an acceptance of things that came as a result of what he was doing. He felt the lack of sleep from the night crossing too and went back down to the cabin, closing and locking the hatch. He drew the bankside curtains all but a couple of inches and lifted the girl's case off the studio couch. Briefly he thought about opening it but he didn't. He stretched out on the couch and fell asleep after a while.

NINETEEN

The sun began to set into a mild evening and Larne sat on part of the raised transom at the stern of the boat. The water of the canal didn't move. On the far bank the white stone edges of the cobbled path were set with black railings and regular, old-fashioned street lamps. One or two people walked past them, still lightly dressed. On his side most of the cars and vans he'd looked at earlier had gone and the canal side was almost empty.

Half an hour earlier, while he was still down below, he had heard two people come on to the other side of the boat. From then on their voices had come and gone as they moved about, and ten minutes ago he'd caught the sound of rattling pans and then the faint smell of cooking. Next to him now he had a sweater, and under it his pistol. The cold, cynical mood of his crossing and arrival had abated – perhaps because he had slept, or because he was no longer travelling – and now he was waiting, again. Not everything was certain, though; that was why he had the gun by his side.

There was a movement at the front of the boat. A slim man in his early thirties emerged above the roof and glanced at Larne, then averted his eyes as he came along the narrow edge of the boat to the stern. He paused at the corner of the cabin before coming on to the small deck.

'Hello,' he said. 'I'm Peter – Christina's friend. You must be Joe.'

'That's right,' Larne said.

'Pleased to meet you.' He took a short step forward to shake Larne's hand. 'Christina told me you were here for a few days on business and the hotels are all full. Please stay as long as you wish.'

'Thank you. It'll only be a couple of days.'

'My wife Anne and I both work,' he said, 'and there's little room here. Please, if you want to take a – *shower*, come to our side.' He felt in his pocket and took out a key. 'You're welcome.'

'Thank you.'

'Is Christina here?'

'No, she went to see some friends.'

'Ah. Anyway I hope you enjoy your stay. I must go back for our meal.'

They shook hands again and the man went back along the boat.

When he'd gone Larne looked along the bank and then at his watch. There was no sign of the girl. He pushed the pistol into the back pocket of his jeans and tied the arms of the sweater round his waist so it hung down at the back and covered the gun. He closed the hatch but didn't lock it and stepped off the boat.

Turning left, so he didn't pass the windows of the forward cabin, he walked fifty yards to an arched bridge over the canal. On the other side there was a square, recessed place in the bank, like a lay-by, with steps down to the water. He turned left again there and paralleled his course until he was opposite the boat. In the shadow of a tree beside an empty car he rested against the rim of a litter bin and watched.

Ten minutes later he eased himself back even further out of sight. On the far bank Christina Rümer was walking briskly towards the boat. When she got to it she went aboard, opened the hatch and went below without a pause. The reflection on the windows of the cabin made it impossible to see inside, but Larne wasn't watching. Instead he moved his gaze steadily from left to right along the opposite bank, looking for movement.

He kept looking for a minute or so, and then the girl came up from the cabin. She also looked around – at one point seeming to stare straight at him. Then, showing no reaction, she retreated into the cabin.

Larne shifted. Unhurriedly he started to walk again, away from the boat in the direction the girl had come from and he hadn't yet covered. For the first thirty yards he stayed close to the roadside buildings, but after that moved into the open; as far as the next bridge, across it, then back. He saw nothing to bother him, and in reality he knew he was wasting his time. All he had proved was that the girl hadn't led anyone there.

There was a smell of frying onions as he went down into the cabin. Christina was prodding and turning two steaks in a

frying pan. By the sink there was salad and two bottles of wine
– red and white – and a French loaf.

'Hello,' she said. 'You're not vegetarian, are you?'

'No, I eat steak.' He made no move to pass her in the narrow
space.

'Good. Is there anyone out there?'

'Like who?'

She shrugged. 'You were looking weren't you?'

For a second he was quiet. 'You'll cut yourself.'

'I don't understand.'

'You're too sharp. Did you see me over there?'

'No.' She looked back at the steaks. 'You can please
yourself, you know. I'll leave.'

'Maybe you should. You've no reason to be here.'

'You think I do too much – organise you too much? There's
no point in being sloppy.'

'I appreciate your help.'

'*But;* there's still no reason why I *should* help you. If you
had a reason you would feel more comfortable.' She left the
steak and began to cut up lettuce and tomatoes. 'Don't you
believe people do things without reasons? No? Well, sometimes the reasons come afterwards, sometimes they're small
and don't mean very much. I was bored in The Hague.
Enough?'

Larne didn't answer, but after a moment he moved past her
into the cabin.

When it was ready she brought the meal and the wine to the
table. They ate for a while and eventually she said, 'I told you
I knew you were a transporter, didn't I?'

'A carrier.' Larne nodded.

'You deliver things to other people and they put them to
use?'

'That's right.'

'And the same with the detonators Pat is making?'

Larne kept her eye, but he also kept silent, chewing.

'Don't you have someone who could make them in England?' she said. 'So you wouldn't have to take the risk of
moving them? Pat takes a risk, too. If he was caught they
would have grounds to extradite him.'

'And you?'

'Perhaps, yes.'

'So the risk's even: everyone knows.'

'You don't think about it?'

'Not a lot.'

She ate again and drank some wine. 'What do you do at home? Do you live alone?'

'Why do you think that?'

'I don't know. You seem that way. You don't talk much. I think people who live alone grow like . . . No, I can't think of anything. Something that circles – *encloses* – itself. Have you been to America, the United States?'

'Once.'

'Did you like the people?'

'They're just about the same as anyone else.'

'Maybe I suppose; if you look at everyone in a certain way. I don't like them. They are the opposite of that self-contained person. They always act as if they are on a game show, they play to the audience, always for approval. They think it is being open and friendly, but it's just shallowness. The Dutch are different, they wait. I think they are even more reserved than the British.'

'What about the Germans, your people?'

'They think they have an excuse for greed because they lost two wars,' she said simply. 'And that greed is all right if you don't flaunt it like the Americans. Most countries in Europe use America as a standard of some kind – good or bad – and that makes their influence greater.'

Larne thought about it, but he didn't have an answer. Christina finished eating and perhaps because she didn't want or hadn't expected a response, she changed the subject. 'Will you see Pat before he's finished the work?'

'No, there's no need.'

'And you'll go home on Wednesday.'

'Yes. That was a good meal.'

'Good.'

She glanced at the window. The sun had gone now and it was half dark in the cabin. Standing up she lit a gas lamp fixed to the wall and it burned with a hiss, yellow-white. 'Do you want to go out to a club or a bar?' she asked, drawing the curtains.

'Maybe, later on.'

'All right. I don't mind.' She said it as a statement that at the same time acknowledged an escape route.

Larne stayed by the table, smoking and intermittently

drinking wine. She moved to the studio couch and for over an hour, then, they sat in near silence. Occasionally she said something or asked a question, but never in a way that implied a lead to conversation. On the other side of the bulkhead the people played records, but the sound wasn't loud and it didn't need to fill a space.

Later still, Christina got up and took a polythene bag from her coat pocket, then used a sharp kitchen knife to chop green marijuana. She rolled a joint and offered it to Larne. When he shook his head she took it back to the couch and smoked, leaning back. Larne got up and locked the hatch.

They had sex in the cramped space below the other cabin's floor, but it was Christina who came to him after turning the lamp to half its former brightness, she who came first and fell asleep afterwards. Larne lay awake and watched his mood through unfocused eyes.

TWENTY

It was raining the next morning; slow, steady and grey out of a washed-out sky, set in for the day. It dampened the air and the soft sound of it falling on the water and the canalside was a constant background. Car tyres made slick, wet sounds as they passed on the cobbles.

Larne had no plans except waiting. If he had been alone he might not have left the boat at all, but although Christina didn't disturb him, her presence made a difference. Perhaps she'd been right last night when she said that when Larne was alone he enclosed himself. In some way she broke the circle by being there. There was no element of intimacy in her presence, either; there hadn't been last night. It seemed their only match was a sameness in not needing each other, of being separate, and maybe a tacit agreement that she was staying. At eleven o'clock she suggested a walk and Larne didn't object.

There seemed to be fewer tourists on the streets, and those that there were wore bright nylon kagouls and had their camera cases closed. They didn't carry umbrellas and often they had sodden making-the-most-of-it expressions, as if to see the city in the rain was to see it closer to reality.

Larne and the girl stopped at a café and drank coffee with pastries as he looked at a copy of the *Daily Express*. Christina had bought a copy of *Le Monde* at the same stall but it stayed in her bag.

On page two of the paper a small piece of news caught Larne's attention. Under the headline BODIES FOUND it reported that two men had been found dead, apparently from gun shots, by the side of a Peak District reservoir late in the afternoon of bank holiday Monday. The police had no comment to make until the bodies were identified. Larne folded the paper and thought about that.

In the end he said 'Have you got Pat Kavanagh's phone number?'

'At home or at work?'

'Home. That's where he'd better be.'

'Is anything wrong?'

'I want to check when the stuff will be ready. Do you know the number?'

'Six eight one, seven three one.'

He got up and went to a phone at the back of the café, enclosed by a plastic dome. The number rang four times and then Kavanagh said, *'Ja?'*

'Pat, it's Joe. Did you get everything?'

'Sure, Joe, no problem. I did the shopping yesterday afternoon and I'm doing them now.'

'When will they be ready?'

'Don't know.' His voice faded as if he'd looked away, then it came back. 'Probably tonight. I've got the day off to do them. It's not difficult, just takes time.'

'Okay, tonight's all right.'

'Do you want to come here to collect? It'll be clear. One twenty-seven Oudedokstraat. Eight o'clock?'

'Okay. Thanks Pat.'

He hung up and went back to his seat. A waitress had just moved his cup to wipe down the table.

'Is it all right?' Christina asked.

'Ready tonight.' He told her where they were meeting and she nodded.

'I know it,' she said. 'What then?'

'I'm flying back tonight, from Schiphol.'

'Isn't that dangerous? Why not the ferry?'

'It takes too long and I haven't got time.'

'Do you want to tell me why not?'

He looked at her consideringly, then nodded. 'We'll get back to the boat.'

'I've got the explosives to go with the detonators Pat's making,' he said. 'But two men were killed to get the stuff.'

'Not by you.' It was more a statement than a question.

They were walking along the bank of the canal that would bring them back to the boat. He flipped his cigarette into the water and put the hand in his pocket. 'No,' he said. 'A man called Hagen. But I was there. I left with the explosives and he didn't. The paper says the bodies have been found.'

'And Hagen?'

163

'No.'

'You think he'll talk if they do find him?'

'I think he could have talked already.'

Her step slowed for a second. 'Ah, I see.'

Larne continued to walk, without making a reply. After a time Christina said: 'You weren't supposed to have the explosives, and you think Hagen could have given your name to the police because you took them. Is that it?'

'Maybe, yes.'

'He doesn't like you?'

'He's got plans of his own.'

'But if you think the police could be looking for you, why go back?'

'They might not be yet.'

'Even so, why risk it?'

'Because I want to.'

'So you have plans of your own too.' She paused. 'Do you want me to come with you?'

'To do what?'

'Help. You are on your own, aren't you? You take explosives and buy detonators, then you plant bombs. You do it because you want to and I'll help you because *I* want to. I think you know what you're doing, so you have a reason, whatever it is. Your reason can be mine, I don't need to know it. I trust you, that's all.'

'What about Klaus Bethmann?'

She shrugged. 'Nothing. I left because it wasn't right, for me. You do what you think is right until you change your ideas, don't you?'

After a moment of silence Larne nodded. 'All right.'

Christina parked the car about a quarter of a mile from Oudedokstraat and they walked. The rain was lighter now, a fine drizzle, and sounds in the dark streets had a faint metallic ring. They were beyond the Zeedijk, not far from the wide cut of the Oude Schans canal. Larne let the girl lead and every so often he glanced round casually. He saw nothing.

They approached the house from the back. It was tall, thin and steep gabled and at the rear there were narrow concrete steps leading up to a door on the first floor. The windows at ground level were dark and barred and the door looked strong.

At the top of the steps the door was ajar by an inch and opened into a lit corridor with a stairwell beside it. There were six mail boxes on the wall and no furniture. They followed worn red carpet to the stairs and climbed another flight. In the background there were vague sounds of habitation.

The door to Kavanagh's rooms was almost opposite the top of the stairs and Christina stood aside and let Larne knock. A few seconds later Kavanagh opened the door on a chain, saw Larne and released it with a rattle. He stood back as the couple went in and bolted the door after them.

'All done, Joe,' Kavanagh said. 'Go in, on the right.' He was wearing a baggy cardigan and his hair was untidy.

From a narrow entrance hall they went into a high-ceilinged room with a moulded Victorian fireplace against one wall, its grate covered by a piece of board. The room looked faintly dowdy and there was nothing about its furniture or contents to hold the eye for long. On a coffee table in the centre of the room Kavanagh had lined up the detonators like a display. Larne went over to them and Christina sat down in a corner, just watching.

'These are the timers,' Kavanagh said, coming to stand next to Larne and picking one up. It was rectangular, about four inches long by two wide and deep, covered by a grey plastic top. He turned it over to show the base as the underside of a circuit board, drilled near one end for the extrusion of a detonator case about two inches long.

He turned it again, his fingers familiar with it, and eased off the plastic top. Now Larne could see the other side of the circuit board, spot-soldered with wire and various components in a tight maze. A nickle-cadmium battery was fixed at one end and joined to the wires of the detonator, a liquid crystal timer and a glass bubble with silver-grey mercury inside.

'It's pretty simple,' Kavanagh said. 'The battery runs the clock and then triggers the detonator. You set the clock here' – he put a finger nail by a small rod of plastic under the clock – 'press it and the clock runs forward, however long you want up to twenty-four hours. If you want five hours you set zero five zero zero and as soon as you let your finger off the clock starts running down.'

'What about the trembler?'

'A mercury switch, but it's sensitive.' He tilted the device a little and the mercury in the glass bubble slid from one end to the other. 'You couldn't carry it with the timer set so I put that thing in. It's a standard timer; always runs the same length of time before cutting in. It's a bit like those snooze buttons on alarm clocks. I've jigged this one about a bit so what it does is cut in twenty minutes before the bomb's set to go off and makes the mercury switch sensitive. It's not foolproof, but I reckoned if they wanted radio control as well then the timers wouldn't be sitting around long enough to be found accidentally. It'll be best if you keep the timers horizontal on the bomb – that way the mercury's most sensitive to move-ment – but it doesn't matter if it's on the top or the side.'

'Is it ready to set now?'

'No.' He picked out a short yellow wire. 'Fix that to that blob of solder, then it is.'

He put the top back over the components, took a screw-driver from his back pocket and used it to secure the case with two screws.

'The radio control's a bit simpler,' he said. 'There's no mercury switch so it's safe to move any time. Connect up the yellow wire in each one and then press the button.' He showed Larne a small steel box with a button and a telescopic aerial. 'You'll get a light on the circuit board to show it's okay and when you press the button again the thing goes off. It's got a range of a mile or so. You're using the same transmitter for each bomb, so you could set off all three together if you wanted to, but you'd have to plan it right.'

Larne nodded. 'Okay. Did you leave the stuff clean?'

'No way to do it; you can't wear gloves when you're building circuits. Just give the case a wipe and the explosion'll take care of the rest.'

'Can the pieces be traced?'

'No, they're from all over the place.' He put down the transmitter and lit a cigarette. 'The covers are off some fuse boxes I found in a skip. I thought they'd come in handy. Some of the other bits are secondhand at least.' He moved away, as if handing it all over to Larne. 'When do you leave?'

'Tomorrow morning, early flight. What's the bill?'

'Hundred and twenty quid. Say four eighty guilders.'

Larne paid him and he fetched an old sports bag to put the things in. 'Do you know when they'll be used?' he asked.

'Not long,' Larne said. He was already putting the detona-tors in the bag.

'I'll watch the papers. Tell them to do a good job.'

Larne straightened, the bag in his hand. The girl rose at the same time. 'Thanks, Pat,' Larne said.

'No trouble. Any time, you know that.'

With a nod Larne made for the door.

Outside on the steps of the house Christina said: 'You don't trust him?'

Larne kept moving. 'Why?'

'Telling him you were leaving tomorrow, letting him think you were only collecting the things for someone else.'

'He didn't need to know the truth. It's safer.'

'And he might not have made them if he knew you weren't, ah – *official*.' She kept up with his quick, clipped stride, away from the house.

'No,' Larne agreed. 'He might not.' He tilted his wrist towards a street light and looked at his watch. 'We've got forty-five minutes to get to the airport.'

'Plenty of time,' she said. 'Don't worry.'

She drove, and in the back of the car Larne opened her suitcase and divided her clothes down the centre. He put in the detonators in a single line, packed up to one another, and put his gun next to hers. He moved clothes over the top of them and finally closed and locked the case.

'Okay?' Christina said.

'It should be. Buy some cigarettes and whiskey and have them in your shoulderbag, just showing.' He studied the girl's pale reflection in the mirror, washed out by the road lights. 'Are you sure you want to carry them?'

Her eyes flicked to the mirror. 'I said I would do it. I will.' She laughed. 'Thank God they don't tick.'

Schiphol was like all airports at night; tile and glass held in the greenish yellow light of strip lights, with the echoing sound of tannoy and rubber trolley wheels on the shiny floor. It was still quite busy, but around the edges of the information desks and under the departure boards cleaners were starting to sweep out the corners.

Larne went in first, carrying his holdall. The flight was British Airways and there was a man at the desk doing paperwork. Larne gave his name and after consulting a list he produced the ticket. 'They'll call the flight in about an hour, Mr Larne,' the man told him. 'Have a good trip.'

Away from the counter Larne waited, hardly seeming to watch. It was fifteen minutes before Christina Remer went up to the counter, her suitcase in one hand, bag over her shoulder. Larne looked away, without interest. Two or three minutes later Christina walked past him towards the Duty Free shop.

Larne sat in a lounge. He appeared to doze, but he heard the first call for the flight, stirred himself and picked up his bag. He walked slowly in the direction of the departure gate. Thirty yards ahead of him, near the centre of the first influx of passengers he saw Christina in line. Without seeming to, he hung back and watched. She handed her ticket to the uniformed girl, put the suitcase on the conveyor. The girl at the desk looked up, smiled, said something. Christina nodded, picked up her ticket, moved off. Larne joined the queue.

' At the final passport check before boarding he was still ten yards behind her, but the official hardly looked at her papers. She passed on and the first part was over.

The flight landed at ten forty at Leeds-Bradford airport, and this time it was Larne who moved first towards the Customs and Immigration. He didn't look for Christina, but as he took the long walk towards the baggage collection point he felt the carriers' squeeze, tight in his chest and belly and like a cold flannel between his shoulders. And the ringing hard hollowness of the place, the sound of people's feet around him, made it worse. It was the girl, the fact that he wasn't alone, that made this run different. It pressed on him, blinding and deafening, closed and trapped. He was lost, with no way out.

He didn't have to wait to collect luggage and he was the second person to Customs, even though his legs had seemed to slow and stumble. He tried to concentrate on the man at the counter, the procedure, but then it was gone and he was moving again, towards the exit.

He didn't remember getting there, out of the glass doors on to the littered kerb outside, but as he stood he wondered if that was it, to have lost the nerve to do it again. He turned and he could see the girl coming. He turned back, glanced left and waved for a taxi.

As it started up and moved forward Christina came beside him. 'It went well,' she said. 'What now?'

'A hotel,' Larne said and stepped down to the taxi.

TWENTY ONE

They spent the night in a bed and breakfast hotel on the outskirts of Leeds. The place had been half asleep when they got there and Larne had paid for one night and signed the register under the name of Donovan. In the morning they found the dining room empty except for a sales rep and a young couple who discussed family problems in half-muted voices. The landlady had a sharp nose and dark, deep-set eyes that watched every time someone reached for a cruet.

Back in their room Christina said, 'When do we leave?'

She was standing by the washbasin and long yellow curtains drawn back from dusty windows that looked down on a main road. Larne zipped up his holdall and set it on the bed. 'We need some transport, then we'll pick up the explosives.'

'A hire car?'

'No, they're too easy to trace. I'll buy something cheap.'

'You've got enough money?'

'Enough for the time being.'

'I've got some, but when it's gone, what then?'

Larne licked the end of a cigarette paper and folded it round tobacco. He put the cigarette in his mouth and lit it. There was a steady, timeless air about him and when he spoke his voice was matter of fact. 'This won't go on for ever. I've got five hundred pounds of explosives and ten detonators: ten bombs. It'll last a week, maybe a couple of days more.'

'That's fast.'

He nodded. 'It has to be. After the first two or three they'll be watching for us – everyone.'

'You know your targets?'

'London to begin with, then we'll see how it goes. All right?'

'Okay.' She came away from the window to pick up her coat.

'No,' he said. 'You stay here while I get the car. I'll pick you up.'

A frown crossed her face, briefly, then she moved away from her coat. 'All right. Whatever you want.'

He nodded.

The car was an Escort, twelve years old. He bought it from one of three small used car lots on a road half a mile from the hotel. The tax disc had a month left to run and the MOT certificate was valid for six weeks. He drove it round the block a couple of time with the salesman beside him and in the end he got it for one hundred and seventy pounds cash. He had about two hundred pounds left, but he didn't dwell on the fact. He picked up the girl from the hotel and they headed south.

It was half past eleven when they reached the lay-by where he'd left the explosives, but the first time he drove past, watching the roadside walls and the slope of thin trees on either side. He went for half a mile, then turned in a gateway and drove back.

The car rolled to a halt on the road verge five yards past the lay-by and he killed the engine straight away. He sat still for a moment, then took out the ignition keys and gave them to the girl. 'Open the boot and keep an eye on the road,' he said.

They got out.

There was no traffic in sight and Larne climbed the wall and walked back a short way on the edge of the ditch. It was three days since he'd been there but there was no sign that anything had been disturbed. Some of the bracken he'd broken was turning brown but he couldn't see the first ammunition box until he was directly over it. He pushed the undergrowth back and glanced up at Christina. She was standing beside the open boot. 'It's clear,' she said.

Larne crouched to the box and took hold of its handles. He got a grip and with a grunt of effort he straightened, took a step across the ditch and the box hit the stone wall. He pushed again and then Christina was there, pulling. The box tipped and fell on the other side.

'How much is in there?' she asked.

'A quarter of it. We'll take two. What about the road?'

'Still okay.'

He moved on to the next box and in the same way they got it

over the wall and Larne was left panting. He climbed back and together they lifted the boxes into the car's boot.

'Will the rest be safe there?' she asked as they got into the car.

Larne started the engine and looked in the mirror. 'It'll be all right for a couple of days yet.'

He put the car into gear and pulled it round in a circle.

They stopped twice on the motorway, once to eat and the second time off a slip road where Larne transferred thirty pounds of explosives into his holdall. The box it came from also contained the Ingram machine pistol, but he left that where it was.

Christina didn't say very much, either during the stops or as Larne drove. It wasn't a cold silence, but there was more of a reserve about it than there had been before, perhaps as if she was waiting for Larne to work something out. There was no doubt that he was preoccupied by his thoughts, but it was impossible to tell if they went beyond planning what they were going to do. Sometimes when she spoke to him after a long silence his answer was abrupt, as if caught off guard from a strange direction.

By four o'clock they'd reached north London, and Larne seemed to have emerged at least part way out of his preoccupation. On Seven Sisters Road by Finsbury Park he waited for traffic lights to change. 'There's a hotel on the left just further on,' he said. 'We can try for a room there.'

'You know this area then? Did you live near here?'

'No, but if you carry on that way there's a lot of bedsitters – flats. No one cares who comes and goes. Some of our people used to live round there.'

'And the hotel will be all right?'

'For tonight, maybe tomorrow.' The lights changed and he moved the car off behind another. 'The tube station.' He pointed it out. 'You'll need to know it.'

A minute or two later a sign showed over the pavement on the left and he slowed, indicated and turned in just before it.

The hotel was fronted by a tarmac apron behind the pavement, divided up by white parking lines. The building itself had been rendered in white that was now turning grey and the sign across its frontage said Pardoe Hotel. Another sign on the corner of the building pointed out car park and reception.

Larne took the car on, down the side of the hotel next to a tall red brick wall. The ground sloped away and at the rear the hotel had been extended to make an L-shape. Through mock-Georgian windows there was a dining room set for about thirty people and in a corner there was a porch and double doors next to a small booth-like window marked Night Reception.

Larne took all that in for a second, then let the car roll forward past the side of the hotel and finally backed it up to a wall in the rear corner. There was a small garden and a couple of rustic tables on the opposite side of the tarmac and a steel fire escape at the back of the hotel. He switched off the engine and turned to Christina. 'You know how it goes,' he said. 'Yes?'

She nodded. 'We don't want to be remembered.'

'No. You do the talking. After tonight they'll look twice at anyone with an Irish accent. Book the room for two nights, just bed and breakfast.'

'Okay.'

They got out and walked to the door of the hotel and as Christina opened it a bell rang somewhere inside.

The reception area was decorated in moss green and gold and the small formica-topped desk backed into an office through a doorway. There was a wire rack of postcards at the end of it, next to a long wall mirror. Beyond that there were stairs and a door to the dining room. They waited for a moment and then a tidily dressed woman in her forties came along a corridor beside the stairs, smiled at them and said, 'Just a minute.'

She went around the back and emerged through the office with a pair of gold-rimmed glasses in her hand. 'Now, can I help you?'

Christina was closest to the desk and Larne stood slightly back, watching but separate. 'We'd like a room, for two nights,' Christina said. 'Do you have one?'

'You don't have a booking?'

'No, we're touring, but we also want to see London.'

'You're not British then?'

'No, I'm Dutch, but my husband is. We live in The Hague.'

'Just back for a visit?' she looked at Larne.

'That's right. For a month.'

'Nice to see home.' She put on her glasses and consulted the register. 'For two nights you said? Yes, that's all right. Mr and Mrs—'

'James,' Larne said.

'Will you want breakfast, or evening meal as well?'

'Just breakfast, thank you,' Christina said.

'Good. If you'll just sign I'll show you your room.'

Larne signed and they were taken upstairs, with the dining room and lounge pointed out on the way.

The bedroom was on the front corner of the hotel, with a double bed, wardrobe, dressing table and a small television. It smelled of perfumed air freshener and hoovered carpet. There was also a sink, but the toilet and shower were shared between two neighbouring rooms.

'Breakfast's between seven thirty and nine thirty,' the woman told them as she made to leave. 'And we also have a bar if you'd like a drink in the evening. I hope you enjoy your stay.'

'Thank you,' Christina said.

The door closed and Larne moved to the window. He looked at the road for a while and when he turned back Christina was sitting on the edge of the bed.

'We'll fetch the bags up,' he said. 'Then you can go out for a walk. We need a few things.'

'You're not coming with me?'

'No.'

'You still think the police might be looking for you for the murder of those two men?'

'They'll be looking soon enough: all their files on the Irish in London. When they don't find me at home they'll want to know why.'

'So you won't be able to go home at all.'

'I haven't been home for a long time.'

'You mean Ireland?'

He nodded. 'We'll get the bags.'

The woman from reception had gone and there was no one around to notice the awkward weight of Larne's holdall. Back in the room he wrote out a list of things he wanted and Christina went out without waiting to unpack.

Larne waited fifteen minutes and then went back downstairs and followed a sign to a telephone enclosed in a glass and wood booth beneath the main stairs. Inside he dialled the number of the scrap-yard.

The phone rang six or seven times before it was picked up and then Wally Osbourne said: 'Yeah?'

'It's Joe.'

Wally's voice lightened a little. 'All right, kid? Where are ya?'

'The back of beyond.'

'You ain't ready to work then?'

'Not yet. Has anyone been round there?'

'What, lookin' for you you mean? Nah. A couple of phone calls, though. I told 'em you was on 'oliday. Bleedin' 'ell, it's me needs the fuckin' 'oliday.'

'No message or name?'

'No, kid. Asked if I knew where you was 'an I told 'im I didn't. An' that's the truth 'cause I don't.'

'Was it the same man calling each time?'

'Sounded like it. You got trouble?'

'No, it's okay.'

'An' you ain't comin' back yet.'

'No.'

There was silence for two or three seconds; just the sound of Wally's breathing, then he said: 'Good luck, Joe.'

'Same to you. I'll see you.'

He hung up and went back to the room.

He was watching the news from the bed when Christina returned. She had two plastic carrier bags as well as her own and put them on the bed beside Larne. He sat up. 'Did you get everything?'

'Yes, no problem. Do you want a drink? Coffee?' There were coffee and tea making things on a small table by the wall. 'I bought some biscuits and chocolate, too.'

Larne opened the bags and took out the items he'd listed. The largest were four nylon sports bags; cylindrical, with zips and carrying handles. They were in various dark colours and Christina had squashed them up to fit in the carrier bags. The other things were loose: rubber gloves, a packet of dusters and an A-Z of London, an evening paper, a tube of liquid solder and a screwdriver.

'All from different shops,' she said, spooning coffee and powdered milk into cups.

'Good.'

He got up and drew the curtains and switched on the bedside light, although it was hardly dark with the evening sun on the window. He unzipped his holdall, then put on the rubber gloves and picked up a duster. As the kettle boiled Christina watched him take out blocks of explosives one at a time and wipe them down with the duster before lining them up on the floor.

'Are you always so careful?' she asked, making the coffee and bringing a cup to him.

He nodded. 'Other people can leave fingerprints if they like. Don't open the bags once I've closed them.'

'Are you going to tell me your plan? I can't help if you don't.'

'Have a look in the paper. Find a West End cinema with a film that starts about half past eight tonight.'

She moved round the bed and sat on the other side with the newspaper open on the quilt. After a time she picked up the A-Z and looked through it. 'Eight forty-five, the Odeon Leicester Square. It's a science-fiction film I think.'

'That'll be good enough.' He began to put equal amounts of explosive in to three of the nylon bags. 'We'll set three tonight.'

'Together?'

'No, separately. I want them to go off in a row. The cinema first, then a pub and a car in the street. You'll do the pub.'

'Why that way?'

'The pub's easiest.'

'I didn't come because it would be easy.'

'Easiest for you to do.' He looked up. 'You've got to walk in with a bag, put it somewhere out of the way where it won't get kicked or knocked, then leave. They might look twice at a man, but you can leave the bag as if you're going to the toilet.'

'What's the pub called?'

'You'll have to choose it yourself, you'll have time, but you want it near a phone box.' He finished packing the bags and picked up a timer to unscrew its cover. 'Leave the bag about twenty-five minutes before it's due to go off. Go to the phone box and call the police. Tell them where the bomb is and when it'll go up, then walk away. By the time they've cleared the place they won't be able to touch the bomb without setting it off.'

'Do I tell them who planted it?'

'Two words: Legend and Sword. Legend is who you are and sword is the code word we'll use each time.'

'So you want them to think the IRA is responsible, isn't that what the words mean?'

Larne reached for his coffee, took a sip and put it back. 'Does that worry you?'

'Not if that's what you want.'

'It is.' He looked at his watch. 'We'll have to be on the way by eight o'clock. If you want to take a shower you'd better do it now.'

She nodded and stood up. 'Will you make love to me when I come back? For luck.'

'You make your own luck.' Then: 'If you want.'

She gave him a thoughtful look, then picked up a towel and went out, closing the door quietly. Larne set the timers.

TWENTY TWO

Larne didn't want them to be seen leaving the hotel with three bags; it would look odd if they were supposed to be going out for an evening drink, and stranger when they came back without them. He had a look at the fire door on the first floor, but it was connected to an alarm and the only other way out was through the reception area.

In the end he solved the problem by putting all three bags in Christina's suitcase and as they passed the receptionist she asked if it would be safe in the parked car. The receptionist, a girl in her twenties, wasn't really interested but she said she thought it would be.

Outside it was almost dark and the number of cars behind the hotel had risen to over a dozen. At the Escort they took out the bags and locked the suitcase in the boot.

They walked to the Manor House tube station together but on the platform they split up – not far apart, but enough not to be connected. Larne carried two of the bags and on the train Christina sat on a side seat in front of him, her bag under her elbow. Once she glanced at her watch, but her eyes looked blind and the movement was automatic, without meaning. She didn't look at Larne, but his gaze moved on and off her like a regular pulse, varied only when other people left or entered the train. He seemed calm, relaxed, but inside he had a feeling he kept tamed, held hard, and all the harder when he remembered the airport. He had been taken by surprise then, but now he lay in wait.

For the last two stops before Leicester Square the train became more crowded, and when they got off most of the other people seemed to follow them. He lost sight of the girl as he walked towards the exit, along with the sound of feet and the tunnelled echoing of a busker's violin, but as he stepped out into the blue night background and the noise of traffic he saw her again only a couple of yards ahead of him. She turned back, looking for him, and when she saw him she gave a faint acknowledgement and moved off, gone in as long as the look had lasted.

It was twenty-five to nine. Larne moved to the kerb beside a couple of other waiting people and crossed Charing Cross Road into Cranbourne Street. There was a smell of fried hamburger and chips in the air; stale, warm and all pervasive – the scent of the city. He hadn't eaten since midday but he wasn't hungry. People milled around him in an eternal flow, constantly changed and replaced. The sign above the Odeon was white with red letters. The doors were open. As he approached he shifted his right-hand bag to the hook of his left. Side by side the two bags looked almost like one. The air inside the cinema was cleaner. A short queue of five people stood by the ticket counter and his feet were soft on the carpet as he joined them. He paid for the ticket and followed the same carpet inside with his ticket in his hand, then taken and torn. There was no way to stop anyone seeing the bags and remembering later on. He knew that, but now it wasn't like the airport, he didn't think about being stopped. He was distanced from the threat; it was only later that people would single him out, when memories worked and descriptions were put together. He knew it and he'd accepted it when he first thought of this place. That was why the pub was easier. Here people filed in one at a time.

Beyond the thick wooden doors the cinema was already dark and there were trailers on the screen. The place was quiet, like a cushion for the sound from one direction; squealing tyres, gun shots, a voice-over. He paused while his eyes grew accustomed to the dark. About two-thirds of the seats were full, near the centre. He turned and walked up a side aisle, counting the rows. Six from the back he moved in sideways, away from the main block of seats with no one alongside him. The bags went to the floor in front of the seat to his left. He sat down and moved the bag he'd carried in his left hand close up to the bottom of the seat. He settled then. Eyes raised to the screen he became motionless.

At twenty-three minutes past nine Larne picked up the bag by his feet and stood up. He stepped out of the row of seats and walked down the aisle, not fast but not lingering to follow the film. He went out the same way he'd come in. There were no usherettes inside the cinema but in the foyer two stood talking to the woman in the box office.

Back in the night outside he turned right and crossed the road towards the railings of the square. As he looked at his watch the time was nine twenty-five.

There were three phone boxes at the top of the square, faced by the dead light of an amusement arcade. A gang of skinheads stood close by. Larne went into the first box, his back to the door. Lifting the receiver he dialled nine nine nine.

'Emergency. Which service do you require?' A woman's toneless nasal voice.

'Police.'

The voice of the police operator had the same toneless sound. 'This is the police. Can I help you?'

'Listen carefully. This is Legend. The code is Sword.' He paused. 'There's a bomb in the Odeon Cinema, Leicester Square. It has an anti-handling device and will go off in eighteen minutes. Eighteen minutes.'

He listened and there was a moment of silence, as if the operator had gone away. Then: 'Caller, would you repeat that please?'

Larne hung up, wiping his hand down the receiver as he did. He left the box and headed away towards Wardour Street.

On Shaftesbury Avenue he turned left in the white light of the theatre fronts and the cars. He felt less obvious with one bag, and it was lighter. As he neared Piccadilly Circus the people were thicker, gathered and sauntering in front of the electric shop caves of brassware and red white and blue. There were urgent sirens behind him. He skirted the circus and went down the steps to the tube.

On the train it was like the cinema again. He settled, subsided and waited. But this time the waiting only filled time; it was a marginal thing and he was not quite as still as he had been in the cinema dark. He watched the stations and matched them to time. Green Park, Hyde Park Corner, Knightsbridge. He was only going outwards to come back, because it was safer out of the way, underground. At Gloucester Road he got off the train and waited for one the other way. It was quarter to nine. The first bomb was due, perhaps had already gone off just as he looked at his watch. He had no desire to know, to hear confirmation. Perhaps that was strange, but he didn't think about it.

This time he got off at Green Park, rode up the wooden elevator from the new blue and white tiles of the platform. Outside he crossed Piccadilly and walked into Mayfair. And this time, unlike the cinema, he had no pre-set plan. He was looking for an opportunity but he didn't know how it would come. He walked, but not fast, and he watched. Occasionally he looked at his watch. It came close to ten o'clock and he realised he was waiting for the second bomb – Christina's. Waiting but not to hear it, just for its time to be past, as if to keep up a sequence.

Then, at two minutes past ten, as though the timing was linked to the place, he was in a narrower street than the others and there were cars lined up in a bay, front wheels to the kerb. He knew without looking that for the moment there was no one in sight, no one watching, that it was all right. He stepped off the kerb between two of the cars, took a couple of steps and lowered the bag to the ground. As he straightened again his foot pushed the bag under the car and then he moved away, increasing his pace only slightly.

Free of the weight of the bag he made right to emerge on Regent Street and the plate-glass light of its windows. In daylight when he'd walked down this road it had seemed out of proportion, built too big, but he didn't look up now. He turned again on the wide pavement, perhaps walking faster, still not hurrying but running down time in his head without feeling. He followed the curve of the street, back towards Piccadilly again because there were phone boxes there.

He made the call as he had done before – just the name of the street and the time – but this time when he left the phone box it was finished. And for a second he felt it, like a pause, a missed beat, a moment of nothing. He felt as if he'd been walking for a long time. He felt empty and very little else. He started towards Shaftesbury Avenue, but after only a few yards he flagged a cab.

They'd arranged to meet on Euston Road, between Gower Street and Woburn Place, not standing but walking between the two. By then the girl should be there. He'd told her to walk after leaving the bomb. Taxi drivers could remember fares, and it was better that she fill the time than be seen hanging around for too long. For his own part the taxi didn't matter.

Like the cinema it was something he'd already accepted; the possibility of being remembered, identified later on. It wasn't that he didn't care about the risk, but certain things were less important now than they had been once. It was as if he could regulate the risk now, as it suited him, as needed to do what he was doing. The girl was different. He knew that in some ways he had worked things to protect her, to minimise her risk; not at the cost of his own, but certainly not to his own best advantage. She hadn't asked for it, but he'd done it. And yet, because he would meet her, and because he would be coming in after she'd arrived, he would be able to make sure she was alone. He didn't probe that trace of suspicion but he knew it was there.

He paid off the cab at the corner of Gower Street, opposite Euston Square tube station, and waited until it had gone before he crossed the road. It was quarter past ten and the trembler on the last bomb was already armed.

He looked in the entrance to the tube station as he passed, just in case the girl was there, then he followed the road on the south side. A group of black youths coming the other way separated on the wide pavement and he passed through the middle of them. He kept an even pace and in the washed out sodium light from the tall street lights he watched the far side of the road as much as his own. Along the frontages of shops selling office equipment and city services there were few recesses. The pavement felt open and long.

It took him no more than three minutes to reach the turning point at the corner of Woburn Place but he didn't see the girl. He knew he hadn't missed her. She wasn't there.

For a moment he thought about the possibility that she was lost, but she had the map with her and the road wasn't difficult to find. He knew about meetings not kept and Danny Mallon crossed his mind. He looked at his watch, turned and moved to the kerb.

He crossed the road and started back in the direction he'd come, measuring his pace, watching the other side of the road. He saw people, but none of them Christina. By the time he was opposite the tube station again it was nearly twenty-five past ten – forty-five minutes since she should have left the bomb: too long.

Then he saw her, coming towards him on the opposite side, from the direction of Tottenham Court Road; not hurrying as if she was late, just walking steadily. He recognised the cut and colour of her hair and the coat she was wearing. And at the same time she looked round, nearing the road junction. She saw him because her head was turned for longer than it would have been if she hadn't, but she didn't signal. She slowed slightly and then moved closer to the building beside her. He glanced at the pavement behind her and crossed towards her, speeding up half-way to avoid the traffic.

He came up behind her and she had almost stopped. She looked sideways at him. 'Joe—' she began.

'The tube station,' he said. 'King's Cross and change for Manor House.'

She turned full on to him. 'What about you.'

'I'm here aren't I?' He pushed her arm almost roughly and moved as she moved, but there was a distance between them, there as much because he didn't look at her again as from the physical space.

They crossed to the tube station and went down to the platform. He let her lead, stayed a pace behind her, eyes running over the people who passed them either way. On the platform he stood back against the wall, reading the posters across the track as she stood close to the edge. The wind from the tunnel caught her hair and the train came, and again he moved only when she moved, entering at a different door, then standing for the short distance to King's Cross.

When the doors opened he stepped out and looked both ways along the carriages, waited for her to appear. When she did he followed again, this time further back as she walked towards the Piccadilly line. When she reached it he finally came back to her side.

The platform was quiet, only a couple of dozen people waiting, and she'd gone to stand at the far end, quite close to the circle of the tunnel. The draught was cold. He stood beside her for a moment, then he said: 'Are you all right?'

She nodded, looking straight forward.

'Why were you late?'

'I couldn't get away.'

He glanced down the platform. 'Why not?'

'There was a man.'

'Doing what?'

'Don't interrogate me!' Her voice rose slightly, a snap. Then there was the pre-arrival noise of the train.

Larne stayed beside her but he said: 'Wait till we get off now.'

She nodded.

They rode together in silence, and at Manor House he climbed the steps close to her, as if he thought she might stumble. She didn't look at him very often, not even glances to make sure he was still there. It was a remote quietness.

Outside they walked for about ten yards before she spoke. 'It was a pub called the Griddle; the second one I went in. I put the bag under the seat, quite far back. I had a drink, but when I was about to leave a man came over and started talking to me.' She paused but Larne didn't say anything. Their pace was a stroll.

'He wouldn't go away. If it had been earlier I would just have got up and left, but I couldn't move the bag then and I was afraid he would see it and pick it up if I tried to leave. So I stayed. I waited and let him buy me a drink, then I said I was going to the toilet to do my makeup. The toilets were round a corner of the bar and I got out without him seeing me.'

Larne broke their step, stopping to light a cigarette. 'What time was that?'

'Three minutes before ten.'

'So there was no warning.' He said it quietly.

'There was no time.'

'No.' He drew on his cigarette, still not making a move to start walking again. 'How many people were in the place?'

The girl shrugged slightly. 'I don't know. Twenty or thirty I think. I didn't count.'

Larne's eyes were thoughtful and then he started walking again, the same pace. 'They won't like it,' he said.

'Who?'

'The police for one.'

'There was no other way. I told you – if I'd left earlier he could have picked up the bag before I was outside. Even if he hadn't, a warning to the police would have told them who had left the bomb. They would have got the man out and he would have described me. He was as close as you are.'

'Then he'll be dead now.'

'He was stupid.'

Larne gave her a strange, hard look and she caught it. 'What do you expect?' she said, almost demanding. 'Did you think you can plant bombs and not kill people? Is that what you wanted? I didn't think you were stupid too.'

'I didn't say anything.'

'No, but you thought it. I know. You want me to be sorry for that man, or feel guilty. It was his own fault. Stupidity has its price, you know? Listen, I sat for twenty minutes beside that bomb when just to knock it would set it off. I did that for you, because *you* wanted it. All right?'

Larne nodded, accepting and silent. The silence seemed to still her, slowly. 'Will you stop now?' she asked.

They stood at the kerb, waiting to cross the road back to the hotel. 'No,' Larne said.

TWENTY THREE

Breakfast television showed pictures of the bombings. Only one sequence carried pictures and sound of a bomb going off. It was the final one in Mayfair; a dark view down the length of an empty street, a brief flare of light and then the delayed sound, oddly distant and soft, followed at once by the ringing of a burglar alarm. After that the reports showed the debris as the dead and injured were carried out of the Griddle pub through broken glass and white and blue lights. Then, in the early morning light, the interior and exterior of the cinema, the burned up wreckage of the car in Mayfair, the broken windows of the pub being swept off the pavement. The reporter said: 'There were twenty-minute warnings for two of the three bombs, and without them the death toll would certainly have been higher. As it is, with three dead and twelve people detained in hospital, there is already speculation that last night's bombs may mark the start of a fresh campaign by the IRA on the mainland of Britain.' In the studio the newsreader gave more details, but it was almost abstract now the pictures had gone: 'The police are looking for two people – a man and a woman – thought to have been seen close to the scenes of last night's explosions. The man is described as dark-haired, medium build in his early forties and carrying a holdall. He was seen going into the Odeon Cinema about an hour before the bomb went off there. The woman, with shoulder length blonde hair and in her twenties, left the Griddle pub only a few minutes before it was wrecked. Police are anxious to interview them and are appealing for witnesses who may have seen them between eight thirty and ten thirty last night. Meanwhile, Commander John Moore of Scotland Yard's Anti-Terrorist Branch urged the public to be on their guard and report any unattended bags or suspicious objects to the police immediately.'

Larne turned off the television.

'Is it safe to stay here?' Christina said. She had damp hair

186

and a towel in her hands, standing a few feet from the sink in jeans and a bra. She'd watched the pictures as silently as Larne, but unlike him her eyes had moved once or twice, to look at his face.

Larne reached for a cigarette in the ashtray and relit it. 'They got descriptions sooner than I thought.'

'They're not very accurate. Who remembers a description ten minutes after they've heard it?'

'We're booked to stay tonight.'

'All right, but then what?' She dropped the towel over a rail and put on her shirt. 'Do you know?'

'They'll want to talk.'

'Who, the Irish?'

Larne nodded. He seemed distanced, even out of phase. What he said had a heavily punctuated feel about it, as if it had escaped from another line of thought. He smoked absently.

'Will they want you to stop?'

'Perhaps.'

'So, will you?'

He stood up from the bed, dropped his cigarette in the ashtray. His face had a closed look. 'It depends on their offer.' He moved past her to the sink and ran water to shave.

'Offer? What do you want?'

'Nothing.'

'Then it doesn't make sense. If you won't do what they want where does that leave you? You have bargaining power but you won't use it. What good is that? I thought you wanted to make them talk to you, listen to you.'

'Not really. I know what they'll say.' He put shaving foam on his face and as he wet the razor he said: 'You can catch a flight home tomorrow.'

'I don't want to do that.'

He looked in the mirror, but not at her. 'There's nowhere to go after here,' he said simply. 'You might as well go home. You don't want to be on the run.'

'What are you going to do?'

'Today? Set another bomb.'

'No, after that, when you've talked to them. I don't understand you, you don't make sense.'

'I want you to go home.'

'You want to be on your own, is that it? You didn't ask me to come, so now you can tell me to go because you feel like it.'

'I didn't want you to come.'

'You didn't stop me, and that's the same as agreeing. You can't treat me like a whore.'

'I won't argue with you,' he said. 'I'm staying till tomorrow. You can leave when you like.'

She watched him shave for a moment, then picked up a brush from the dressing table and began to pull it through her hair.

They went down to breakfast quite late to avoid the other guests. It had rained during the early hours of the morning and outside the car park was sheened with water and the trees that hung over the wall around the hotel dripped slowly. The sky was white grey. Larne sat facing the mock-Georgian window, quiet again and withdrawn, except once when he asked what day it was. 'Thursday,' Christina said. 'The thirtieth.'

He nodded. 'I'd forgotten.'

They left their room clean, taking the detonators out in the girl's bag because Larne didn't trust the cleaners. Outside, as he unlocked the car, Christina said, 'Do you need me to come?'

'If you want to.' He got into the car and unlocked her door. After a pause she opened it and climbed in.

'Are you being like this so I'll leave?' she said. 'You haven't told me what we're going to do.'

He pushed the keys into the ignition and turned his head sideways to her. 'I told you, I won't argue. This isn't your business.'

'It could be.'

'Until you get bored, like you were in The Hague? No.'

'That's unfair. I helped you.'

'Nothing's fair. Blowing up people in the street isn't fair. If you want to help you can bring the car back here when I've found another. That's all.'

'That's *not* all. What are you going to do?'

'Leave a car bomb. Now close the door or get out.' He turned the ignition and as the engine fired she closed the door.

He drove for a full half hour, along main roads and side streets, turning almost at random, as if following hunches, before he found a car park that suited him. It was a long-stay place on a slope running down from the pavement of a three-lane carriageway. The entrance was off a side street and manned by a grey machine on two steel poles. There was no one around and although there were factory-like walls on three sides, all their windows were high up and opaque.

He pushed coins into the machine and drove the car round the outside ranks of the cars. There were about thirty with space for another dozen or so, and most of them had been left pointing uphill on the damp red shale. He went right round the park, running his eye over the cars, then on the second circuit he stopped and reversed the car up to a brick wall between two others. He cut the engine and pulled on the hand-brake.

He glanced at the girl, but when she didn't respond he shifted his gaze. 'See the dark blue car over there? Fourth on the top row.'

'I see it.'

'I'll go over and open it. When I look at you bring this one along and back it in beside it. I'll open the boots and shift the explosives from this one to that.'

'Why not park over there now?'

'Because if someone gets nosey I might have to run. You wouldn't get out without them getting the number. If there's trouble you wait and drive away later.'

'And when you've moved the explosives?'

'Take the car back to the hotel and wait, or go for a drive around. I'll be a while. Maybe two or three hours.'

He reached into her bag and took out a detonator, then opened his door. 'When I look at you,' he said.

He walked across the slope of the car park and Christina slid across into the driver's seat. There was a light rain in the air that pricked against Larne's face. He had his coat closed and the detonator in his pocket. In his hand he had two pieces of slim steel that he'd taken from his wallet.

Beside the blue car he checked the ticket on the windscreen, then bent slightly and worked the picks in the lock of the rain-wet door, probing, easing and finally turning. It only took a little longer than using a key would have done. He opened the door and glanced in at the dashboard, but only briefly, then he went round to the boot and repeated the work on its lock. As the lid came up he looked over to Christina and nodded.

She started the car, came up the slope and along, then stopped and reversed. She wound down the window a little way and kept the engine running as Larne opened the boot.

He didn't waste time, but there was no self-conscious hurry in his movements. He took hold of the handles of the box that the last night's explosives had come from, and with his back straight he heaved it on to the edge of the boot. It weighed just less than a hundredweight now and he re-firmed his grip, then sidestepped to the back of the other car, letting it down inside. With that done he banged down the boot lid and did the same to the other.

'Joe—' Christina said.

He went to the window. At the car-park entrance another car had stopped by the ticket machine.

'Are you going to give them a warning?' she asked.

'I don't know. I don't think so.' He glanced at the other car. 'You'd better go.'

'Good luck.'

She let in the clutch and turned the car out of the space. Its wheels slid a little on the wet ground.

Ten minutes later Larne stopped about a mile from the car park, pulled in by the kerb in a residential avenue lined with broad-leaved trees. He took out the detonator. Making the final connection and setting the timer didn't take long and when he'd done it he went to the boot and put the device in the centre of the explosives, leaving the lid off the box. Nobody watched, nobody moved. For a while in that avenue it was as if no one existed outside the quiet, semi-detached houses. There wasn't even a dog using the trees.

He'd been generous with the time. It was eleven o'clock and the bomb was set for one, but as he started the car and moved out of the stillness of the avenue he was aware in a way that seemed to loom out of nothing that it didn't make any difference any more. Three bombs or four, it didn't matter. It was odd, the realisation that it had happened last night and he hadn't even thought about it then. He knew now, though; it would only have taken one bomb and it would have been done. He tried to think back to how his reckoning had worked, to what had made him think in terms of several instead of just that one. He couldn't. All he could think of was that it was like being stuck on one track once started, that somehow it was like a kind of sleep, and that from the moment you fell asleep you no longer had control over when you'd wake up. But thinking of that was only a secondary thing; what occupied him most as he drove towards the centre of London was not having seen last night as the passing of something. It seemed odd to have missed it, forgotten it, not thought about it, when in reality he'd been moving towards it for days.

And now it didn't matter, or did it? He wondered. There was no reason to go on but equally there was no reason not to. For a moment he felt trapped by his own momentum, but then he realised it was no longer a matter of achieving something. The bomb could – would – serve a purpose. He needed to leave it because it would be a means of confirming what he'd done this far – a conscious affirmation. And in a way he saw this as more real than the supposed reality he'd been living till now. The bomb did make a difference, and he was glad of that.

Dawn

TWENTY FOUR

'Mr James.' The girl on the reception desk called to Larne as he came in. She was young, with fashionably untidy hair and a cluster of rings on her right hand.

'Yes?'

'Your wife left a message. She said she's gone to visit her friend and would you ring her this evening.' She reached under the desk and brought out a white envelope. He took it.

'Thank you.'

'Mrs James did say she might be staying at her friend's house tonight. She had her suitcase with her. Will you still be using your room till tomorrow?'

He nodded. 'Yes, till tomorrow.'

He put the envelope in his pocket and went up to the room. It was tidy and the bed was made. The carpet looked newly hoovered. He opened the drawers that the girl had kept some of her clothes in. They were empty. The car keys were on top of the dressing table. He took them and went down to the car. The car park was almost empty, quiet in the damp air. It was as if he was the only person free.

The detonators and his pistol were in the glove compartment and the last box of explosives was in the boot. He didn't look because he mistrusted the girl. Now she had gone he trusted her more. He took the pistol and went back to his room.

There were pictures and a report from the scene of the car bomb explosion off Oxford Street. When they had finished, the picture switched to the studio.

'This new wave of IRA bombings appears to have caught the police and security forces off guard. Unlike many previous mainland bombing campaigns there seems to have been no warning of what the IRA were planning, and in some quarters it's being said that the police may have been too complacent after the arrest and charging of nine people allegedly involved with IRA cells in London. At the time of the arrests it was widely believed that the police had made a major coup against the Provisionals, but now the Anti-Terrorist Branch must be left wondering if they did such a thorough job as previously thought.

'With the death toll since last night now standing at twelve and the number of injured at over twice that, the explosions – two of them without warning – must be seen as calculated to have the maximum public effect. The fact that the fourth bomb was placed and timed to explode when many people were in the streets during the lunch hour is said to be particularly worrying to police in case it indicates a trend away from political and military related targets to indiscriminate attacks on civilians. Also worrying the police is the fact that so far they have no idea whether these attacks have been carried out by a single active service unit in place for some time, or whether the IRA has specially detailed the bombers to come here from Northern Ireland as a measure of reprisal.

'This afternoon in a statement to the House of Commons, the Home Secretary said that terrorism of this particularly vicious and callous kind would not succeed in changing the Government's hard line on subversive organisations, nor on the problems of Northern Ireland. There was agreement from all sides of the House, but at the moment one wonders if that is the IRA's aim. Undoubtedly, in certain quarters these recent attacks are seen not so much as political means but as a demonstration of the IRA's continued determination to keep themselves in the eye of the general public as a force which cannot be ignored.'

'We've been looking for you, Joe.' Hagen's voice was quiet, slow, listening.

In the hotel telephone booth Larne said nothing. He hardly moved. Every so often people walked past him, but he had his back to the corridor, leaning slightly against the folding door.

'Was it your work?' Hagen asked.

'Where's McGiven?' Larne said.

'He's out. There's only me here. Was there something you wanted, Joe?'

'Have they sent someone yet?'

'Sure, and you know him. His name's Ryan. A big man they say. I haven't met him yet but I know he wants to see you.'

'I'll see him. Where do I call?'

There was silence for a moment, then Hagen said: 'Tell me, Joe, I'll see he gets the message.'

'Tonight?'

'As soon as you like.'

'There's a multi-storey car park near the bus station in Croydon. Do you know it?'

'He'll find it. Tomorrow?'

'Tonight. Half past two on the top floor. It'll be open.'

Again there was silence. Then: 'All right, Joe.'

Larne said nothing but he made no move to hang up. His eyes tracked across the back of the booth, the emergency services instructions and the mini-cab cards.

'Will you bring the stuff?' Hagen asked.

'Some, the rest's buried.' His eyes kept their movement and still he hung on.

'You've still got your gun, though. You're a wise man, Joe. Don't worry, Ryan'll be there.'

'I'll call again at ten. He can tell me himself.'

Hagen chuckled. 'A wise man. He'll do that all right.'

Larne hung up.

In the flat Hagen put the phone back in its cradle and moved from the room, down the hallway to the kitchen. The air there was a mixture of cigarette smoke and coffee, unease and waiting. The blind on the window was drawn down and the light shade focused light on the table below. McGiven sat at one end of the table in shirt sleeves, his collar undone. His back was to the sink and the window and all he could look at was the man opposite him, still dressed as he had arrived, in a light raincoat and a look that held him apart.

The man was Ryan. He was clean-shaven, well dressed, and the sense of his separateness went deeper than anything he could make his expression do. He hadn't a hard face, but it didn't belong, and not belonging had set in it, as if he had spent a long time in kitchens like this, with people like McGiven who had a whiskey bottle by his right hand.

'It was Larne,' Hagen said. It seemed to mean something

that he looked at Ryan not McGiven as he said it. He sat down on a chair close to the door.

Ryan's head came up slightly. 'Why didn't you call me?'

'He didn't want to talk to you.' Hagen got a cigarette from a pack on the table and lit it.

'What *did* he say?' Ryan's voice had no accent at all, but it carried a note that made Hagen react.

'He wants a meeting, tonight in a car park in Croydon. Half past two on the top floor. He'll ring again for you to say yes.'

'Did he say why he wanted to talk?'

'No, that was all.' He drew smoke. 'You'll want a driver.'

Ryan considered. 'A driver, not a gunman. There'll be no shooting on top of a car park. They'd hear it for miles and there'd be no quick way out. You said Larne lived in Croydon. He knows what he's doing.'

'Aye,' Hagen said, then tilted his head at McGiven. 'But he's got a gun for the job if you want it, though he's no guts to use it.'

Ryan's gaze shifted briefly to McGiven, then back to Hagen. Then he seemed to be waiting. He said nothing.

Hagen scraped his chair back and stood up. From a drawer he took McGiven's Hush Puppy with the silencer screwed to its muzzle. McGiven watched but made no move to stop him. Then, as Hagen deliberately formed his hand round the gun's grip and the muzzle moved past McGiven, McGiven lurched up.

'Fuck you,' he said. 'Fuck the both of you.' He smacked the whiskey bottle into his hand and pushed past the table, out of the kitchen.

Hagen watched him go with dispassionate eyes, then looked at Ryan. The older man was thoughtful, then he nodded. 'When I say so,' he said.

In the hotel room Larne sat without moving for a time he didn't measure. His breathing was shallow and regular. He sat on the edge of the bed and his back was curved forward, his weight settled. His hands lay thoughtlessly; the right on the bedspread an inch from the grey box of a detonator, his left crooked on his thigh. He wasn't waiting, and that was all.

The car stopped, just past the corner of the road, still ten yards short of the turn into the car-park building. Its lights were dipped and its engine made only a low sound, almost lost in the light breeze that blew cold over the damp black of the road. Smoke from its exhaust caught a little of the red wash from the rear light before it dispersed.

For a moment nothing happened. Then the passenger door opened and Hagen got out. He wore a dark leather bomber jacket, zipped up to the neck, and as he looked round at the empty side street he turned up its collar against the wind and shivered slightly. He bent again and spoke into the car.

'It'll take a couple of minutes to get up there.'

In the driver's seat Ryan nodded. 'There's no hurry. He wants to talk.'

'Yeah, but will he listen?'

'You do nothing unless I tell you.' Ryan's voice was definite, giving no leeway. 'If you see me fasten my coat, then he's yours, but not before.'

'You're the boss.'

'Go on then.'

Hagen straightened and pushed the door closed, lightly, with only a click. The car moved away and Hagen crossed over behind it, into the shadow on the far pavement.

The car stopped again in front of the barrier arm into the car park. The small hut between the entrance and exit was unlit and locked up. The light under the concrete floors was a dirty white, hollow and flat like the empty parking lots. The car's headlights were too bright against the yellow paint of the barrier and the steel railings which filled the gaps between floors. Ryan reached forward and turned them to sidelights before he took the slip of card from the vending machine. The barrier rose and the car idled forward.

He didn't increase its speed as he turned it right, into the long low corridor, guided by crack-painted arrows marked UP. There were three cars there; empty. Nothing moved except the enclosed tick of the car's engine.

The first ramp was twenty yards from the entrance and Ryan swung wide for it, only putting on speed at the last moment, boosting the car up the slope, but then just as quickly letting it slow as he came into a new straight. And now, in the narrow gap between wall and ceiling, the sky was visible; dark but haloed by orange without source from below.

Another car, solitary, looking cold and abandoned. Ryan watched it for a moment as he moved past it.

He took four more ramps and each time the darkness of the sky became fractionally lighter, to blue-black, and the cast of the street lights became thinner. Then the last ramp took him up to the open and as he turned the wheel at the top he saw the Escort, backed up to the parapet, and he let his own car come to rest for a moment.

There was no light there; none from the strip lights inside the car park, none from the thin crescent moon, just shades of darkness and shadows without source. It was quiet and the stillness seemed sharper, more solid, for the light sound of the wind passing the walls. Then the stillness moved and beside the Escort a man separated himself from its form.

Ryan watched him, but he didn't move far, perhaps two steps and then nothing. Ryan let the car roll forward again and brought it round to park away from the parapet, facing the gap between that floor and the one below. He turned off the lights and the ignition and sprung his seat belt free. As he opened his door he undid the two buttons that held the front of his raincoat together.

He stepped out, letting the door close, looking over the roof of his car towards Larne, then he started to walk. The wind was stronger there and it pulled at his coat. He didn't put his hands in his pockets. As he came closer to Larne his eyes moved briefly along the skyline of single lights, but then they came back to Larne's face. It seemed like part of the darkness and was impossible to read.

Larne took one pace as Ryan halted about four feet away. His hand slid along the bonnet of the Escort finally to light on the Ingram laid flat there. He only touched it and he didn't look down.

Neither did Ryan. He seemed to draw in his shoulders against the cold. 'You said you wanted to meet,' Ryan said. 'So I'm here. I didn't bring a gun.'

'From the Council?'

Ryan nodded.

'Do they want it to stop?'

'What do you think?' Ryan's voice was neither hard nor sarcastic. He stood like a man who had been sent, without hostility or sympathy; just to listen and talk.

'What did they say?'

Ryan made a gesture as if the question was too broad to be answered. 'The wrong targets, the wrong time, the wrong way. You've got no backing.'

'So what'll they do?'

Ryan repeated his last gesture. 'Maybe nothing, if you came here to stop.'

Larne nodded, understanding, and shifted his stance slightly. 'Tell me something, did you claim the last one, today? I didn't, but somebody did.'

'We called them,' Ryan said. 'It was too late to do anything else, but they don't like claiming what they didn't know about. You were still wrong.'

'So what did they tell you to do about it?'

'Find you and stop it – for the time being. You've got the explosives so maybe we'll use them later, but there's a lot to sort out first. If you do what you're told it could be forgotten.' He glanced away for a second, as if letting that sink in, then he said: 'Who was with you?'

'No one,' Larne said.

'The police want a girl.'

'They've made a mistake.'

'Okay,' Ryan said. 'Why not? Tell me what sort of a deal you want for the explosives, then we can both go to bed.'

'Deal?' Larne shook his head. 'If you want it the stuff's in the boot – about a hundred and twenty pounds. The rest's buried up north but it'll be easy enough to collect. Here—' He held out the car keys with his left hand, not moving his right from the bonnet.

Ryan looked from Larne to the keys but he didn't move to take them. For a couple of seconds Larne kept his arm outstretched, but when Ryan still didn't move he flipped the keys into his palm and lifted the Ingram in simultaneous actions. He turned on his heel and walked back beside the car to the boot. He worked a key in its lock and when the lid came up he stood back and faced Ryan again.

From the opposite side of the car Ryan looked in at the shape of the ammunition box. Larne watched him, then after a moment he reached in and lifted the lid of the box. In the darkness it revealed nothing more – the explosives were invisible inside – but Larne had been making a point.

'No tricks,' he said. 'If I booby-trapped it they'd just send somebody else.' He let the lid fall, backed up and closed the boot. 'Take it,' he said and dropped the keys on the boot with a rattle. 'You can pick yours up in the morning.'

'And where'll you be?' Ryan said.

Larne started back towards the front of the car. After a slight pause Ryan took up the keys and followed him, but with the car still between them.

Larne stopped by the front wing, turned slightly. He strung out the silence for just a while longer and then he said: 'I'll be at home. Ask David Hagen. He can come for my stock and I'll tell him where to pick up the rest of the stuff.'

Ryan's head made a small, sharp movement. 'So that's the deal. You want to get out.'

'If you like.' Then his voice was jaded. 'Take the stuff, you know where I'll be.'

For a moment Ryan was still. He had an arm across the front of his coat, holding it to his body against the wind. By the centre ramp Hagen stood in the darkness on the floor below. He saw over the floor of the top level but the sound of the men's voices didn't reach him. In his hand he had the Hush Puppy.

The light colour of Ryan's coat stood out pale, better than Larne who was just a shape without form. Then Ryan shifted and his coat blew free from around his body. He moved back a step and opened the car door. The interior light came on for a couple of seconds and washed him paler. When it was gone there was a pause before the car's engine started and Hagen ducked, anticipating the headlights.

They came, then swung as the car moved, turning left towards the down ramp twenty yards away. Hagen rose again slowly. He looked for Larne and could see him more clearly now against the sky and the faint whiteness of the parapet without the car in the way.

The car reached the edge of the ramp and Ryan turned the wheel, braking. The rear lights shone more redly for a second as the car started downwards and then they were gone as the white light of an explosion tore up the car and the night.

Hagen bent out of instinct, covering his head, but for a time out of proportion it seemed that the noise and the shock wave were too great to be withstood or escaped and they battered him into the concrete corner. In the open Larne staggered back, turned sideways, blinded and deafened until the hard rain of debris started to fall and he drew his head down low.

Something struck him a blow on the shoulder and he recoiled, but by then it was gone and he could hear the pebble-like sound of gravel falling around him. Then slowly the rain stopped.

As it did Hagen opened his eyes and lowered his arm from his head. On the ramp there was nothing left of the car or of Ryan; just a misshapen lump of metal – perhaps a wheel – that had come to rest on the lower floor and flickered with small orange flames. The air smelled of smoke and dust and Hagen coughed and wiped his arm across his face, then as if he'd remembered, he looked towards Larne.

The man had looked at the ramp too, but now he turned away and started to move, as if stiff, towards a small tower in the corner of the parapet where a door led to stairs downwards. He didn't walk fast but even so he seemed to cover the distance quickly and Hagen pushed himself out of the corner, staggering at first then in a bent-over trot. He rounded the rail on the side of the ramp, fending it off with his gun hand. He went up the ramp and as he came out into the open there were sirens below and distant and clear. He reached the top of the incline and his breathing was hard, dry. Bringing the gun up he made to call, but the sound wasn't a word. He tried again.

'Larne.'

By the door to the stairs Larne appeared not to hear. He was pushing the door inwards against the pressure of a spring and it grated on the concrete floor. He put more weight against it with the side of his right hand that held the Ingram.

There was the sound like a soft spit, but he didn't hear that. Instead he felt a shove, as if by a hand at his back, which then seemed hot in the back of his chest. The blow urged him forward and his hand slid along the wood of the door and his shoulder touched it, more heavily than he'd meant. Then he felt the second and third blows almost together in his kidney and spine and their dull heat seemed to combine with the first and he knew as he fell.

He couldn't see in the darkness. He could only feel himself falling, but when he hit the concrete that hardly seemed real. None of it was real, or else it was too real; like the hard rattle of steel on stone that came as the Ingram fell down the stairwell. As if his blindness added to the sound it was sharper than anything he had heard before. Then the pain grew sharper, half its edge in its suddenness; intense, flowing, but then it became soft, almost warm, and he realised he could feel warmth on his hand. He moved it slightly and its numbness didn't feel odd because he was used to its unnatural shape. In the darkness, now without sound, his hand pushed the thick pool of blood he was losing, smearing it outwards. Then it stopped and the reality was, he felt nothing.